"Who are you, really?"

"Bank robbers aren't edgy and taciturn. They don't make jokes. They don't take hostages on the spur of the moment unless they're trapped. And they're certainly not considerate of their captives. You're having way too much fun." Her remarkable eyes narrowed. "I suspect you've got an agenda."

"Relax. You're safe with me. But the less you know, the better."

"Let me guess. You could tell me, but then you'd have to kill me." She glanced out the window, her conflicted body language telling him she wanted to believe him but didn't quite dare.

Dear Reader,

As always, Silhouette Intimate Moments is coming your way with six fabulously exciting romances this month, starting with bestselling Merline Lovelace, who always has *The Right Stuff*. This month she concludes her latest miniseries, TO PROTECT AND DEFEND, and you'll definitely want to be there for what promises to be a slam-bang finale.

Next, pay another visit to HEARTBREAK CANYON, where award winner Marilyn Pappano knows *One True Thing*: that the love between Cassidy McRae and Jace Barnett is meant to be, despite the lies she's forced to tell. Lyn Stone begins a wonderful new miniseries with *Down to the Wire*. Follow DEA agent Joe Corda to South America, where he falls in love—and so will you, with all the SPECIAL OPS. Brenda Harlen proves that sometimes *Extreme Measures* are the only way to convince your once-and-only love— and the child you never knew!—that this time you're home to stay. When *Darkness Calls*, Caridad Piñeiro's hero comes out to…slay? Not exactly, but he *is* a vampire, and just the kind of bad boy to win the heart of an FBI agent with a taste for danger. Finally, let new author Diana Duncan introduce you to a *Bulletproof Bride*, who quickly comes to realize that her kidnapper is not what he seems—and is a far better match than the fiancé she was just about to marry.

Enjoy them all—and come back next month for more of the best and most exciting romance reading around, right here in Silhouette Intimate Moments.

Yours,

[signature]

Leslie J. Wainger
Executive Editor

Please address questions and book requests to:
Silhouette Reader Service
U.S.: 3010 Walden Ave., P.O. Box 1325, Buffalo, NY 14269
Canadian: P.O. Box 609, Fort Erie, Ont. L2A 5X3

Bulletproof Bride
DIANA DUNCAN

Silhouette®

INTIMATE MOMENTS™

Published by Silhouette Books

America's Publisher of Contemporary Romance

SILHOUETTE BOOKS

ISBN 0-373-27354-1

BULLETPROOF BRIDE

DIANA DUNCAN

Diana Duncan's fascination with books started before she could walk, when her librarian grandmother toted her to work. Diana crafted her first tale at age four, a riveting account of Perky the Kitten, printed in orange crayon. The discovery of her mom's Harlequin Romance novels at age fourteen sparked a lifelong affection for plucky heroines and dashing heroes. She loves writing about complex, conflicted men and strong, intelligent women with the courage to dive into the biggest adventure of all—falling in love.

When not writing stories brimming with heart, humor and sizzling passion, Diana spends her time with her husband, two daughters and two cats in their Portland, Oregon, home. Diana loves to hear from her readers. She can be reached via e-mail at writedianaduncan@msn.com or snail mail at P.O. Box 33193, Portland, OR 97292-3193.

For Berny. Who shanghaied me on a wild and crazy adventure—the best time of my life. Thanks, kiddo. Your unshakable faith dared me to dream.

For Darol, Danielle and Natalie. Who ate canned, frozen and takeout until it came out their ears, and went without clean socks and sometimes my time and attention—with nary a complaint. Thanks, gang. Your love and support enabled me to pursue the dream.

For Cindy and Deb. Who dried my tears, cheered every small step—and, when necessary, kicked my fanny. Thanks, sistas. Without your encouragement, there would be no books. You made the dream a reality.

I love you all.

Chapter 1

"You have stolen my heart with just one glance of your
eyes."
—*The Song of Songs*

"*Another* bad omen. You have to call off the wedding!"

Tessa Beaumont glanced up from her desk in alarm as her
best friend and maid of honor, Melody Parrish, stormed into
Tessa's office at Oregon Pacific Bank, a large garment bag flung
over one shoulder. Tessa's stomach pitched. *What now?* "Mel?
What's wrong?"

Her sapphire eyes snapping, Melody shoved the door closed
with her foot. "Every time you progress with your wedding
plans, something terrible happens. A freak fungus down south
wiped out the orchid farm. Your photographer slipped on a stray
gefilte fish at a bar mitzvah and broke his arm. The caterer went
belly-up after food poisoning flattened three hundred gastro-
enterologists at a hospital benefit."

"Coincidences," Tessa soothed, setting her paperwork aside
in a neat pile. "Stuff happens. And we found replacements."

Melody thrust the garment bag under Tessa's nose. "You think so? Well, maybe *this* will convince you."

Tessa glanced at the clock. It was after 1:00 p.m. They'd been two tellers short all week, and she hadn't taken a break or even lunch in days. She rose and circled the desk. "Ten minutes, then I have to get back to work."

Mel unzipped the bag. With a flourish, she whipped out two dresses and hung them on the brass coat rack beside the door. "I hope you haven't eaten."

Tessa's jaw dropped. Speechless, she stared at the ugliest ruffled white monstrosity she'd ever seen, accompanied by a hideous bluish-purple bridesmaid's dress. "Wha—what's *that?*"

"Lucille changed your order. Imagine my surprise when I picked up our dresses today."

"Oh, no!" Tessa hurried over to finger one of the hundreds of flounced organza ruffles on the horrible bridal gown. "I'll look like a refugee from *Gone With The Wind*. A hoop skirt, for Pete's sake. One misstep, and I'd give a whole new meaning to the term *flash photography*."

"Not if you were Little Bo Peep." Mel snickered. "At least your fashion holocaust is white. My 'elegant eggplant' number looks like a black eye. What was Lady Stalin thinking?"

"I don't know, but she went too far this time." With quick, efficient movements, Tessa zipped the awful dresses back into the bag. "These are going right back. I jumped at Lucille's offer to help with the wedding because my mother couldn't care less. But I refuse to let her bulldoze me."

"Yeah. Your future mother-in-law has the personality of a Zamboni."

"Well that's no reason to meekly lie down and let her shave my...ah...ice." Tessa tucked a wayward auburn curl into the gold clip at the nape of her neck. "I hope the bridal shop can deliver our original choices in less than two weeks."

Her friend grew somber. "That's the least of your worries. You know, you still have plenty of time to change your mind."

Tessa winced. "You think I should? I chose the candlelight empire satin gown because of the high waist, but I was afraid my big caboose sticks out way too far anyway."

"You've been comparing yourself with the models in those bride's magazines again, haven't you? There is nothing wrong with your butt." Mel sighed. "Not the gown. The wedding. Please don't marry Dale just because you think he'll give you the security you crave. Do you really want to spend the next twenty years trying not to rock the boat with Lucille?"

For a moment, the only sound was the muted hum of voices from the outer lobby. Then Tessa shuddered and forced a strained laugh. "You know better than to mention boats to me."

"Don't change the subject. You don't really love him. Admit it."

"I *do* love him. For two years, Dale has been my closest friend, besides you. The wild, passionate version of 'love' is just an attack of raging hormones. Ten minutes of pleasure—a lifetime of consequences. My mother for instance—"

"Yeah, you had a new 'uncle' every time you phoned home, but Vivienne is a bad example. Lots of actresses have revolving doors on their bedrooms."

But Vivienne's unfaithfulness had caused the death of the only person who had ever loved Tessa. Her dad. Her mother's flighty lifestyle was the reason Tessa had chosen a financial career. Numbers never lied, never changed and never let you down. "Dale and I are perfect together. He's an accountant and I'm a banker. We both enjoy books, music and playing in Lucille's charity concerts."

Mel snorted, making her short blond locks bounce. "I admit, I've never had a relationship longer than two dates, so I'm the last person to give advice. But don't settle for blue-eyed bland. You deserve the best."

"Maybe Dale isn't as exciting as 007, but he's loyal, responsible and sweet, and he loves kids. I'm getting my heart's desire." She frowned. "In two weeks, I'm going to marry Dale and have a family of my own. Children to cuddle. A dog shedding hair on the carpet. Noisy, bustling holidays. And nothing on this earth will stop me."

"Okay, have it your way. I just don't want you to wake up in thirty years and realize you've wasted your whole life with a man who doesn't trip your trigger."

Tessa chuckled. "Gee, don't hold back. What do you really think?"

"After twenty years, you're more than my best friend—you're like my sister. We've been soul mates since our teary eyes met that first awful day of boarding school and I want you to be happy."

"No tears, see? I am happy. Very happy. Everything is on track and according to plan." She glanced at the clock again and a groan slipped out. "Except I'm out of time. Trask has been on my case all week because we're so far behind. And he'll relish throwing it in my face at the promotion interview."

"He's lucky to have you. Any woman who alphabetizes her spices and arranges her canned goods by expiration date is a pillar of organization." Mel grabbed both Tessa's hands in hers. "I'm telling you, this dress fiasco is another sign. Mark my words, Tessie, Dale is not your destiny. If you don't wise up, The Man Upstairs will resort to something drastic."

Her friend's pronouncement resonated in the throbbing pulse at Tessa's temples. *Dale is not your destiny.*

A shiver crawled up her spine. She shoved the eerie feeling aside. Practical and steady, she didn't believe in destiny. A person made her own fate, and her course was perfectly charted and firmly set. She wouldn't let anything thwart her lifelong dream for a family and security. Not now, not when it was finally within her reach. Tessa gave her friend a reassuring smile. "It'll be fine. Everything will run smooth and well-oiled from now on, you'll see."

The door flew open and her vault teller, Carla, burst inside. "Sorry to interrupt, but everything just went to hell. We've got customers lined up to the door. The cash shipment arrived, and needs to be verified. The kiosk ATM isn't working again, the newbie on window three is having a panic attack, and Darcy went home with that flu that's going around." She groaned. "Oh, and Mr. Trask pitched a fit because he didn't get your weekly report yet. He wants it ASAP."

Tessa sighed. As operations supervisor, her job was to ensure the branch ran efficiently, especially during Mr. Trask's frequent absences. With customers up the wazoo and another teller gone, she'd have to keep Carla at a window and manage the vault herself. That meant spending an hour after work trapped in the vault counting stacks of bills. And she had a dinner date with Dale and Lucille to discuss wedding plans. At the thought of confronting Lucille, her heart sank. According to *Modern Day Bride,* newlyweds fought about three major topics: money, sex and in-laws. She grimaced. Her hopes to be the exception didn't look promising.

"Give the newbie a pat on the back, tell her to take a deep breath and focus on one thing at a time. Then go back to your window. I'll count the cash."

Carla shook her head. "That's my job. You've already got your hands full."

"Maybe so, but I need you out front."

"Don't you think you should go out front? That newbie looks pretty shaky, and with Darcy sick, we're now three tellers short. And don't forget, today is payday for the biggest companies in town. I'd better do the count."

Tessa frowned. Carla usually obeyed without question. "Exactly why you belong at a station. I'll get it done as fast as possible, and I can pop out if needed in the meantime."

"But—wait—" Carla's brown eyes widened in near panic.

"I know how much you despise manning a window, but it can't be helped. Buzz if you need me."

Her face clouded with reluctance, Carla departed, and Tessa turned to Mel. "I've gotta run."

"Yeah, I know. Trask is such a bozo!" Mel huffed. "He's always gone, and he works you like a six-handed cherry picker while stalling your promotion for months." The tiny blonde planted her hands on her hips. "For five bucks, I'll take him out for you. Lucille, too. I learned two killer moves in kickboxing class last week. I'd do it for free, but I'm dead broke."

In spite of her exasperation, Tessa chuckled. "You might have defended me all through boarding school, but I'm a big girl now. I'll work things out with Trask and Lucille. Negotiation and logic."

"Negotiation and logic. Right. And sometimes, a good swift kick in the chops." Mel picked up the garment bag. "I'll return

Bulletproof Bride

these and demand the originals back. I wouldn't have accepted them in the first place, but I knew you'd have to see 'em to believe 'em.'' With a wave, she headed out the door. "Bye. And think about what I said, okay?''

"I doubt I'll have time to breathe, much less think." Her friend left, and Tessa's stomach grumbled, reminding her she'd gone without lunch. Again. Since she had to stay late, she needed something to keep her on her feet. She rushed to the break room and gobbled two stale chocolate doughnuts before hustling into the vault.

Inside the locked room, she cut the first bag's seal to remove a bound package of twenties and then placed it in the money counter. The machine whirred as the crisp bills spilled into a neat rectangle. Humming "Jailhouse Rock," she picked up the next package.

The process went smoothly until the very last package, when she found a number of client payroll checks mixed in with the cash. How odd. Frowning, she flipped through the pile. The checks amounted to fifty thousand dollars and belonged in the main vault downstairs.

She had to report this serious security breach immediately.

After replacing the checks in the bag, she stepped out of the vault. An eerie silence shrouded the room, everyone frozen in place. "What's going—"

The sight of a tall man in black, his face concealed behind a black quilted nylon ski mask choked off her words. With a sick, breathless lurch, her stomach bottomed out. She had just stepped into the middle of a robbery.

Gabriel Colton watched the vault gate swing closed. The faint click echoed like a gunshot through the hushed lobby. He sized up the woman frozen in the doorway. The baggy cut of her plain brown suit nearly disguised her curvy figure, and her long chestnut curls were clasped at the nape of her neck in a conservative ponytail. This little kitten wouldn't give him any trouble.

Then his eyes locked with her sharply intelligent gaze, her golden-brown eyes wide with horror. A jolt of recognition slammed into him. For a split second, his concentration splintered. *Impossible.* He'd never even seen her before. He shook his head to clear it. "You the vault teller?" he snarled in his best bad-guy voice.

Her face blanched fish-belly white and she nodded.

Man, he hoped she wasn't about to pass out on him. "Get the cash delivery." His jaw clenched at the fear shimmering in her big amber eyes, but he didn't have time to reassure her. He needed to grab the goods and get out.

She stood rooted to the spot, stunned and staring.

Feeling as low-down as the guy who shot Bambi's mother, he dropped his voice to a menacing rumble. "Now! Move it, sister!"

Kitten squared her shoulders. Color flooded her cheeks. She raised her chin and shot him such a blazing glare he needed asbestos boxer shorts. He got the message loud and clear.

Uh-oh. His kitten had morphed into a lioness. *No heroics, sweetheart. Please.* He glared at her. "Do it!"

She hurried inside, quickly returning with six canvas bags. She stalked toward him and tossed the bags at his feet.

Gabe reached for the money, but the sight of the cut seals brought him up short. *Damn!* This operation was going to hell on a torpedo. "Did you look through these?"

After a heartbeat's hesitation, she nodded. Then understanding flashed across her face.

He was too late. She must have seen the checks! Gabe assessed the situation with the speed of experience and reacted on instinct. His gloved hand shot out and grabbed her wrist, hauling her up against him. She stiffened. "Pick them up," he growled into her ear. As she complied, her softly rounded bottom brushed intimately against his groin and her warm vanilla fragrance teased his senses. He shook his head. *Get a grip, Colton, before all your brains rush south and get you killed.*

What the hell was wrong with him? He never lost his focus. Ever. Especially not over a woman. Consciously tempering his strength, he yanked her out the entrance, hustled her to his black Corvette, and flung open the driver's side door.

His captive tried to wrench free. "What are you doing?"

"Sorry, sweetheart. You're now my hostage."

"No!" Her elbow stabbed his solar plexus.

The breath slammed out of his lungs. Gabe lost his grip and she slipped under his arm. She sprinted toward the bank and he lunged, grabbing her jacket to yank her back. "Nice try." He shoved her into the car, tossing the money behind the seat.

She tried to climb out. "I can't be your hostage. I have an important appointment this evening."

He frowned. Poor Kitten probably didn't even realize what she was saying. Damn, he hated scaring her, but if she knew anything and he left her behind, she was dead. He pushed her back inside and threw himself into the seat. As he twisted the key, she scrambled away from him, over the console.

"I won't hurt you," he attempted to reassure her. Sirens screamed, and the sweet, heady rush of adrenaline glittered through his veins. He grinned. A conscientious employee had tripped the alarm. Now life was getting interesting. Exactly the way he liked it. He turned to his wide-eyed passenger. "Fasten your seat belt." The engine roared, and he tore out of the parking lot.

The ski mask interfered with his vision, and he ripped the mask and gloves off. He'd deal with the repercussions of letting her see his face later. Right now, he had to get them out of here in one piece. He wasn't about to add either of their names to the long list of casualties on this one. His foot slammed down on the gas pedal.

"Hey!" his captive squeaked. "You're running the red lights!"

"No kidding." Chuckles burst out of him. "A traffic citation is the least of my worries, honey."

"You've committed robbery, don't add kidnapping," she said in a reasonable tone, though her shaky voice gave away her panic. "You're lengthening your sentence by at least five years. Let me go. Please."

"No time to explain. I'm taking you for your protection." He ignored the screaming sirens behind them. The 'Vette responded to his touch like a familiar lover as he wove from side to side. Revved up to sixty, the car screeched around a corner. He skidded and spun into another sharp turn and they nearly rocked up on two wheels.

A moan leaked out of his passenger and Gabe glanced over at her. Stiff and unmoving, she clutched the armrest like a life preserver, her face a bilious pea-green. Unless he missed his guess, she was about to yodel in living Technicolor. "You okay?"

"Motion sick," she murmured through white lips.

Wonderful. Just what he needed. "Take deep breaths." He stabbed the window button. Fresh air. Get the lady some fresh air.

The window slid down and Tessa leaned out like a wind-drunk poodle, gulping in cool autumn air. She clung to the armrest, fighting her terror and the nausea pitching in her stomach. This was all a crazy nightmare. Any minute, she'd wake up, call Mel and have a good laugh. Right after she threw up. Distraction—she needed a distraction.

The police would want a description. She forced together her scattered concentration and studied her captor. Six foot one, around a hundred and ninety pounds. All hard, male muscle in a black jacket, T-shirt and snug jeans. His thick black hair was cut military-short at the sides and back and left just long enough in front to stand straight up. Long, sooty lashes fringed light-colored eyes. She couldn't see the shade in profile and the slits in the ski mask had concealed them in deep shadow before.

The shifting light played over a tanned classical face with strong cheekbones and a Roman nose. His sculpted lips were quirked in a smile over even white teeth and his square chin cradled a dimpled cleft in the center. Her gaze followed his wide shoulders downward. His lean, tanned hands—musician's hands—controlled the wheel with grace and power.

She knew firsthand how much strength those hands possessed.

Suddenly his eyes narrowed and he sucked in a sharp breath.

She jerked her gaze to the front. A thousand yards ahead, two police cars charged toward them, blocking both lanes and thwarting their escape. She was saved! But instead of slowing down, the bank robber shifted gears, his muscled thigh tensing beneath the tight denim as he stomped on the gas. The car leapt forward at a blood-curdling speed. "What are you doing?" she yelled.

An unholy grin of pure joy split his face. He looked like he was having the time of his life! "Playing chicken."

Was he insane? Dumb question. He'd robbed a bank and was attempting to outrun the cops in a high-speed pursuit. Of *course* he was insane. Fear clutched at her chest as they closed the distance with incredible speed. *Stay calm. Humor him.* Wrestling down her dread, she tried negotiation. "Do you know how unlikely that is to work?"

He chuckled. "Never tell me the odds."

"Han Solo."

"Huh?" He flicked a quick, puzzled glance at her.

Common sense told her to shut up. Screaming nerves made her babble on. "You're quoting Han Solo."

"You are one nutty broad." The handsome felon shook his head. "Don't worry, I know exactly what I'm doing. They'll blink."

Obviously he was delusional, too. So much for negotiation. She gripped the dash with fingers gone numb. Her entire body felt numb. Her mind struggled in slow motion, her thought processes clogged by fear. *For heaven's sake, talk your way out of this.* Logic. Logic never failed her. "Have you tried this demented maneuver before?"

"Yep, twice."

"And it worked?"

He urged the car even faster. "Not the first time."

Tessa took a fortifying breath. "And the second?"

He chuckled. "I'll let you know in about five seconds."

The car rocketed forward, the tires skimming over the highway. The force pushed her back against the seat. Tessa stared at the police cars hurtling toward them and her stomach rolled, bitter bile rising up in her throat.

Her life flashed before her eyes in a horrifying squeal of tires and blaring horns.

The thief's deep laugh rang out. "See? No problem."

"Who are you, the Angel of Death?" she croaked. Her stomach lurched in warning. "Oh, no." Frantic, her gaze spun wildly around the car.

The robber glanced at her and groaned. "Here we go."

The car was swept clean, nothing to get sick in. Her desperate gaze locked on the money bags behind his seat. If she could get one open in time...

"Oh, no you don't. I need that. Uncontaminated." He thrust the ski mask at her.

She snatched the quilted cap and turned away from him, mightily regretting those chocolate doughnuts. After several horrible minutes, she felt much better. Holding the ruined mask between two fingers, she looked at the door handle, then at the scenery flashing by. "Um..."

"No evidence." His right hand reached past her to open the glove compartment.

She deposited her burden and slammed the door. Out of sight, but definitely not out of mind. She heaved a short-lived sigh of relief. One problem solved. Kind of. She glared warily at her captor. Served him right for driving like the lunatic he was.

She glanced into the side mirror at the empty street behind them. Her kidnapper had evaded the police. Her heart stumbled into an uneven gait.

She was on her own.

Chapter 2

The thief pulled over in front of a warehouse in a run-down neighborhood. A fresh rush of adrenaline surged through Tessa. Now that they'd stopped rocketing through space at warp speed, maybe she could escape. Negotiation and logic were out. Time to try Mel's swift kick in the chops, or anywhere else she could manage. As her captor exited the car, she tensed, waiting for an opportunity.

He sauntered around to open her door, offering his hand.

Now or never. Make your move. Heart pounding, she leapt out, rammed the door into him and tore down the sidewalk.

She made it five yards before his arm snaked around her waist and yanked her against his hard body. Even as her mad dash for freedom crashed and burned, his clean male scent invaded her senses, and she blinked away dizziness. Who knew a wild-and-crazy bank robber would smell so good?

"That door hit a little too close to my favorite part of my anatomy, honey. Unless you want to find yourself bound and gagged, chill out." But his silky threat sounded more amused than angry. For a bank robber, he seemed amazingly easygoing.

He marched her into the building. Every nerve ending she

possessed jittered in alarm, making her breathing much too rapid. *Hold it together. Stay alert, you'll get another chance to escape.* They climbed three flights of broken stairs and then her captor followed her down a gloomy corridor. He lifted the bar on a steel door and the screech of rusted metal echoed in the hallway.

The fine hairs on the back of her neck prickled, then stood on end as she reluctantly preceded him into a large, dim room. A storage facility from the looks of it.

The robber grasped the back of a dusty wooden chair. "Sit," his deep voice ordered.

Annoyance burned away some of her trepidation. Who did this cretin think he was, anyway? "I am not a dog," she huffed.

His chuckle rumbled out again. "Plant yourself in the chair. *Pretty please,*" he added in a sugary tone.

Seeing no other choice, she obeyed. Behind her, his jacket rustled. Aware of her vulnerable position, she stiffened, her short choppy breaths not conveying nearly enough oxygen to her lungs. So far, her captor had been good-natured and surprisingly gentle. Even when he'd used his superior strength to control her, she'd sensed him holding back. But what would he do now that he had her alone, and at his mercy?

Without warning, his hands gripped her shoulders. In spite of herself, she flinched.

"Easy." His voice moved closer to her ear. "I'm not going to hurt you." His low reassurance slid out, rich and mellow.

His deep baritone wrapped around her like the hot darkness of a sultry summer night, blanketing her uneasiness in warmth. A tingling ripple spiraled up her spine, sparking a shiver.

"Are you cold?"

Her muddled thoughts focused on his question and she shook her head. Tense, jumpy and anxious, you bet. But whatever unfamiliar mixed cocktail of emotions had made her shiver, she wasn't cold.

"Listen up. I've got some loose ends to deal with. I should tie and gag you...."

Her every muscle clenched. *Over my dead body!*

He gently squeezed her shoulders. "But I won't. There's no

way out, and if you've got any brainy ideas about screaming for help, eighty-six them. Any 'help' you attract in this neighborhood won't be the kind you want. I'll be back soon. You'll be safe if you stay put and don't do anything stupid. Got it?''

She nodded. As he walked away, she heard the whisper of clothing. The door creaked open and then slammed shut. The bar clanked into place, leaving her alone in the gloomy silence.

Relief swirled through her. Like a dream, a sense of unreality clouded her mind. Crazy surprises didn't happen to Tessa Beaumont. She kept her life ordered, predictable and controlled. Being kidnapped was *not* scheduled in her planner in neat script— blue for daily schedule, green for appointments and red for urgent matters.

What would happen when the thief returned? He'd said he wasn't going to hurt her, and so far, he'd kept his word. But rule number one in the Deranged Kidnappers' Handbook was probably, ''Keep the victim calm and obedient.'' Unfortunately, she'd been too busy with wedding plans to take that kickboxing course with Mel last month.

Though the roguish robber seemed more than capable of handling a whole class of self-defense graduates. With his looks, one of his sunny smiles was enough to disarm any female between nine and ninety. Glowing with a combination of sensuality and mischief, his infectious grin had incited a flood of response deep inside.

Tessa straightened. What was wrong with her? The shock must have unhinged her mind. No way would she meekly wait for him in this dump like an expired certificate of deposit.

As if to drive home the thought, rustling and sharp squeaks erupted from the corner. She gulped. Rats? Yelping, she scrambled onto the chair, her gaze skittering around the room.

Bundled newspapers littered the floor and three cardboard boxes leaned drunkenly in a corner. Not much to aid a jailbreak, but a small window high on the opposite wall offered some hope.

In one of Tessa's favorite movies, Goldie Hawn thwarted kidnappers by climbing out a window to the fire escape. But even if Tessa could reach the narrow window, it promised a tight fit.

She mentally compared the window to her hips, glad she'd skipped lunch.

After a hesitant glance at the now-quiet corner, she stepped down, and dragged the chair over. Even with the added height, the sill was out of reach.

As her gaze lingered on the cardboard boxes, an idea formed. Tessa grabbed newspapers and dumped them inside a box. She lifted the filled box onto the chair before fetching another carton and more papers. Papers with raggedly chewed edges. A shudder rippled through her. She lifted another stack and uncovered a pile of droppings. Ugh! Inspired to work even faster, she finished the last box and stacked it on top of the others, then stood back to assess her makeshift ladder. Not bad.

Sucking in a breath, she hiked up her long skirt to climb onto the wobbly pile. Her head now reached the bottom of the sill. A grin creased her face. She could do this! Her jacket hampered her movements, and she had to unbutton it in order to pull herself up and peer out the grimy panes.

Her fingers tightened on the sill as her hopes unraveled. No fire escape. "What now, Goldie?" she muttered.

Refusing to knuckle under to despair, her gaze swept the outside of the building. A drainpipe bolted to the bricks with metal brackets ran clear to the ground like a miniature ladder. Her palms grew slick with perspiration. The rusty pipe looked much too fragile for her peace of mind.

More squeaks and shuffles burst from the corner and a rat the size of a house cat skittered across the floor. She shrieked and tried to scrabble onto the windowsill, but her calf-length skirt and flapping jacket made gymnastics impossible.

She had no choice. Teetering on the swaying boxes, she stripped off her suit. Nothing would stop her from going out that window now. Not with a pack of giant rodents eager to tear her to shreds. She'd never be able to climb wearing her slippery half slip, thigh-high stockings and pumps, so they came off, too. She tied her clothing and shoes into a bundle.

Dressed in a purple satin bra and matching panties, she clamped the bundle between her teeth, levered her knees up onto the sill, and shoved open the filthy, peeling window frame. The alley below was empty, so she dropped her clothes to the ground before shimmying out the opening headfirst.

Her stomach jittering, she stretched out her arms, grabbed the pipe and swung over. With sweaty hands and shaking limbs, she clung to the slender pole, the only thing between her and a three-story fall. If this were a movie, she'd be at the police station drinking a cup of coffee with Chevy Chase by now. "Don't look down," she muttered, and began to hum to boost her courage. She arched her foot and felt for the first bracket, gingerly testing her weight. It held! Inch by terrifying inch, she climbed down.

She stepped onto the asphalt and pumped her arms in a victory salute. *"Yes!"* she crowed. Now, to get her clothes, find a phone, and call the police.

"Going somewhere?" a silky male voice asked.

Tessa's heart bucked and then lurched into an unsteady gait. She whirled, her arms shielding her half-naked torso.

Her handsome captor leaned against the wall with her bundle of clothes dangling from one finger. A wide, wicked grin lit up his face. "A tad informally dressed for an escape, aren't we?"

Clear, cool, rain-forest-green eyes sparkling with amusement studied her intently. Her breath hitched in her throat. The world stopped, frozen, as she fell into those jade depths. Realization hit. Caught. Again. Half naked. Her body went ice cold. Then heat whipped into her face.

"You could have died during that gutsy stunt," he drawled.

"Rats." She wrapped her arms around herself and scowled at him to disguise her apprehension. He'd told her to stay put. Would he punish her for trying to flee? "You locked me in there with giant killer rats."

His lips twitched. "I didn't know about the mutant rats. Sorry." He thrust her clothes at her. "Get dressed."

She snatched the bundle from him, and Gabe turned to give her some privacy, chuckling to himself. He wouldn't have missed that for a million bucks. Dressed in purple skivvies, with a halo of chestnut curls rioting over her shoulders, clutching the drainpipe for dear life and humming "Be My Teddy Bear" at the top of her lungs, Kitten should have looked ridiculous.

But she hadn't. She'd looked sexy as hell. Desire snaked through him, heating his blood. He wanted to run his fingers through her thick, shiny curls. Kiss those luscious pink lips. Cup her generous breasts in his palms—

Whoa! Where did that come from? She's your prisoner, Colton, and under your protection. You might have taken her hostage, but that's all you're taking.

"I'm dressed." Her indignant voice broke into his thoughts, again only a slight tremor revealing her distress. In spite of the fact that she had to be terrified, she was a pretty cool customer. Not to mention her ingenious jail break. If he'd arrived two minutes later, she'd be nothing but a memory. His admiration grew, encompassing not only her physical attributes, but her mental ones as well. He must be losing his mind.

With confusion throbbing in his temples, he gripped her arm. "Come on, Houdini." He hustled her down the alley to a gray Jag and helped her inside before climbing in himself.

"You changed vehicles."

The engine roared to life and Gabe maneuvered out of the alley. "Very observant. Yes, this is a Jaguar XK8, and you'll never find a sweeter ride. Except..." He grinned at her. "One other." She scowled at him again and Gabe chuckled. Damn, she was cute when she scrunched up her nose like that. He fished a bottle of motion sickness pills out of his pocket and tossed the vial to her. "Take a couple of these. I don't have any more ski masks, and we're in for a long drive. There's soda in the cooler behind your seat and some sandwiches if you're hungry."

"Look, you seem reasonably intelligent." She'd regained control over her voice, but a lingering edge of apprehension clouded her lovely eyes. "Be sensible and let me go. You can move faster, and the police won't hunt you as intensely without a hostage."

"What's your name?"

She eyed him warily. "Tessa."

Gabe shifted gears and the car roared past an oil truck. "For your own protection, I can't turn you loose. Unfortunately, you've stumbled into a bad situation, which I can't explain." He wished he could. But if he could find out how much she knew and still keep her in the dark, he might be able to safely release her. For her sake, he hoped so. The scum he'd just thwarted with his rip-off played for keeps, and they'd already left too many bodies in their wake. Whether either of them liked it or not, Gabe had been thrust into the role of guardian angel. He covered her hand with his. "I'm Gabriel. Call me Gabe."

She slapped his hand away. "Keep your hands to yourself. So, who are you, really? Bank robbers are edgy and taciturn, they don't make jokes. They don't take hostages on the spur of the moment unless they're trapped. And they're certainly not considerate of their captives. You're having way too much fun." Her remarkable eyes narrowed. "I suspect you've got an agenda. The misplaced payroll checks in the bags you asked about, maybe?"

He bit back a grin. The lady was way too smart for her own good. His impulsive decision to grab her had netted him a lot more than he'd bargained for. "Relax. You're safe with me. But the less you know, the better."

"Let me guess. You could tell me, but then you'd have to kill me." She glanced out the window, her conflicted body language telling him she wanted to believe him, but didn't quite dare. "Where are we going?"

"A place where I can protect you until I sort this mess out."

"And how long will that be?"

"Ah, yes. You mentioned an important appointment?"

"I'm getting married in two weeks and I have a million details and an overbearing future mother-in-law to deal with."

"Why do you want to do an idiotic thing like get married?"

"I beg your pardon?"

"A rolling stone gathers no chains." Gabe shuddered. "I can't imagine anything worse. Except being locked in prison."

"Try being kidnapped, taken on a roller-coaster car ride by a lunatic and jailed with giant rats. Not to mention having your promotion blown to kingdom come." She frowned. "You *are* disturbed. But I suppose your attitude shouldn't be surprising for someone who robs banks for enjoyment."

He threw back his head and laughed. "You've got a point.

Now swallow a couple of those pills. I don't want to have to run the inside of the Jag through a car wash, it's a loaner.''

"Or stolen. A thrill a minute.''

"Why, Tessa, I'm hurt.'' Gabe fluttered one hand over his heart. "You have such a low opinion of me.''

"If the ski mask fits...''

He grinned. "Hand me a couple sandwiches, would you? I'm starving.''

Tessa woke disoriented on a double bed in a paneled room. She remembered trees streaming past the car window and then fading to a blur. The pills must have knocked her out, a normal side effect. But everything was swaying, *not* a normal side effect. She blinked, but the room continued to roll. High-pitched squawking scraped across her eardrums. The rhythmic slap of water caught her attention, and terror clawed up her spine.

She tore open the door and raced upstairs, then skidded to a horrified stop. Endless blue-green waves crashed across the horizon of the Pacific Ocean. A scream ripped out of her and she collapsed, shaking. Her chest heaved in labored breaths.

Pounding footsteps vibrated the boards, and then Gabe's strong hands gripped her shoulders. "Tessa, what's the matter?''

She tried to speak, but couldn't. Head spinning, her vision darkened. Her lungs convulsed and her heart galloped.

"Listen to me,'' Gabe's deep voice commanded. "You're hyperventilating. Take slow breaths, in through your nose and out your mouth.'' He pulled her into his embrace and his warm hand rubbed her back. "Easy does it. Slow your breaths down, honey.''

She obeyed, and as her breathing slowed, her vision cleared.

"That's it.'' His arms tightened. "Now tell me what's wrong.''

Trembling violently, she clung to him. "Off the ocean,'' she gasped. "Get me away from the ocean—off this boat.''

"What the—? This is my yacht, *Serendipity,* and she's entirely seaworthy. Nothing's going to happen to you here.''

Tessa burst into tears, involuntarily digging her nails through the nubby white cotton of his sweater, into his arms. "I want off," she begged. "Now!"

"All right." He stroked her hair. "Let go of me so I can get the launch."

She managed to unclamp her fingers, and he rose. Arms wrapped around herself, she huddled on the deck, trapped in the nightmare that had haunted her since age six. She squeezed her eyes shut, struggling to breathe.

"Hang tight, sweetheart." His footsteps faded. Thumps, a metallic clang and a dull bang sounded. Minutes later, he returned. "I take it you don't swim."

She shuddered.

"Yeah, big surprise. Put this on." He helped her into a neon orange lifejacket. "All set, let's go."

"Aren't you going to wear one?" she gasped.

"I'm more at home in the water than in my own bedroom." He chuckled. "And I've got the big ol' frog's feet to prove it."

With his hands supporting her, she pushed upright on wobbly legs. He urged her toward the rail. She caught sight of the dark, churning water and jerked to a stop, digging in her heels.

"Tessa," Gabe spoke with quiet patience. "The only way to get to dry land is to climb into the launch."

"I can't." Caught between two agonizing, impossible choices and crazed with terror, she whimpered. "Hit me."

"What?"

"Hit me; knock me out. I'll never make it to shore."

He sighed. "Close your eyes."

Desperate, she obeyed. But instead of the blow she expected, he swept her up into his arms.

"I've never hit a woman in my life, and I'm not about to start with you," his satin voice murmured into her ear. "Even we bank robbers have our principles. Hang on."

Eyelids squeezed tight, she clung to him. His rock-hard biceps bunched, a door creaked, and then holding her with one arm, he stepped downward. The splashing grew louder. He lowered her to a cold metal bench that rocked wildly. She gripped the edge so hard her fingers ached.

"Keep those eyes shut," he commanded before moving away.

Ragged breaths raced in and out of her dry throat, but she obeyed, even as a new round of sobs shook her.

The motor chugged on. Gabe's warm, solid body pressed against her side. She eased her eyes open and he slid one arm around her. As the boat leapt forward, the sharp sea breeze slapped her face. Shaking, she flung her arms around his neck and buried her face in his shoulder, clinging to him.

"It's all right," he murmured. He stroked her back in a soothing caress. "When I was a little boy and I would wake up scared in the night, you know what my foster mom did?"

She gulped down her sobs and pulled away to gaze up at him.

"She used to give me kisses to hold in my hand. That way, I always had her love with me." He touched his soft lips to her forehead in a sweet, comforting kiss.

Her fear receded, replaced by a shocking awareness of the man holding her so protectively.

The boat leapt upward, then plunged sickeningly down. The bow crashed through a huge swell and icy spray stung her skin. She lurched sideways, an involuntary scream bursting out.

Gabe's arm tightened around her. "Whoa, it's okay."

She huddled in his encircling arms as he whispered words of comfort, until the boat finally slowed and he moored alongside a weathered wooden dock. He jumped to the pier and lifted her out beside him, but her trembling legs collapsed. Holding her, he sank to the dock and pulled her into his lap. "You're safe, sweetheart," he murmured, tugging the lifejacket off.

She let him hold her until the tight bands around her chest eased and the sick, shaky feeling faded. "Now, what was that all about?"

"I'm afraid of the water."

"No kidding." He brushed her damp hair away from her face, the clasp that had held her curls in order long gone. "Why?"

"Wh-when I was six, my brother pulled me into the ocean and I went under. I almost drowned. The lifeguard rescued me. Sh-she had to perform AR and I spent the night in the hospital."

He cupped her face in his hands. "Your fear is a normal response to trauma. But," he hesitated, "I'm trying to help, not put you down, okay? You shouldn't have to feel that the fear overpowers and controls you. Being terrified is no way to live.''

''I've tried to conquer it. Intellectually, I understand. But forcing my emotions to obey is another story.''

''This sounds simplistic, but concentrate on something else. Stay focused, so you don't have time to panic.''

Maybe he was onto something. For a few minutes in the launch, she *had* forgotten her terror. That had never happened before. But she'd been focused on him. Bewildered, she shook her head. ''Is that what you do?''

He was silent for almost a full minute. ''Yeah.''

''You don't seem like you're afraid of anything. What scares you, Gabe?''

A dark shadow clouded his eyes for a second. Then the mischievous sparkle returned and he gave her a dazzling smile, deepening the cleft in his chin. ''Martha Stewart's 'to do' list— now *that's* scary.'' He stood and helped her to her feet. ''Nightfall will hit soon. C'mon.''

She recognized a distraction when she saw one. ''Where?''

''I always have a Plan B.''

He supported her while they navigated the dock and toiled up a rocky path bordered by pines. But instead of his touch making her his captive, she felt protected. Her bewildered gaze scanned the thick Oregon forest. A scarlet maple leaf drifted down to land on her shoulder. Inhaling a breath of crisp fall air sharpened with tangy wood smoke, she brushed it off. From the shadows, crickets chirped a singsong chorus.

The setting sun stretched long gold fingers of warm light across the path by the time they finally reached a log cabin at the top of the bluff. Below, hungry white-capped waves hammered the shore. With a shudder, she jerked her gaze away. ''Where are we?''

He unlocked the door. Instead of answering, he waved at a green-and-navy plaid sofa. ''Have a seat. I'll start a fire.''

Perfect. While he was busy, she'd summon help. She didn't give a rip who he was, or what he was mixed up in, she wanted out. ''I'll make a pot of coffee.''

''Sure. But don't go climbing out the window. The kitchen

overlooks the bluff.'' He grinned. ''There's canned soup in the cupboard and bread in the freezer. You didn't eat in the car. You should get some chow in your stomach.''

Tessa strode into the cozy, spotless kitchen. Red-checked curtains framed the window, accenting the wooden walls and navy-tiled countertops. Her gaze darted around the room, looking for the phone. *Oh, no.* No phone. Her hopes flatlined. She squared her shoulders. Fine, she'd devise another plan.

She made the coffee and then opened a cupboard. The sight of Road Runner mugs inspired a reluctant smile. The cartoon cups fit Gabe's mischievous, faster-than-a-speeding-bullet personality to a T.

As she filled his mug, a daring idea hit. Her hand slid inside her pocket and gripped the bottle of anti-nausea pills. Two had knocked her out for several hours. If he ingested enough…

She stood there, the plastic lid cutting an imprint into her clenched palm. What if she accidentally killed him? Drugging him felt like a sneaky, dirty trick. He'd treated her very decently. *Get real, woman, the guy kidnapped you.* She quickly smashed six tablets and stirred them into his coffee.

In the living room, a cozy fire crackled in the hearth. She couldn't meet Gabe's eyes as she handed him the mug. Perching stiffly on a navy chair near the fire, she cradled her own warm drink.

With a contented sigh, he propped his stocking feet on the coffee table. Dressed in a fisherman's sweater and snug, faded jeans, he looked relaxed and comfortable. And not at all like a bank robber. As he took a sip, guilt pierced her heart and she steeled herself not to flinch. She felt like she'd given him a cup of hemlock. He grimaced. ''I wonder how old this coffee is?''

Her gaze jerked sideways to the flickering flames. Would he realize what she'd done?

''You're still jumpy. You're not afraid I'll hurt you?''

''The ocean scares me. You don't.'' In spite of a lingering edge of doubt, some primal instinct deep inside insisted he wouldn't harm her. After his gallant response to her irrational terror on his boat, she was almost sure of it. Wanted to believe it. However, she had a life to get back to.

Gabe shook his head. "You did go pretty ballistic on me there for a while." He took several more swigs. "I'm sorry about having to detain you."

"You *don't* have to detain me. I don't have any interest in whatever skullduggery you're involved in."

"Skullduggery? Now there's a word." He chuckled before drinking again, then rested his head against the back of the sofa. "Unfortunately, you're already involved." He yawned. "I'm starting to fade. I'd better make us some sandwiches."

No! She had to keep him quiet in order for the medication to kick in. She jumped up. "I'll do it."

His dark brows lowered and he flashed her a puzzled look.

"I was going to fix myself something to eat anyway."

"Go ahead then. And thanks for being such a good sport." He flashed her one of his heart-stopping smiles. "You've held up damn well considering what I've put you through."

Feeling unaccountably like Benedict Arnold, she stalked to the kitchen.

The snap and crackle of the fire was the only sound in the cabin as she made a tuna sandwich and carried it to the small table near the window. Chewing slowly, she managed to draw out her meager meal. Twenty minutes later, she poked a cautious head through the doorway.

Gabe lay stretched out on the couch, the mug still clutched in one hand. His sooty lashes rested against his cheeks and his full lips were parted. He was motionless, not even appearing to breathe.

Had she given him too many pills? Her stomach flip-flopped. Pulse racing, she stared at his broad chest until she saw the rise and fall of his deep, rhythmic breaths. "Gabe?" she whispered.

He didn't move.

"Gabe?"

Still no response.

She tiptoed across the room, and then carefully turned the doorknob. The door swung open with a slight creak. She stepped across the threshold.

"Don't leave me!" Gabe begged, his voice husky with anguish.

Her heart rocketed into her throat. She whirled.

Still asleep, but restless, he flung out his arm and the empty mug fell to the rug. Heart pounding, she stood frozen until her muscles cramped, waiting for him to resettle into deep slumber. Finally, she crept outside.

"No!" he cried. "Please don't go!"

A choking lump lodged in her throat. Who was he pleading with in his dream world?

Her chest tight, she eased the door closed and crept out into the darkness—feeling oddly as if she had left something precious behind.

Chapter 3

Enveloped in blackness, Tessa paused. The ocean roared on her left, loud in the quiet night. She turned in the opposite direction and broke into a run. Blindly, she stumbled through the woods, clawing aside rough branches and wet leaves. Finally her burning lungs grew unbearable and a stitch caught in her side. Gasping in the damp air, she clutched her aching ribs and slowed to a walk.

The night closed around her like a predator cornering his prey. An eerie screech rang out, echoed through the fog-shrouded forest. The hairs on her arms prickled. The bushes beside her rustled, and she swallowed a scream. Gabe's advice to focus on something else popped into her mind.

She hummed ''Don't Be Cruel'' as her thoughts spun. Gabe— what a puzzle. Even when she'd tossed her cookies in his car and whacked him with the door during her escape attempt, he'd kept his good humor. And when she'd been terrified in the boat, he'd comforted her with a story about his foster mom. And a tender, calming kiss.

Obviously, he'd been in the juvenile care system, not always the best environment. His foster mom sounded loving, though.

What had caused the flash of anguish in his eyes? And to whom was he crying out in his sleep? Her heart contracted at the memory of his desperate plea.

The irony of the situation struck her and a grim smile tightened her mouth. Not only had she taken the advice of a man she was running away from, thoughts of *him* provided the distraction that kept her panic at bay.

Suddenly, pain exploded in her forehead. Reeling backward, she plopped down in the damp grass. Brilliant stars crackled in front of her dazed eyes. She blinked, peering upward into the darkness. The twisted shape of a low-hanging branch loomed above her. She must have smacked into a tree limb.

Tessa gingerly explored the swelling knot on her forehead. It wasn't bleeding, but the throbbing sting made tears stream from her eyes. She clenched her teeth against a whimper. Throwing a pity party wouldn't accomplish a thing. The only way out was to keep going. She blinked again and then clambered to her feet. Shivers crawled up her spine, and she wrapped her arms around her middle. Warily peering into the gloom for any more of Mother Nature's ambushes, she doggedly put one foot in front of the other.

Hours of cold, lonely progress later, she stumbled out of the smothering thicket of trees and onto a highway. The long ribbon of asphalt loomed black and empty. On a guess, she turned right and kept trudging, praying she was headed toward a town.

Her plodding steps in tandem with her pounding head, she trudged along the gravel shoulder. She'd quit humming hours before. Her pinched, empty stomach grumbled in the silence. The pale morning sun peeked over the horizon, weaving golden strands through pink-and-lavender clouds. Another round of shivers rattled through her and she hunched over, too forlorn to appreciate the beauty. The unexpected rumble of an engine behind her sent her spirits soaring. She whirled and waved, but the car sped past. Sharp disappointment speared through her. Her despair deepened when she saw the taillights of a green sedan. Why had she expected a gray Jag?

The miles dragged by in an icy-cold blur before she finally spotted a weigh station with an Oregon State Patrol car parked in the turnaround. Her knees weak with relief, she staggered toward the welcome sight.

A tall, square-jawed trooper jumped out and helped her to the car. "Sit down, ma'am." He opened the back door. Shaking, she sank onto the seat. He squatted down. "What happened?"

"I'm Tessa Beaumont. I was...kidnapped yesterday during a bank robbery in Riverside."

The officer studied her forehead. "Did the perpetrator assault you?"

Tessa drew a ragged breath. "No. Please take me home."

"You were in the woods all night?"

At her nod, he rose and walked away. The car bounced as the trunk popped open. In seconds, he returned with a foil blanket. "There's a small hospital in Forreston, ten minutes away."

"No hospital. If you can't take me home, please call a cab."

The cop patted her hand. "After the doctor checks you out." He climbed into the front seat. The engine rumbled and flashing blue lights reflected off the car's hood. She huddled into the blanket, her teeth chattering.

Before long, he hustled her into the hospital. Ignoring her objections, a burly nurse stripped off Tessa's damp suit and underwear and strong-armed her into a hospital gown. Draped in a white blanket, she perched on the exam table, her uncontrollable trembling making the paper covering crackle.

The door swung open, giving her a whiff of the sharp, medicinal smell from the hall. A tall doctor with salt-and-pepper hair strode into the room. He wheeled a stool to the exam table and sat down. "I'm Dr. Maxwell." His kind hazel gaze studied her. "I understand you've been through quite an ordeal. Would you like to tell me about it?"

"I'm cold, that's all. I'm going home." She tried to climb off the table, but her wobbly limbs refused to obey.

"Not the best idea, Miss Beaumont. You've sustained a head injury. You're weak and shaky because you're suffering from hypothermia." The doctor probed at the knot on her head, flashed a bright light in her eyes and asked questions about double vision and nausea. "The laceration on your forehead isn't serious, but you do have a concussion. We'll take a CAT scan and keep you overnight for observation." He glanced at his clipboard. "The nurse said your clothes were disheveled and torn. Did your abductor sexually assault you?"

Tessa jerked upright, a gasp bursting out of her. "No!"

Doctor Maxwell's bushy brows pinched in a concerned frown. "Don't be afraid to tell me the truth, Miss Beaumont. There's nothing to be ashamed of, and your life could be at stake. There are diseases—"

Dizziness washed over her and the room whirled. "He didn't even *hint* at anything like that! My suit got ruined when I ran through the woods."

"You're in shock." He patted her hand. "Completely understandable considering the circumstances. Will you consent to a thorough exam and lab tests?"

"You're not hearing what I'm saying. There's no need." She ordered her weak, trembling body to climb down, but couldn't summon the strength. "*He* listened to me better than this."

"You've suffered a blow to the head combined with a traumatic event. But don't you worry about a thing; we'll take good care of you. I'll send the nurse in with an IV." The doctor again patted her hand. "After the scan, we'll settle you into a room. You'll feel much better after you've had a chance to rest. Would you like me to notify your family?"

Tessa gave him Mel's number. The nurse returned with an IV bag and a needle so huge she could have knitted an afghan. Tessa gritted her teeth and focused on the only thing that helped. The image sustained her through the endless, claustrophobic CAT scan and was the last thing she saw before she fell asleep.

Gabe's rain-forest green eyes.

Tessa woke to Mel's angry hiss. "What do you mean you can't find her clothes? What is she supposed to wear home, one of those idiotic gowns? She'll get arrested for indecent exposure!"

"Mel?" she mumbled.

Mel's worried blue gaze met her own. "Are you okay?"

Dazed, Tessa struggled to sit up, blinking at the painful stab of sunlight. "Nothing eight or nine aspirin won't cure." She pressed her palm to her forehead, where the Philadelphia Philharmonic Orchestra was conducting cymbal practice. "What time is it?"

"Barely past dawn. You've been out for almost twenty-four hours." Mel grabbed her hand and squeezed Tessa's fingers. "I've been so worried."

"I feel like I'm trapped in Oz. I keep demanding to go home, but can't get there. Did you say they lost my clothes?"

"Yep, I was just butting heads with Nurse Ratched. Apparently, they were ruined, and someone threw them away by mistake."

Tessa huffed out an exasperated sigh. "Another violation on top of everything else."

"Oh, Tess!" Tears brimmed in Mel's eyes. "He didn't—"

"No! He was actually kind of...sweet."

Mel shook her head, making her short blond curls bounce. "A sweet bank-robbing kidnapper? Obviously, you're still under the influence of your lovely purple and green lump there. Did they take X rays?"

In spite of her pain, Tessa couldn't stop a chuckle. "A CAT scan. Other than a headache, I'm fine. And I want out of here."

"Okay. I'll rustle up some clothes and be right back."

"How? Nothing will be open at this hour."

"I'll find something. Oh, Dale and the Dragon Lady are outside. Nurse Ratched wouldn't let them in your room. Apparently, a fiancé doesn't count as family."

"How did *you* get in?"

Melody grinned and buffed her nails on her red turtleneck. "I told her I was your sister."

"You're impossible!" Tessa smiled. "But I'm glad you were here when I woke up."

"A tiny white lie for the benefit of everyone isn't that terrible. What Nurse Ratched doesn't know won't hurt her. I'm outta here. Do you want me to send in the clowns?"

Tessa groaned. "Melody Parrish!"

"Mea culpa. Do you want your blue-eyed bland and his fire-breathing mamma invited in?"

"Yes, send in my *fiancé* and *future mother-in-law,* please."

Mel hurried out. Seconds later, Lucille glided in, followed by Dale. Immaculate in a beige Chanel suit, the petite woman shook her head. "Tessa! We've been worried sick, and the nurse wouldn't let us in!" Lucille peered at Tessa's forehead. "Oh, dear! I hope that fades before the wedding, or the photographs will need to be retouched."

Concern darkening his sky-blue eyes, her tall, broad-shouldered fiancé stepped forward, dwarfing his tiny mother. "Are you all right?"

"Only a bump, nothing major."

"Dale, darling, wait outside for a moment." Though phrased as a request, Lucille's steely tone brooked no argument.

"Why?" Dale cocked his head. "I just got here, and I want to make sure Tessa is okay."

"I'd like a word alone with her. You know, woman to woman."

"Ah." Dale nodded. "Tessa, you're probably thirsty. Would you like some water, or a soda? Do you feel up to eating anything?"

She ran a dry tongue across her teeth. Her mouth was as nasty tasting as if the French Foreign Legion had marched through and left their boots behind. "Nothing to eat, but a Sprite sounds great, thanks."

"Okay, let me know when you're done with your girl talk." Dale departed.

While Tessa appreciated her fiancé's considerate offer, her skin prickled with annoyance at his easy capitulation. She'd always thought a man who treated his mother with such respect was charming. Girl talk or no, Gabe wouldn't stand for being ordered out. She frowned. Now why had she thought of *him* at a time like this?

Lucille's ice-blue eyes narrowed to slits and she dropped her voice to a murmur. "Did that criminal attack you?"

"Why does everybody ask me that? He behaved like a perfect gentleman." Tessa's frown deepened. "And frankly, I don't appreciate your intrusion into my privacy."

"Tessa! You've never spoken to me with disrespect." Lucille patted her hand. "It must be the head injury."

Tessa snatched her hand away. First the cop, then the doctor and now Lucille. If one more person patted her, she'd scream.

Lucille sighed. "I was so excited about having grandchildren immediately, but now I suppose a baby will have to wait until there's no doubt about diseases."

Though she'd never hit anyone in her life, the desire to slap Lucille's elegant face burned through Tessa and she clenched her fists. She'd always thought of marrying Dale as gaining both a husband *and* a mother. Her own mother had been obsessed by her lovers, the New York soap opera scene and Tessa's brother Jules's tennis career. Vivienne had hidden her awkward, overweight daughter at a boarding school on the opposite coast and never discussed her. Tessa had believed Lucille's involvement in Dale's life was motherly love, but now it seemed motherly love had become blatant interference. No way would she let Lucille control her marriage, including when to have children.

She forced herself to take slow, deep breaths and relax her hands. Now was a fine time to have second thoughts—the wedding was less than two weeks away.

I can't imagine anything worse. Except prison. Gabe's heartfelt anti-marriage sentiment echoed through her throbbing temples. Did a green-eyed bandit have anything to do with her sudden enlightenment?

The door opened, and Mel strode in carrying a paper bag. "I'm back, with a change of clothes. Hey, Lucille. How come you're in here and Dale is out in the hall?"

"Hello, Miss Parrish." Lucille's voice dripped icicles. "That's really none of your business." She inclined her head at Tessa. "I'll give you privacy to dress."

Mel giggled as Lucille swept out. "What did the queen vulture want?"

Her daughter-in-law dancing on a string? Tessa struggled to corral her anger and confusion long enough to spout a coherent answer.

Mel's gaze locked on hers. "Hoo boy, what did she say that upset you so much?" Her blue eyes shot sparks. "Should I punch her in the snooty nose?"

Tessa straightened. "We're not six, and you don't have to

fight my battles anymore. I'll set Lucille straight. And if any punching goes on, I'll wear the boxing gloves.''

Mel's brows shot into her hairline. ''Wow, I've never seen you talk back to the Dragon Lady. I've never seen you threaten to get physical, either. It's about time. I don't know what the 'sweet' bank robber did that pumped up your attitude, but I like it.'' Giggling, she fished a bright orange garment out of the bag. ''Better get dressed first, though. Courtesy of Al's Truck Stop, the only place open. I caught a waitress going off duty and she happily sold me this.''

Tessa stared at the stained dress with *Al's* stamped in neon green on the pocket. ''I can see why.'' She chuckled. The sound gonged through her skull and she winced. ''However, it's better than baring my assets to the world. Thank goodness the nurse at least found my shoes.''

Balanced on wobbly legs, Tessa put on the ugly uniform, wrinkling her nose at the lingering odors of cigarette smoke and stale French fries.

The instant they stepped into the hall, Lucille swooped down on them. ''The BMW is out front. During the drive home, we can plan the postponement.'' Her meticulously groomed brows rose a fraction. ''What are you wearing?''

Dale offered a sweet, encouraging smile. ''She looks good. I'm glad to see her on her feet.'' He glanced at his mother and his smile slipped. ''What postponement?''

Tessa squared her shoulders. ''I'm riding home with Mel.'' She kissed Dale on the cheek. ''Don't worry, the wedding's on schedule. No delay.''

''I think it would be better for everyone if—'' Lucille huffed.

Tessa cut her off. ''I'll get in touch tomorrow.''

Dale enfolded her in a gentle bear hug. ''I'm glad to hear that. But we'll do whatever is best for you. Call me later if you need anything, Tessa.''

Tessa and Melody ambled to Mel's ancient red Volkswagen bug, leaving Lucille in the lobby sputtering like a defective tea-kettle. Mel jiggled the key into the rusty lock. ''About this 'sweet' bank robber.'' She shot Tessa a sparkling glance. ''What's his name?''

Tessa wrenched open the squeaky door and swept a crumpled Taco Man bag off the duct-taped seat before she settled in. "I have no idea, and could care less."

After all, sometimes a little white lie for the benefit of everyone wasn't that terrible. Was it?

The next morning, Tessa sat in a bleak room at the Riverside police station scrutinizing mug shots. She closed the third book and pushed the heavy volume across the table to the redheaded police officer who had popped in to check on her progress. "Still no luck."

"Okay. I'll get more books and bring you some coffee."

As the officer left, she rested her tender head in her hand. She doubted Gabe's picture would show up in any mug books. In spite of the robbery and kidnapping, his protective, considerate behavior wasn't consistent with a criminal's. Who knew? In any case, she wasn't about to let him hold her against her will, especially without an explanation.

The door opened and a huge, dark-suited man the size of a soda machine slipped inside. He flashed a gold badge. "Gregson, FBI." He slid his hulking form into the seat across from her and bobbed his head in a curt nod. "We're taking over this case."

The man's flat, hooded gaze locked on hers. A chill crawled over her and instant dislike prickled across her scalp.

Gregson pulled a pen and small black notebook from inside his jacket pocket. "Have you given your statement?"

She shook her head. "They're short handed. The flu epidemic that's going around. They asked me to look at mug shots first."

His nearly black eyes narrowed into slits, the reptilian gaze of a snake hypnotizing its prey. "So, you can identify him?"

Her instincts screamed mistrust. An intense desire to protect Gabe from this predator rose within her and she straightened in her chair. "No. He had on a ski mask."

His bushy black brows furrowed. "The entire six hours?"

She stared into those malignant eyes and lied. "Yes."

"Then why are you looking at mug shots?"

"I tried to tell them." She shrugged. "They're keeping me busy until they can get to me, I guess."

"What about his voice? Can you describe it?"

Every nuance of Gabe's warm, silky drawl burned in her memory. "Just a man's voice, nothing special."

"Do you know where he held you? Could you find it again?"

"It was dark. I stumbled onto the highway by sheer luck."

"Did he have the bags with him?" Though Gregson's tone remained level, he leaned forward, betraying his interest.

Goose bumps crawled over her skin. Something was very wrong. "I have no idea."

He steepled his thick fingers and stared at her over them. "You're not being very cooperative."

She managed another casual shrug. "I can't tell you what I don't know."

"A teller went home sick that day and you took over the vault." His eyes glittered as coldly as black ice. "Did you open the shipment before the perpetrator arrived on the scene?"

How did he know that? This had to be about the misplaced payroll checks. But why? And in order to know about the checks, he had to be involved. Her nerves thrummed on a surge of adrenaline. The bags had been sealed before she got them, and afterward, no one had seen the contents except Gabe. But this man was no friend of Gabe's; she knew that as well as her own name. "I didn't have a chance."

His fleshy lips compressed into a cruel line. "Stop the games. Your vault teller confirmed you counted the shipment. What was in the bags?"

He'd obviously done his homework. She swallowed down her rising unease and managed a dry chuckle. "Money, of course."

With surprising speed for a man his size, Gregson surged to his feet. He stalked over and stood behind her chair, silent and unmoving. She could feel his cold-blooded gaze drilling into the back of her head, and she clutched the edge of the table.

"Time for a private discussion." He gripped her arm and jerked her up. A gun barrel stabbed into her ribs. "We're leaving, without a fuss. There's a silencer on this piece, I'll drop you and disappear before anybody knows what happened. One squeak and you're dead, understand?''

Numb with disbelief and fear, she nodded.

The giant yanked her to the doorway, and peered out. She fought to control her breathing. Surely he wouldn't be able to abduct her from the police station! Someone would notice. Especially if she made a *help-me* face.

''Don't even think about trying to attract attention,'' he said as if he'd read her mind. ''I have a buddy who works here. He tipped me off to your presence, and he'll make sure nobody sees us.''

So much for someone noticing and coming to her rescue. Time to switch to Plan B. Problem was, what *was* Plan B? Her palms grew damp and her heart raced as Gregson hustled her down the deserted corridor and out the back. She needed a plan!

Outside, a motorcycle cop lounged on his bike with a paper cup of coffee, his white helmet and sunglasses reflecting the bright sun. Gregson muttered an obscenity. ''The coast was supposed to be clear.'' He rammed the gun tighter into her ribs, and a sharp ache pierced her side. ''Smile and walk,'' he growled into her ear. ''If you involve the cop, I'll kill him.''

With a frozen grimace pasted on her face, she managed to stay upright and totter what felt like miles to a black van. Gregson opened the passenger door, and the dark interior loomed in front of her. *Think!* Maybe she could convince him to let her drive. A low-speed crash might allow her to escape.

''Sir,'' the cop called. ''Your taillight is broken.''

Tessa's heart gave a wild leap. She'd know that silky voice anywhere! Then her throat constricted. Gregson had said he wouldn't hesitate to kill, and she believed him.

Gregson jerked to a stop. ''Not a word,'' he threatened. He slid the gun into his jacket pocket, keeping his hand on it as they turned around.

Gabe sauntered toward them. Dressed in the tight navy uniform, tall black boots, helmet and sunglasses, his lean, muscular body emanated a barely leashed power. Danger hummed under his graceful movements and careless smile. She slanted a glance at Gregson, but he didn't seem to notice anything amiss. Then again, the behemoth holding her captive had a loaded gun in his hand and Gabe's pistol was securely strapped to his side.

"Probably vandals." Gabe gestured. "Better take a look."

She had to tell him about the gun!

"Yeah." Gregson reluctantly lumbered toward the rear of the van.

Tessa opened her mouth to speak.

Gabe lowered his sunglasses a fraction and his eyes flashed a warning before he pushed the glasses back.

She snapped her mouth shut.

As Gregson rounded the back bumper, Gabe's arm shot out. With a bone-crunching thud, his fist smashed into the hulk's nose. Before the other man could react, Gabe grabbed him by the shoulder, spun him around and slammed his head into the van. Gregson crumpled to the asphalt like a deflated beach ball.

Her rescuer flashed a sardonic grin before he grabbed her arm and hustled her toward the motorcycle. "We've got to stop meeting like this, Houdini." They reached the bike and he swung a long, muscled leg over the seat. "Hike up that skirt and hop aboard."

As she bunched the winter-white skirt of her suit up her thighs, Gabe slid the sunglasses down his nose and his verdant gaze grew warm and smoky. "I ought to arrest you." He shook his head. "It's definitely a crime to hide those legs under a granny skirt, sweetheart."

Her stomach flip-flopped at the expression in his eyes. *Hunger?* No, impossible. He must be joking again. She climbed on behind him and flung her arms around his waist. The machine roared to life between her legs. The roar grew deafening and the bike sped out of the parking lot. "Are you a cop or a criminal?" she shouted over the throaty growl of the engine.

His broad back shook with laughter. "Well, honey," he tossed over his shoulder. "I guess that depends on who you ask."

Chapter 4

Tessa clung to Gabe as the scenery flew by in a blur. For the second time in three days, she'd been stolen away by this green-eyed pirate.

She hugged his waist, her face pressed against him. Heat from his broad back radiated through the dark blue uniform and warmed her breasts, making them tingle. The bike tipped to the left and her locked hands convulsed.

He shifted. "Leave me a little breathing room, would you?"

"Sorry," she mumbled, loosening her stranglehold a fraction. His hips were wedged closely between her spread legs, his hard thighs pressed against hers. Belated awareness of their intimate position dawned and embarrassment washed over her.

He squeezed her clenched fists reassuringly. "Trust me, honey. I'm not going to let you fall."

Twenty wild, hair-raising minutes later, Gabe leaned to the right, and the bike shot down the airport exit. He pulled up to a helipad and killed the engine. The motor spat out a metallic ping. He jumped off, offering his hand. "Watch the hot muffler."

"What are you up to now?" she accused.

He grinned, deepening the cleft in his chin. "We're going for a helicopter ride."

She gripped the motorcycle seat. "I'm not going anywhere."

Gabe crossed his arms over his chest. His tanned biceps bunched under the short sleeves of the navy-blue uniform. "You are boarding this chopper. Either on your own, or with help."

"Try it." Her gaze swept over his square, set jaw and glittering eyes. "I'm not getting aboard without a darned good reason. I'm through being grabbed by strange men and ordered around—you included."

His grin disappeared. "I tried to warn you."

She flipped her tangled curls over her shoulder. "You robbed my bank and kidnapped me, and I'm supposed to take your word for it? How did you know where I was and that I was in trouble, by the way?"

"Mr. No-Neck will wake up and come looking for us soon. You want to hang around and wait?" She regarded him silently, and he sighed. "Your life is in danger. You'll get an explanation *after* you plant your cute little six in the chopper. No time to waste."

She studied the self-assured man in front of her. Strangely, her instincts assured her she *could* trust him. Hopefully, they were right. He hadn't hurt her before, and had just rescued her from what promised to be an ugly fate. She sure as certain didn't want another encounter with the Incredible Hulk. Especially since he'd be waking up with the mother of all headaches. "I'm warning you, you better have an airtight story, or I'll shove you out in midair."

Gabe's grin bounced back. "In that case, I hope you have a pilot's license." He opened the door with a sweeping gesture and a bow. "All aboard."

She settled into the padded ivory seat. He leaned across to fasten her seat belt, and his fresh, outdoorsy scent teased her senses. His face a mere breath away, he placed a pair of miked headphones over her ears. He gently touched her forehead, and his eyes narrowed with concern. "What happened?"

She gazed into the lush, rain-forest depths of his eyes, inches from hers. Her heart stuttered, and her palms grew damp. Probably a delayed reaction to the close call with Gregson. She gulped. "I bumped my head on a tree."

He frowned. "It looks serious."

"It's not. Mild concussion."

Gabe climbed in and fastened his seat belt and headphones. He flipped several overhead switches. The rotors whirled, vibrating the cockpit.

As the ground fell away beneath her, Tessa braced herself. But instead of a stomach-lurching ascent, the machine gently floated upward. Was there anything this man couldn't do? "I expected this to be scary, but it's fun."

His white, wicked grin flashed. "Flying is the second-best out-of-control feeling there is."

Her toes curled in her shoes. She looked away from those knowing eyes, focusing on the endless expanse of blue sky.

"Trust your pilot, honey, his knowledge and experience." His husky, mellow voice floated into her ears. "Trust him to send you soaring as high as you can go and then float you safely back down. Relax and let yourself enjoy the ride."

Her insides melted at the intimate promise in his tone. Flying had never sounded so tempting. Warm, quivery sensations she'd never felt before shimmered through her. She shifted uneasily. "About that explanation?"

Gabe glanced over at Tessa's flushed face, and his groin tightened. What the hell was he doing? He'd better keep his mind on the job and his hands off the woman. Life on the edge was one thing, but playing with the safety off got a guy shot in the heart. He'd already had his heart blown to pieces. He wasn't about to trust another female with it. "I'm a federal agent."

"Oh, please. That's the oldest line in the book. Next you'll spout a British accent and claim your name is Bond, Gabe Bond."

He threw back his head, roaring with laughter. Still laughing, he handed her a leather wallet from his shirt pocket. "License to kill, sweetheart."

She traced her graceful fingertips across the smooth surface. He pictured those fingertips trailing over his skin, and a rush of desire scorched his blood. He jerked in a breath.

"The Incredible Hulk had ID, too, FBI, in fact."

Jaw tight, he shifted his gaze out the windshield. "Did he hurt you?"

"I thought I was going to die." Out of the corner of his eye, he saw her touch her ribs in a subconscious gesture.

Gabe's knuckles whitened on the stick. If the big lug had put his hands on her, he would pay. "You saw a badge and documentation?"

"He flashed his shield so fast, I couldn't see much. He said his name was Agent Gregson."

"What did you tell him?"

"Nothing."

Not for the first time since he'd met her, admiration surged through him. The goon had had her inside for thirty minutes. Though Tessa was as soft and sweet as a woman could be on the outside, she had inner fortitude of tungsten steel. "Nothing?"

"I didn't trust him, he had rattlesnake eyes. Reptilian." She shivered. "He didn't care about the money. He knew about the checks and wanted to find out if I did. The only way he could have that information is if he was involved, because the bags were sealed. I doubt he was really FBI."

His kitten was one smart cookie. But then he had already glimpsed the sharp intellect behind those big golden eyes. "You've got good instincts, Houdini. Check out my ID."

Tessa opened the wallet. "Well, this is interesting. No wonder you use your middle name. I'm sorry, I know it's not polite, but you, of all people, to be named—" she broke off in a gale of husky giggles.

"Valentine," he finished, enjoying her laughter. "Valentine Gabriel Colton, FBI Special Agent, at your service."

"Okay, you have ID. Like I said before, so did Gregson. How do I know it's the genuine article?"

"Hey, if I made something up, I sure wouldn't conjure up *that* name."

"Maybe so, but when we get where we're going, I want to call the local FBI office for confirmation."

"I'm not affiliated with the locals, I'm working out of D.C.

on a special interagency assignment. At the moment, I answer to one guy, work alone and go where I'm needed, doing what's necessary. Even if that means coloring outside the lines.''

''The hired gun, cleaning up Dodge City all by himself?''

''And when the job is over, I ride off into the sunset. Alone.'' He was warning her, but also reminding himself. Keep everything on the surface, keep it superficial. Keep it safe.

''How does one get a job like that? Did you go to super-secret spy college?''

''I was a frogman for ten years.''

''A what?''

''Sorry, Navy SEAL.''

''That explains the affinity for water.''

''My love affair with the ocean began long before that. I grew up in San Diego, started surfing when I was only seven.''

''*Seven?*'' A shudder wracked her. ''Then why did you leave the SEALs? You're landlocked now, I take it.''

He considered her question. ''It stopped being fun.'' Blurting out the honest reply startled him. He was always careful not to reveal his true feelings.

''So you quit.'' Her brows arched. ''What happened?''

Guilt wrenched inside him. *You don't want to know.* That's what he got for following his crazy impulse to open up to her.

Thrown off balance by his out-of-the-blue lapse of control, which seemed to happen too often around her, he focused on the business at hand. ''As you've realized, this...situation concerns the checks. But it's complicated. Gregson may or may not be genuine FBI. Too much information has leaked out. Cops are involved and we're not sure how high the betrayal goes. That's why I had to pull the bank job. I couldn't just waltz in and ask to see the checks. I'd have blown my cover. The robbery got me the checks without arousing suspicions. From the local cops on up, nobody can know I'm working for the good guys. Two of our agents are already dead. We can't trust anybody. Including our own.''

''But you trust me?''

Gabe had discovered the hard way he couldn't trust anyone. He'd learned the lesson early, and learned it well. He survived by holding people at arm's length, substituting adventure and excitement for relationships. A clever quip and a ready smile kept deeper emotions where they belonged. Buried.

Every day was a party. But it was a party for one.

He'd run a thorough background check on Tessa and discovered nothing incriminating. Defying logic, his gun-shy instincts urged him to trust her all the way. If he couldn't get her out of this mess, he might have to. A suffocating fist gripped his lungs. He might be forced to include her—to a minimum—on a professional level, but he'd make damn sure it didn't get personal.

"Obviously if they're after you, you're not in on it. And you saw the checks, which puts you in jeopardy." Quashing his inner turmoil, he grinned at her. "I need your cooperation, and I can't be afraid to eat or drink when you're around. Very clever, by the way. I couldn't see straight for twelve hours. Which made surveilling you since you left the hospital a little difficult. Luckily, I managed, or Gregson's abduction attempt would have succeeded."

Her cheeks flushed. "I'm sorry. I felt badly about drugging you, but it seemed like a good idea at the time. I wanted to go home. But even after I escaped, nobody would let me."

He frowned. "Why not?"

"The doctor made me stay in the hospital overnight and then I had to wait for Mel to get me some new clothes."

"What happened to your clothes?"

"They were ruined and someone threw them away." Her voice dropped to a murmur. "Then the doctor wanted to do an exam and lab tests. He wouldn't believe you didn't rape me."

Nausea slammed into him at the thought of anyone violating her that way. His jaw felt too tight to get the words out. "I would *never* force myself on a woman."

"I know," she replied softly. "I know you wouldn't."

He squeezed the stick to keep from ramming his fist into the door. She'd been hurt and humiliated because of his actions. Her head injury was also on his account. In spite of his devil-may-care attitude, he went out of his way to make sure no innocent bystanders took any flak. This time he'd failed. And Tessa had suffered the consequences. It ate at him like acid. "I'm sorry you had to go through that because of me."

"Everybody kept patting me until I wanted to scream. I told them you were *nice,* and they stuck an IV in my arm," she huffed. "Mel was the only one who believed me."

His stomach rolled again, for an entirely different reason. He didn't want to analyze why he suddenly felt proprietary and protective toward this woman, when he'd never before felt that way about anyone. *Step back, Colton.* "Is Mel your boyfriend?"

"My best friend since first grade, we're like sisters."

"Funny name for a girl."

"Her name is Melody. Mel's a nickname. You should talk...Valentine." A grin sneaked out before remorse erased it. "I'm sorry, teasing you is mean."

An answering smile curled Gabe's mouth. "You're not the first. How do you think I learned to fight? I was battle-hardened long before Navy martial arts training, believe me. Anybody who called me Valentine got clobbered."

"Why did your parents choose something so unusual? Is Valentine a family name?"

Gabe's face shut down, his eyes darkening, his expression shifting into neutral. "I have no idea."

Tessa frowned. Obviously, she'd hit a nerve. Too late, she remembered he'd mentioned a foster mom. "I'm sorry, I didn't mean—"

"Look, there's our destination ahead."

Her gaze followed his pointing finger out the windshield. She gulped. "That microscopic patch of grass between the trees?"

His grin reappeared, banishing his wariness. She studied his deliberately casual profile. This complex man wasn't what he appeared, in more ways than one. The grin that sprang so easily to his lips covered a shadow inside. Compassion flooded her. No stranger to pain herself, she recognized the deep hurt he so determinedly held at bay. In spite of herself, she was drawn to him, to the impudent courage that shielded his heart.

"No problem. Your pilot knows how to hit the sweet spot every time."

True to his word, the helicopter floated gracefully between

the colorful oaks and maples, and then kissed the ground with a slight bump. "Cape Hope. I believe you'll recognize the cabin."

He placed his hand on the small of her back as they walked through the forest. Heat radiated from his hand, through her. Though the path wasn't steep, her breathing accelerated. Baffled, she gulped in the cool, autumn air.

Gabe unlocked the door, and they entered the familiar log cabin. He grasped her upper arms and pulled her toward him. "I want your word you won't run off. These scum are dead serious, and Gregson got too damn close."

"I realize that now. I won't, I promise."

"If I hadn't made it there in time—" He shuddered, swallowed hard. His darkened emerald gaze ensnared hers. As if he couldn't help himself, he fingered a curl that had fallen over her shoulder. "You have hair like a Caribbean sunset. Copper and red and gold. Bewitching. Beautiful."

Nobody had ever called her beautiful. Warmth curled through her, settling around her heart. "I, um, thank you," she whispered.

His callused fingertips traced the shell of her ear, and delicious sensations rained down her spine. His gaze caressed her face, lingered on her mouth, then slipped upward to hold her captive again. "So tempting." He lowered his head, moving closer. "You smell so sweet, Tessie. Makes a man want to eat you up," he murmured, his breath feathering across her temple.

Her heart shimmered. The wonderful things he was saying, the enraptured expression on his face filled her with wonder, held her spellbound.

His fingers slid into her hair, urging her nearer. Resisting didn't occur to her. His warm lips touched hers, and the bright, sizzling jolt of pleasure made her gasp, startled her pulse into a gallop. Shocked by her intense response, she shoved at his chest.

He instantly released her.

She jumped away, pressed quivering fingers to her lips. "Wh-what do you think you're doing?"

A "hell-if-I-know" stunned expression glazed his eyes for several long, trembling heartbeats. Then he shook his head, and the familiar naughty twinkle appeared. "If you don't know, I must not have been doing it right." His shaky chuckle vibrated through her. "That was a kiss."

It certainly was. A startling, amazing, set-me-on-fire kiss. She'd enjoyed the brief pressure of his mouth on hers far too much. "I am *not* that kind of a woman."

He wiggled his eyebrows at her. "Maybe you are and just don't know it."

Fury burned away the sweet ache inside her. Because maybe, just maybe, he was right. And that would make her the kind of woman she'd vowed not to become. "You...oh! You're a...a...an oversexed gorilla!"

His grin flashed. "I thought you said I was *nice*."

"I've changed my opinion." She stormed into the kitchen. Trembling, she stood in front of the sink, her hands gripping the cold edge of the tile counter. What was the matter with her? She'd basked in his kiss with the greedy thirst of a desert wanderer at an oasis.

Gabe poked his head in the doorway. "Is it safe to come in?"

She whirled. "What do you want?"

He held up both hands. "I shouldn't have done that."

"I happen to be engaged."

"Yes, you are." His impudent grin flashed. "Engaging."

"Get serious. If you can. We've got to plan what to do."

"I'm sorry. You're right. Truce?"

"Well...I suppose. But keep your distance."

"Yes, ma'am. I'm going to grab a shower and change out of this monkey suit. You *will* be here when I get back..." His eyes danced with mischief. "And not traipsing around in the woods in purple skivvies singing 'You Ain't Nothin' But a Hound Dog'?"

She shot him a glare. "I never break a promise. I want to talk to your superior. Then I need to call Mel, or she'll have every cop in the state searching for me. You wouldn't happen to have a phone in your shoe?"

"You watch too many movies, Houdini." He unsnapped his pocket and produced a cell phone. "It's a secure unit, can't be traced." He gave her his boss's name and phone number, and the code name *Falcon Three* so his boss would release the information to her. "When you talk to your friend Mel, make something up. Don't tell her anything about me."

"Of course not. I'm not an imbecile."

"No you're not. You're a very sharp lady, and I'm glad you're on my side." He saluted, turned and sauntered out.

Tessa didn't trust the information he'd provided, after all he could have paid someone to lie for him. She called directory assistance in Washington, D.C. They recited the same number Gabe had given her. Hurdle one conquered. Excitement jittered through her. Feeling disconcertingly like a Bond babe, she dialed, waited through three transfers, and then gave the code name to the gravelly voiced baritone who identified himself as Gabe's superior. At her request, the man supplied a dead-on description of Valentine Gabriel Colton down to the cleft in his chin, and verified that he was indeed a federal agent. Hurdle two. Relief, mixed with an emotion that felt oddly like happiness careened through her. Gabe was who he said he was. Not a criminal. FBI.

After a second call to inform Mel that she'd been delayed at the police station, Tessa hung up and set the phone on the counter. Leaning on her elbows, she stared out the window at the forest, blazing with resplendent fall foliage. What was the strange reaction that overpowered her whenever Gabe was near? Her stomach jittered in horror. Maybe her mother's genes would triumph after all. Tessa wanted stability and a family, but perhaps she was fated to follow her hormones through man after man, just like Vivienne.

She slammed her palms on the counter. No way! Her mother's life was a nightmare example of that tortured path. Tessa refused to follow in Vivienne's destructive footsteps. Her shoulders stiff with resolve, she focused on making coffee and sandwiches. When they were ready, she carried a tray to the small table in the living room. Goose bumps prickled up her arms and she rubbed her hands together. The cabin hadn't been in use, and the room was cold. Kneeling in front of the fireplace, she started a fire.

A pair of long, tanned bare feet appeared in her line of vision. "I was gonna do that."

She swallowed hard. Good heavens, even the sight of the man's feet tweaked her libido. She said the first thing that popped into her mind. "You don't have frog's feet."

His husky laugh bubbled through her veins like expensive champagne, filling her with a warm, sparkling glow. "I didn't mean literally."

"Of course not." She leapt up, backing toward the chair. "I made sandwiches and coffee."

Gabe's brows tilted. "Should I have you taste-test them?"

"I *said* I was sorry about that."

"So you did." One corner of his mouth quirked up. "But remember, honey, payback is hell." He grabbed a sandwich and a mug of coffee and collapsed on the plaid sofa.

She dropped into a chair beside the fire. The damp sheen of Gabe's hair reflected the dancing flames. He'd changed into snug, faded jeans and a black cotton sweater. Trying to ignore the disturbing zings ricocheting along her nerve endings, she doggedly chewed her sandwich. It tasted like sawdust.

"So—"

She jerked, nearly spilling her coffee.

He shook his head. "You've gotta get a handle on that hair-trigger reflex. Do I still make you nervous?"

Not in the way he meant. "I was thinking, and you startled me, that's all. How long will we be here?"

"I don't know. Did you leave the phone in the kitchen?" She nodded, and he rose. "Be right back."

His low voice murmured from the kitchen. In minutes he returned. For once, his face wore a somber expression, without a hint of levity. Dread hung heavily between them.

Sighing, he jammed his fingers through his hair. "There's no sugar-coated way to say this. Gregson may be dead."

Bile swelled in her throat. "Y-you killed him?"

"No." He dropped onto the sofa and stared down at the green braided rug. "Whoever he works for doesn't have a real subtle job performance evaluation. You escaped, and I saw his face, but he didn't see mine because of the helmet and sunglasses.

With his cover blown, he was useless. The local cops found a John Doe in the river, a bullet in the back of his skull. My boss is running his prints. We'll know soon if his real name was Gregson, and if he was genuine FBI." Gabe's intent gaze fastened on her.

The hairs on the back of her neck prickled.

"You should know what we're dealing with." He left, quickly returned and handed her two checks. "You saw these before. What did you think?"

Puzzled, she turned them over. "Sav-Mart payroll checks."

"But one's real and one's counterfeit. Problem is, we can't tell them apart because stolen checks were used as templates to make perfect phonies. Counterfeit checks from big companies are showing up all over the Northwest. The Treasury Department has been tracking them for nearly two years, but every time they think they're making progress, they run into a dead end. The bad guys are always somehow one step ahead."

Tessa frowned. "That's why you suspect someone in law enforcement might be involved?"

"Yeah, plus the fact that our previous agents on the inside were murdered. So I came in deep undercover. Only my boss knows I'm working this, and he's top-level security. A few days ago, we arrested a check passer who gave us some information, but wanted immunity before he'd tell all. While we were working out the details, the suspect 'hung himself' in his cell. We knew the checks were in the cash delivery to your branch. The robbery got them into my hands without tipping off the crooks or burning my cover. The checks confirmed the one common thread we've found."

Every trace of the carefree rogue had disappeared. All business, his cool, serious gaze bored into hers. Tessa stared at a very different Gabe—the dangerous man his enemies faced. Icy fingers crawled up her spine.

"The real checks are being stolen from Oregon Pacific Bank. So far, the crooks have cleared over eight million dollars."

"Eight *million?*"

"A hell of a motive for murder." He grimaced. "And one of your co-workers is up to their neck in blood."

Chapter 5

"What?" Tessa gasped.

"The mole has to have high security clearance. The setup is sophisticated, ingenious, and impossible to trace. That is, until you stumbled across the evidence. If you'd called security—" Gabe's dark brows slammed together, and he clenched his jaw. "You'd be bunking beside Gregson in the morgue."

Her stomach churned. "That's why you kidnapped me."

"When I realized you'd seen the checks, I couldn't risk leaving you behind. I'd hoped to let you go none the wiser. No chance of that anymore."

"So now what?"

"I have to find out who's running the operation, *and* protect you." He tapped his pursed lips with a long finger.

Tessa stared at his sculpted mouth, the memory of his recent kiss burning through her brain. She gulped a swig of hot coffee.

"I can't make you disappear without tipping off the bad guys. I can't trust anyone else with your safety. And your inside connections at Oregon Pacific Bank will come in very handy." He flashed a wickedly sexy smile. "Yeah. Looks like we're gonna be roomies."

The room tilted as every molecule in her body hummed in response to his gorgeous smile. She straightened. She would *not* let out-of-control hormones jeopardize her future. "Absolutely not."

He sobered. "These guys will kill you with less thought than taking out the garbage. Gregson's isn't the first suspicious body to be found downriver with a new view out the back of his head. I doubt they'll risk attracting attention with a public hit, but if they catch you alone, all bets are off."

She scowled. "But my wedding arrangements."

"If they succeed, you won't have to worry about that." He scowled. "Or anything else."

"I refuse to let those criminals ruin my wedding." She crossed her arms over her chest. She was so close to achieving her dream. Nothing short of a nuclear war would stop her now. "You'll have to compromise."

"I could tie you up and lock you in a safe house, you know." His sober gaze didn't look like he was joking.

"You wouldn't dare." *Would he?*

"Don't kid yourself. If I could guarantee your safety, you'd already be there. Okay, I'll figure out the wedding stuff." He shuddered. "But stick close and do what I say, when I say."

She squared her shoulders. "To a point," she warned darkly. "How am I supposed to explain you to my friends and my fiancé?" How would Dale react to the news that she was living with another man? During their two-year relationship, she'd never seen him ruffled. A purely female part of her hoped he'd respond with at least a small show of jealousy. Men in love were supposed to feel proprietary, weren't they?

"Later." He glanced at the complicated gauges on his watch. "First we take the chopper back to the city."

During the trip, he grilled her about the checks and the incident with Gregson. But she thoroughly enjoyed the ride, and his company.

When they landed at the Riverside airport, he turned to her with a knowing smile. "Nice, huh? The first time, fear of the unknown takes away from some of the fun. The second ride is usually much better." He arched a dark brow. "It doesn't take long to get addicted to flying."

She willed away the annoyingly delicious shimmer caused by his double entendre. "Are we taking the bike?"

"No. I've got a Viper here at the airport."

"What happened to the Jaguar?"

"Using different vehicles keeps them guessing. I've also changed plates on the 'Vette, so the car can't be traced to the robbery. Here's the plan. Your place, fifteen minutes to pack, then we're bugging out to my house."

"I can't pack in fifteen minutes!" And she needed a lot more time to get used to the idea of living with Gabe.

"You'd better, because ready or not, I'm hauling your cute little six out of there."

"You said that before. What's a six, or do I want to know?" He chuckled. "Military slang. Tail, rear end—"

She held up a hand. "I get the point."

They climbed into a white Viper with tinted windows and Gabe whisked them to her apartment with his usual Mach speed.

She reached for the handle, but he stopped her. "I check it out first." He thrust out his hand. "Keys?"

She pulled them from her purse and slapped them into his palm. She might owe him her life, but his macho routine set her teeth on edge.

Gabe opened his door. "If anything happens, hit the horn." He sauntered around the front bumper with confident grace. In the blink of an eye, he disappeared into the bushes.

Minutes passed. Tessa fidgeted. Should he be taking so long? Had something happened? Maybe she should go find him. She gripped the door handle.

Before she could open the door, Gabe reappeared and swung it wide. "Are you the only tenant in this building?"

"Yes. There's a small music store on the ground floor but it closes at four. I live in the loft above."

He shifted into "doing business mode." Body taut, his alert gaze scanned the area. With his right hand tucked under his black leather jacket, he escorted her into the elevator. There was no amusement in him now, only deadly purpose. She shivered. Under his carefree exterior lurked a competent, dangerous cop.

The elevator doors slid open. A massive gun appeared in his hand. He preceded her into the one-room loft. "Uh, Tessa? I hate to tell you this, but unless you're a really messy house-keeper, somebody tossed your place."

Her possessions lay strewn about the apartment, everything viciously rifled, and then discarded like worthless trash. Tessa's knees wobbled and she clutched the kitchen counter for support.

"Easy, sweetheart." Gabe grasped her arm to steady her, his eyes dark with concern. "It's okay."

"Those criminals were in my home. They pawed through my things—"

"They're long gone." He squeezed her arm reassuringly. "I'll make a call and have this cleaned up in two hours."

"But—"

Something thudded against the window.

Before she could turn, his foot swept Tessa's legs out from under her. His arms wrapped around her waist and took her down. Holding her on top of him, he hit the floor. In a split second, he rolled her beneath him, the back of her head cradled in his palm. "Don't move," he whispered.

Heart hammering, she lay under his taut body. His clean, male scent assailed her senses. She fought to gasp in air, but her breathlessness had nothing to do with his weight on top of her and everything to do with his nearness.

His gun edged past her cheek. He pressed her face into his shoulder. "Shh. Don't move."

A chorus of plaintive meows shattered the tense silence.

Relieved laughter burst out of her. "Andrew, Lloyd and Webber."

He glanced at her, disbelief etched on his features. "Andrew, Lloyd and Webber?"

"The music store owner's cats." She grinned. "When she leaves, they climb the fire escape and beg for snacks."

"Cats." Gabe breathed out a sigh. His body relaxed.

Intimately joined from shoulder to hip, Tessa stared up at him. The golden afternoon light gilded the planes of his face, emphasizing the cleft in his chin. Her gaze roamed over his sculpted mouth. Remembering his brief, exciting kiss, she licked her suddenly dry lips.

He groaned. She jerked her gaze up and saw his smoky green stare fastened on her mouth.

"Relax, sweetheart," he urged, his voice a hot, husky whisper as he touched his lips to hers. His fingers lightly traced her cheekbones, caressed the curves of her ears. No one had ever touched her with such gentleness, such aching tenderness. Her body melted like warm honey.

His moist breath feathered over her temples, and her lashes floated down in languid surrender. She was rewarded by a soft kiss on each eyelid. His lips journeyed along her jawline, nibbled behind her ears and down her neck, heating her body, heating her blood. She basked in the delicious sensation. Her mouth parted in a sigh.

Gabe teased her lower lip with his velvet tongue. He bit gently, then suckled the sensitized flesh, wringing a moan from her. His mouth tempted, enticed, seduced—and she wanted more. She opened to him and his tongue glided inside, stroking slow and gentle against hers, inviting her response. Her stomach fluttered at the minty taste of him, cool, and yet at the same time, unbearably hot. Fire scorched her nerve endings, every inch of her alive and quivering. More alive than she'd ever been.

Tentatively, she returned his kiss, her tongue meeting his in a seductive duet. His breathing quickened, and he explored her mouth with a sensual, thorough expertise that shattered her control.

She wanted, needed, like she'd never needed before. She couldn't get enough. Her arms slid around his neck, urging him closer. She moaned into his mouth, and his low answering murmur vibrated through her.

Reality slammed into her with a jarring crash. Her heart stopped, then kicked into painful, irregular thrusts. She was kissing a man she barely knew—while engaged to another! She tore her mouth from his and shoved at his chest. "Get off me!"

He frowned in confusion. "Tessie? What's wrong?"

Dazed, and livid with herself, she lashed out with the only

weapon she had. "Maybe everyone was right to question me about you after all."

He froze, his eyes darkening. "I didn't force you. You wanted that as much as I did."

"I most certainly did not," she lied. If she admitted it, that would make her like Vivienne, and she would *not* go there.

He was trembling. Had she done that to him? "Baby, your brain might be clinging to denial, but your body sure as hell knows what it wants." He jumped up and stalked to the other side of the room. "Get packed."

She clambered to her feet. "I'm not going anywhere with you."

He prowled toward her, all lean muscles and dangerous grace. "This is not an optional exercise. Pack, or I'm hauling you out right now without whatever you need."

"I won't—" she started, then thought better of pushing him. He looked furious enough to follow through, and she had no doubt who would win. Provoking a confrontation was foolish. Pivoting, she marched to the closet and grabbed a new suitcase, purchased for her honeymoon. She threw it on the bed, and began flinging in clothing at random.

An echoing note from her baby grand piano made her jerk her head up. He was seated at the oak bench. "What do you play?"

"Music," she snapped.

"Don't be mad." Looking as lost and bewildered as she felt, he gave her a shaky smile. "I couldn't have stopped myself from kissing you right then if my life had depended on it." He cleared his throat and his gaze slid away. "I was out of line. I apologize."

Confusion swirled through her; her muddled feelings tangled in a knot. She shoved a taupe sweater on top of the growing pile. "I'm promised to another man. A good man. You can't just kiss me whenever you get the urge. I need to be able to trust you."

"You can trust me, Tessa." He returned her gaze, his jade eyes dark with suppressed emotion. He held up a two-fingered salute. "I won't kiss you again. Scout's honor."

"You were a Boy Scout?"

His gaze sidled away again. "Not exactly."

He looked so much like a little boy with his hand caught in the cookie jar, she couldn't help herself. She chuckled. "You are something else, Bond, Gabe Bond."

"I believe you used the word nice?" He wiggled his brows at her.

"I *said* oversexed gorilla." Shoving aside the sickness in her soul at the mess the criminals had made of her apartment, and the urgent desire to stay and set things right, she strode to the bathroom to pack her cosmetics. Her safety was more important.

"So, what do you play?" he called, plinking on the keys.

"Classical, mostly." She dropped makeup into a zippered bag. "Dale and I do violin and piano duets in performances Mother Winters organizes. Lucille has a wide circle of wealthy acquaintances and we raise money for children's charities."

"You like stuffy classical junk?"

"I don't dislike it, and classical is what that crowd wants to hear." She returned to the main room.

"What sends you soaring? What do you play when you can let go and pound out what you want?" He hit a discordant chord, making her wince. "You ever cut loose, Tessie? Go wild?"

She avoided the uncomfortable question. Tessa Beaumont didn't do wild. "I need to water my plants before we leave."

As Gabe rose from the piano bench, the phone rang. His eyes sparked a warning. "Let the machine pick up."

She huffed out a sigh, but obeyed.

"My dear, are you there?" Lucille's refined voice, tight with panic, broke into the room. "It's another disaster—"

She snatched up the receiver. "Mother Winters, what's wrong? Has something happened to Dale?"

"You *are* home, thank goodness! It's Frederick. He absconded with the money from his business and fled the country. The deposits were paid, but the balances are gone. We'll never book another wedding coordinator at this date!" Lucille's voice rose. "What are we going to do? The wedding is ruined!"

Oh, no, *another* glitch. A big one. Maybe Mel was right and fate had again intervened to stop her. Tessa banished the horrifying thought and hurried to soothe her future mother-in-law. "We'll confirm the details and repay the balances in person. Let's get together with Mel. Between us, we can fix it."

"Excellent idea." Lucille calmed. "We can meet at the club, at six."

Ignoring Gabe's frown, Tessa glanced at her watch. "Six?"

Gabe shook his head in an adamant no.

"Fine, I'll see you then." After a quick goodbye, Tessa hung up.

He stalked over to her. "What do you think you're doing?"

"Our wedding coordinator flew the coop. It's an emergency."

"Great. Just what I need." His forehead creased in a pained expression. "You mentioned watering your plants." He waved a hand. "I've been in jungles with less foliage. I'll help, or this could take all day."

Thank heavens whoever had searched her apartment hadn't touched her precious plants. "I love plants. I like nurturing them, watching them thrive under my care." Her cheeks heated. "Probably more than you wanted to know." She gave him instructions on watering the kitchen plants and hustled to the bathroom to tend her ferns.

"Uh-oh," he called.

"What now?" She rushed to the kitchen.

He leaned over the counter, peering into a brass pot. Wearing a puzzled frown, he pointed to a shriveled pile of leaves. "I touched it, and the thing croaked."

Tessa chuckled. "That's a Sensitivity Plant, genus *Mimosa pudica*. When touched, the plant wilts. In about thirty minutes, it will look good as new."

"If you say so." He shook his head. "Time to go."

Downstairs, Gabe stowed her bags in the back while she climbed into the front. He settled into the driver's seat. "Want to listen to a CD?"

"Sure." The car roared away from the curb. She sifted through his collection of classic rock and Latin music, choosing a Latin CD. A rhythmic beat filled the car. "I've never listened to Latin artists. The music has a...I can't quite put my finger on the feeling. I like it, though."

"Sensuality?" His smoldering green eyes perfectly illustrated the concept. *Sensuality indeed.*

Her pulse skittered, and she looked away. "It might help if I understood the words."

"Sometimes you don't need words." Mingled with the throbbing drumbeat, his dark, smooth drawl shivered over her, and heat twisted in her belly. She started to tremble.

"But I guess understanding the lyrics *would* help."

"Do you?" she managed to croak, turning back to him.

"Sí señorita," he replied, his eyes sparkling. "Foreign languages come in handy in the super-spy business."

"So, you speak Spanish and what else?"

Gabe shrugged.

"Don't be modest Mr. Bond, it doesn't suit you."

He chuckled. "I can get by in French, Arabic, German, Japanese, Italian and a smattering of Soviet and Chinese dialects."

She'd seen the quick intelligence lurking under his playful demeanor, but had still underestimated him. "I'm impressed."

"Don't be. I like to know what I'm ordering in a restaurant when I travel."

He turned onto a quiet residential street. The space between houses increased, until finally he entered a long driveway flanked by stone pillars. Yellow leaves fluttered down from the oak trees lining the driveway as he drove up the winding path that sheltered the house. He stopped the car in front of a gray stone cottage. "Home sweet rented house."

He ushered her inside. Her shoes sank into thick ivory carpet, the creamy color warming the soft white walls hung with verdant forest paintings. A brown leather sofa and chairs piled with light-blue, emerald-green and ivory pillows sat in an inviting semicircle around a huge beige stone fireplace.

An attached small dining area contained a whitewashed pine circular table flanked by four chairs. She caught a glimpse of emerald-green tiles and matching curtains in the kitchen.

Gabe gestured as he led her down the hallway. "Kitchen, deck on the patio, complete with hot tub. Unless that would freak you out?" He looked over his shoulder, brows raised.

"No, bathtubs and hot tubs don't bother me."

"Head, er, bathroom, to your right, hope you don't mind sharing." He pointed at the first door on the left. "Equipment and surveillance room. Stay out of there. My room," he indicated the last door on the right. "In which you're cordially welcome, anytime." The wolfish grin curving his lips sent an annoying sizzle sparking through her again.

Get a grip.

"Guest room." He opened the last door on the left and stood to one side so she could enter before depositing her suitcase on the powder-blue down comforter. "We've got forty minutes, so don't dawdle." Muttering something about his brain cells going AWOL, he departed.

A seascape hanging over the bed caught Tessa's gaze. A cold, anxious shudder wracked her. Deliberately turning her back on the painting, she slid the mirrored closet doors aside to hang her dresses on the empty rod. Arranging her clothes in the whitewashed dresser took ten minutes.

She changed, grabbed her raincoat, and strolled into the living room. Her new roommate turned from the window. His black tailored suit fit his muscular body to perfection. A heathered gray shirt and jade and gray patterned tie emphasized his striking green eyes. With his thick hair tamed back from its usual tousled state, he looked like he'd stepped off the pages of *GQ*. Very unlike the roguish pirate she'd gotten used to. Her throat constricted. "You look—" *Good enough to take a bite out of* "—nice."

"Thank you. You look nice yourself." Gabe let the drapes fall closed and studied the intriguing woman in front of him. She'd clipped her hair back, ruthlessly subduing her lush copper curls. An oversize, drab gray dress hid her spectacular figure. Clunky "sensible" shoes completed the ensemble.

Desire arrowed through his gut, his skin hot and tight. Damn, what was it about her? He'd never had a reaction like this to a woman. Oh, yeah, he was familiar with lust. This was something more.

He'd wanted Tessa at first sight, but the feeling went deeper than lust, and was much more complicated. Her sharp intelligence piqued his interest. Her quick retorts tweaked his sense of humor, and inspired reluctant affection. Her incredible courage and composure in the face of grave danger had won his respect. Complications he didn't need.

He swallowed the uneasiness churning inside him. He sure as hell wasn't used to being attracted to a woman for her mental attributes. In fact, he never stayed long enough to get to know them, or for attachments to form. On either side. Nothing lasted, nothing was forever.

No matter what starry-eyed romantics claimed, nobody would ever love him enough to stick around. He already knew that. So, he left before they could leave him. That way, he did the walking out. That way, nobody got hurt. He ignored the tightness in his chest, the aching desperation, and shrugged.

C'est la vie.

He'd be the first to admit Tessa was not only smart, she was gorgeous. But he'd hung around with boatloads of beautiful babes, and his brain had never gone renegade before. He stayed in control, made conscious choices of like-minded women. No strings. No nooses. Tessa was the type of woman he avoided. She was too sweet, too innocent. Too full of hope. She would want promises. He didn't have any to give.

Damn it, he knew better, yet couldn't control his attraction. This time he couldn't protect himself by walking away. Not with Tessa's life at stake. His stomach cramped with something that strongly resembled fear.

"Gabe? Are you ready to go?"

He fought his way out of the riptide and redirected his thoughts. Keep it light. Playful. Keep it on the surface. Safe. "Yeah. You know, you'd look really hot in an emerald-green dress."

She shook her head. "I don't like to draw attention to myself."

"You've got an incredible body. You should flaunt it."

"That's not funny." She turned away and shrugged into the olive trench coat she carried.

Gabe squelched the smart retort hovering on his lips. What kind of insecurities was this amazing woman hiding? He closed the distance between them in three strides. With a finger under her chin, he raised her face. Her wide, amber eyes glimmered with hurt.

His heart fisted. "I wasn't teasing. You're a beautiful woman. Don't let anybody convince you differently."

"No worries about my ego. I believe in no-nonsense reality." She pulled back and stalked toward the door. "We're going to be late."

Belted into the Viper and speeding toward Riverside Drive, he tried again. "What exactly is your version of reality?"

"Forget it. How about some music?" She slid a Latin CD into the player and turned up the volume.

Somebody had mutilated the lady's self-image. Brutally. He jammed his fingers through his hair. Concentrating on deep, regular breaths, he clenched his jaw and hardened his heart against the empathy throbbing there.

It wasn't his concern.

Not his problem.

None of his business at all.

Gabe's Golden Rule: never get involved. He was a pro at walking away. He did his job and left. If you got attached, you got in trouble. You got hurt. Mortally wounded. He knew where the line was, and never crossed it.

The fact that he wanted to, for Tessa, shook him to the core. Rattled, and more afraid than he would admit, he concentrated on the road.

At five minutes to six, he escorted her into the glitzy burgundy-and-gold interior of the West Riverside Country Club. "When we get to the table, introduce me as your cousin."

"I don't have any cousins."

"I'm your long-lost cousin, in town for the wedding."

"But Mel knows—"

"Just do it. I'll take care of the rest."

"We should have discussed this," she gritted. "Don't blame me if it doesn't work."

The hostess escorted them to a table in the corner. A giant blond man three inches taller than Gabe rose from his chair with fluid grace. The hulk's designer navy suit emphasized his wide athletic shoulders and narrow waist.

This guy was a violinist? He could play linebacker for an NFL team. Gabe's disconcerted gaze swept over the golden hair, blue eyes and even features. But no, contact sports would ruin Mr. Perfect's model good looks.

"Tessa, you look gorgeous," her fiancé rumbled. His eyes lit with pleasure as he brushed a soft kiss on her cheek. "You're obviously feeling better."

An unfamiliar, selfish urge to snatch her out of the other man's arms grabbed Gabe by the throat. His hands balled into fists. What the hell was wrong with him? He took a deep breath, forcing his fingers to relax. *Focus.*

Tessa gestured toward him. "Dale, I'd like you to meet..." she hesitated briefly. "Valentine Colton."

She must be really torqued about the cousin thing. Nobody called him Valentine and lived.

"Val, this is my fiancé, Dale Winters."

Oh, yeah, *Val* was much better. Gabe arched a "thanks a lot, honey," brow at her before accepting the massive paw Dale offered.

She flushed. "My future mother-in-law, Lucille Winters."

He studied the delicate woman in beige silk and pearls. Her gray-blond hair was winched so tight, he was surprised her hawklike blue eyes weren't crossed. He ignored her sharp, disapproving gaze as he shook her hand.

"And my best friend Melody Parrish. I've mentioned her."

Mischievous sapphire eyes sparkled up at him from an elfin face. The petite, curly-haired blonde beamed him an impish smile. "Well, well, where has Tess been hiding *you?*"

"Val is m-my cousin," Tessa stammered.

Melody's eyes narrowed. "You don't have any cousins."

Gabe pulled out Tessa's chair, one-upping Dale by a satisfying fraction of a second. He sat across from her, and poured a strawberry lemonade from the pitcher on the table.

Tessa sucked in a shaky breath. "Long-lost cousin. From my dad's side. We've only met recently."

Melody's brows drew together. "But—"

Lucille's soft-spoken, cultured tones carried across the table.

"Tessa, where have you been all day? I've been frantic to get in touch about this wedding disaster."

"I'm...staying with Ga— Val," Tessa amended hastily.

She was a lousy liar. Gabe could almost see her squirming in her chair. He grinned into his glass.

"My apartment is, ah, bugs. That's it! They're fumigating my apartment and I'm staying with Val."

Lucille grimaced. "That's not a terribly good idea." She nodded at him, "No offense, young man."

"Oh, none taken," Gabe drawled.

Lucille continued. "Tessa, I insist you stay with us."

How would Tessa talk her way out of this one? Gabe swigged a gulp of lemonade.

"There's no problem," Tessa replied blithely. "Val is gay."

He strangled on his lemonade. The icy drink burned down his windpipe and surged through his nose, stinging like acid.

Melody jumped up to pat him on the back. "Wow, I never saw lemonade shoot out of anybody's nose. Must hurt like crazy."

Wheezing, he grabbed a napkin. His eyes streamed tears as he glared at Tessa over the white linen.

Lucille's eyes brightened. "He could be the answer to our problems!"

"How is that?" Tessa asked, wariness coloring her tone.

"Frederick left us high and dry." Lucille offered Gabe a practiced, insincere smile. "And besides, you must be good at that sort of thing."

Tessa scowled. "I don't think..."

"Now, now," Gabe patted her cheek. "It'll be *fabulous.*" Into her ear he whispered, "Remember, honey, paybacks are hell, and now I owe you two."

It was her turn to choke. Out of the corner of his eye, Gabe saw Melody flick a curious glance at Tessa, then himself.

Dale rumbled out his second conversational contribution. "I think it's nice that your cousin wants to join in. Planning a wedding is a lot of work, and with one thing after another happening, we can use all the help we can get."

Gabe winked at him.

A loud, exasperated breath exploded out of Tessa.

Gabe bit the inside of his cheek and swallowed down the snicker desperately trying to escape.

"I need to powder my nose." She bolted for the ladies' room, Melody hot on her heels. Why did women always visit the head in groups? She probably wanted to grill Tessa about her new-found "cousin." Man, he'd love to be a fly on the wall for that conversation.

Before long, the pair returned, a hectic flush still staining Tessa's cheeks. As the wedding talk continued, sweat beaded on Gabe's forehead and dampened his shirt. His neck wasn't even the one in the noose, and he could barely breathe. He surreptitiously loosened his tie. He needed to take his bike out for a spin and blow out this rat-with-his-tail-in-a-trap feeling.

Two torturous hours crawled by. Lucille tried to manipulate the plans, first with finesse, then pressure, progressing to blatant manipulation. Tessa quietly stood her ground, and Gabe's respect for her grew. Dale automatically agreed with his mother when asked. Finally, Tessa called a halt to the ordeal.

As the group parted ways in the parking lot, Gabe waggled his fingers at Dale. "Bye, handsome."

The blond hulk blanched, and stammered a farewell.

"What a huge disappointment for all womankind," Melody murmured to Tessa.

He could hear Tessa grinding her teeth. "You don't know the half of it."

Gabe grinned. Wait until she saw what he had planned for tomorrow.

She would kill him.

Chapter 6

Tessa's co-workers rallied around her at the bank the next morning, offering sympathy over her ordeal. After several pointed glares from Mr. Trask, she finally settled everyone into the pre-opening routine.

Leaving her office door open, she sat behind her desk and stowed her briefcase underneath. Her personal assortment of ferns, potted palms and fichus grouped around the small room offered welcome relief from the austere gold-and-black decor.

She tuned out the office chatter and sipped tea from her musical Elvis mug as she leafed through a stack of memos. The kiosk ATM machine was still jamming up. She sighed. How many trips would the service reps have to make before they fixed the darn thing?

''Ms. Beaumont?'' Edwin Trask's pompous summons made her jerk her gaze up.

Her stocky, mustached boss marched into her office with another man in tow. The guy shuffled behind Trask, his slumped shoulders covered by a baggy olive suit that clashed with his purple shirt and yellow suspenders. A thick layer of goo slicked back hair of indeterminate color, and Coke-bottle glasses with square black frames shrank his eyes to pinpoints. He offered a shy smile, displaying prominent buckteeth. She stifled a groan. Not another Trask nephew!

Trask cleared his throat. "Carla quit without notice. This is your new teller, and he has impeccable references. I trust you'll train him with the usual efficiency."

Her vault teller had quit? Her stomach sank. If the newbie's I.Q. matched his fashion sense, they were all in serious trouble. She pasted a frozen smile on her face. "Of course." Mentally chiding herself for judging the man by appearance, she rose and offered her hand. "Tessa Beaumont."

He enfolded her hand in lean, warm fingers, and sparks tingled up her arm. What on earth?

She tilted her head, studying his face. Her eyes narrowed in suspicion. *Oh, no!* It couldn't be! She should have suspected shenanigans when Gabe sedately drove her to work in a beat-up mustard-yellow Pinto. Instead, she'd blithely swallowed his explanation of a low profile. When she'd asked him if he was moonlighting at Moore's pre-owned car emporium, he'd grinned. He'd admitted the 'Vette was his, but his desperate-for-results boss had given him a generous expense account for rentals. Gabe had said he'd keep her in sight and she'd assumed he meant surveillance, like before.

Her mistake.

"Bond, Gabe Bond," he answered in a nasal twang, before flashing the wicked grin she knew so well, now partially disguised by buckteeth.

"Ms. Beaumont?" Trask prodded.

Belatedly, she realized she was standing there with her mouth hanging open, and snapped it shut. She suddenly had new empathy for Lois Lane.

Trask shattered the stunned silence. "You can take it from here. I'll be out of the office all morning." He strode away.

Once her boss had left, her muddled senses cleared. "What do you think you're doing?" she demanded.

"This is my 'nobody suspects the nerd' disguise. Like it?"

"You might have warned me."

"And miss the priceless expression on your face?" He

laughed, his broad shoulders shaking under the baggy jacket. "Wish I'd had a camera. Told you paybacks were hell. I guess we're even."

She mentally counted to twenty. "You're going to stick out worse than a hooker in church in those hideous clothes. Aren't undercover agents supposed to blend in?"

"This is better than camouflage. Most people don't bother to look beneath the surface. Everyone will take one look and discount any threat. Nobody will want to know me better. Admit it, what's the first thing you thought?"

"Point taken." She massaged her forehead, where a steady ache pulsed. "Do you know anything about banking, *Mr. Bond?* Or do I have to instruct you from the basics up?"

He swept off the thick glasses. His eyes twinkled with mischief. "Teach me anything you like, sweetheart. I'm a willing pupil, and a very quick study."

In spite of her annoyance, her skin tingled. "Stop the innuendoes!" she snapped. "This will be impossible if you don't behave. You'll get me fired!"

"Speaking of which, Trask said your vault teller quit." One dark brow arched. "Interesting timing."

"Carla?" she gasped. "Involved with murderers? Impossible."

"Nothing's impossible. Anything suspicious about her?"

She nibbled at her lower lip with her teeth. "She tried to talk me out of counting the vault shipment the day you showed up, but I thought she was upset because we were so busy and she hated running a window."

He rubbed his jaw. "Train me as your new vault teller. The more access I have, the better."

She groaned. "Just what I need. I thought you'd keep an eye on me from a distance, like in the movies."

"We're joined at the hip, twenty-four-seven. So if you want to get rid of me, stay alert and help me nail these scum." He shot her a dark look before sliding the glasses back on. "This isn't the movies. One mistake can get you killed."

Her hand tightened on the mug, and she gulped.

Gabe gently extricated the cup from her death grip. "I'm not going to let anything happen to you." He squeezed her hand. "Now, where do we start? You're the boss."

"That'll be the day," she muttered, yanking her hand from his. "Follow me. I'll introduce you to the other staff and get you set up with a training manual and a window."

Two hours later, Tessa bit her tongue to keep from screaming. She scrubbed damp palms over a wrinkle in her brown tweed suit, desperately wishing she could as easily soothe her frayed composure. Gabe's constant presence, their bodies brushing, hands touching, his smooth, deep voice low and intimate in her ear, had set every nerve thrumming. Worse, she didn't know why she felt so unbalanced. He'd stayed in nerd mode and behaved impeccably all morning.

When the money delivery arrived, she picked up the bags and handed half to him. "Let's take these into the vault."

The gate slammed shut behind them. Great. Enforced confinement with a man who drove her insane. She backed as far away as the small space allowed, but his enticing scent and warm, muscled body tempted her as badly as a banquet would tempt a beggar.

"What's the usual routine?" he asked.

Her senses swirling, Tessa unlocked the inner vault. She set the cash next to a shelf holding the money counter and a tray of office supplies. "When you enter or leave, log your initials and time." She grabbed a pen from the tray and wrote on a clipboard hanging next to the shelf. "A guard delivers from the main basement vault around eleven." She tucked the pen in her pocket. "I usually verify immediately, but it depends on how busy we are."

She cut the seal on the first bag, withdrawing a bundle of fifties. "Run them through the counter, rebundle, then the money goes into a locked bin. The vault teller also fills the ATMs." She stacked the bills in the machine and pressed the button. "We have two. One at the drive-through and one in the lobby."

Gabe removed his Buddy Holly glasses and rubbed the bridge of his nose. "Why are you so patient with her?"

Tessa jerked her gaze to his. "I beg your pardon?"

"The pit bull in pearls. Lucille tried to torpedo all your ideas last night." He folded the glasses beside the tray. "I'd tell her to take a flying leap."

She busily repackaged the money. "She's going to be family. One can stand up for oneself without resorting to rudeness."

"Your fiancé is a man of few words."

"Unlike *some* people, he's quiet, but he's a wonderful person. He's compassionate, intelligent and treats me with respect. His father died three years ago, and he takes care of his mother. He's also a very talented musician. Evenings and weekends, he gives free violin lessons to underprivileged kids."

"A paragon of virtue."

"Don't make fun of him!"

He held up his hands. "Hey, I wasn't. He seems like a decent guy. I wonder, though—" Gabe studied her face. "When he kisses you, does your heart race?" He stepped closer and she edged away. "Your skin tingle? Your body quiver?" He took another step and she again edged away. "Like it did when I kissed you?"

Her back hit the wall. All those things were happening to her right now. Horrified by her uncontrollable reaction to him, she went rigid.

"Do you want to crawl inside him and live there?" he murmured, planting both palms on the wall on either side of her head. He lowered his face a whisper from hers.

How could she stand here and discuss her fiancé's attributes, all the while yearning to kiss another man? She was disgusting. "Congratulations, a new record. You managed to behave for two whole hours." She forced in a shuddering breath. "You promised I could trust you."

Gabe froze. "You're right. You can. I won't kiss you again." One corner of his mouth quirked in a lopsided smile as he stepped back. "Until you ask."

Gripping her hands together to hide their shaking, she turned away. "The Dow Jones will hit five million first."

His husky laugh embraced her. "Never say never, Houdini." He cut open the last canvas bag to hand her another pile of bills.

"I assume Trask has the vault log and a master list of teller endorsement numbers. When his secretary takes her lunch break, we can search his office."

She whirled. "If we're caught, I'll get fired, arrested, or both!"

"You forget who you're dealing with. In this situation, I *am* the law. Besides, everything will be legal."

"Talk about the fox guarding the henhouse."

Gabe's lips turned up in that heart-stopping grin. "There you go. Take that sassy mouth and turn it on Lucille."

"I'll work things out with her my own way." She snatched the pen from her jacket and logged them out, then shoved the pen back in her pocket. "We can't search Trask's office. I always take new staff to lunch their first day. My policy is well-known and any break in routine will raise questions. Trask is out more than he's in, so we'll have plenty of opportunity." She glanced at her watch. "It's noon, we might as well eat."

"Okay. We'll discuss tactics and you can tell me about the other employees." With a flourish, he swooped up his glasses. "After you, boss."

Tessa turned on her pager as she led Gabe toward the bank of elevators. "The cafeteria is in the basement, but I have lunch in the courtyard when the weather is nice."

After choosing their meals, they strolled out to the courtyard in the center of the six-story building. Relishing the ripe-apple scent of late autumn, Tessa led Gabe to her usual table in the corner, sheltered by maple trees. She brushed crisp orange and red leaves off the glass tabletop before depositing her salad. "I can't believe nobody else is taking advantage of this beautiful day."

His movements smooth and economical, Gabe slid into the seat across from her. "Getting outside feels great, doesn't it?" He removed his glasses and set them on the table. Closing his eyes, he leaned back and turned his face upward. Gilded bronze by the warm sun, his tanned features radiated peace and strength.

Her heart leapt, then flipped over. Heavens, he was gorgeous in spite of the ridiculous disguise. Desire saturated her limbs, quickly followed by the odd, disconcerting feeling that her fate was irrevocably sealed. Just like when she'd tried to get away from him in the car, the warehouse, then the cabin, there was no escape. She gulped iced tea, the cold burn helping rein in her panic. "You said you wanted information about our co-workers?" she choked out. "What do you need?"

His eyelids floated up, and his smoky, sensual gaze caressed her face. "Do you really want to know what I need, Tessie?" he asked, his low voice sliding over her like warm silk.

Suddenly she couldn't breathe.

"Hello, Tessa."

She jerked her startled gaze to the sandy-haired man striding across the courtyard. "Hello, Peter," she managed to say. Out of the corner of her eye, she saw Gabe thrust his glasses back on.

Peter stopped at their table. His pale, haggard face looked as if he hadn't been sleeping well. "I thought I'd find you here. Enjoying your lunch?"

"Yes. Would you like to join us?"

"For a minute." He took a seat beside her.

She gestured. "This is Gabe Bond, our newest teller. Gabe, Mr. Peter Richards, senior vice president."

"Hi," Gabe twanged out in his nasal nerd voice.

"Welcome, Mr. Bond. Did you come to us from another bank?"

Gabe shook his head. "No, I worked at Moore's pre-owned car emporium. You know, *Come to Moore's, where Moore means less?*" He snorted out a high-pitched laugh.

Peter's lips twitched into a pained half smile. "Miss Beaumont is the best, you're lucky to be working under her."

Gabe tossed her a surreptitious wink. He grinned, displaying his buckteeth. "I'm going to enjoy working under Miss Beaumont very much."

Tessa congratulated herself on her restraint for not kicking the living daylights out of him under the table.

Peter's brows dipped. "Ah, yes..." He cleared his throat as he turned to Tessa. "You've recovered from your ordeal? I was sorry to hear what you went through. When they catch this criminal, he deserves to be strung up by the, er, hanged."

"I'm fine, thank you, and I heartily agree."

Gabe choked out something between a laugh and a cough.

"Will I see you and Dale at the banquet this weekend?"

"We'll be there."

He rose. "Good. I hope to see you also, Mr. Bond. The banquet is an opportunity to get to know your co-workers better."

"I'll have to consult my social calendar," Gabe whined.

With a friendly wave, Peter departed.

"Very chummy with the VP," Gabe commented in his normal voice as he scooped up his thick turkey sandwich.

She'd met Peter shortly after joining Oregon Pacific. He'd taken an interest in her, becoming a mentor as she moved through the ranks. Before she'd started seeing Dale, he'd asked her out, many times. She'd always refused to mix work and dating. Peter had accepted her decision and they remained friends, often lunching or catching a movie. "Peter makes a point to know all his employees. His brother Neil is the other VP and their father, Donald, is the company president."

"Nothing like a little nepotism to get ahead in life."

"He looked stressed. I hope nothing is wrong. Neil and Donald don't get along since Donald remarried, and Neil's daughter has health problems. They seem like a nice family."

"Appearances aren't always what they seem. Speaking of, the report came in on Gregson. Real identity, Greg Fielding, a minor player with a rap sheet a mile long. Definitely not FBI. So we still don't know the police connection." He took a drink of his Coke. "Tell me about this shindig."

"The annual employees banquet. A dinner dance held at the Chantal Ballroom as a morale booster every October."

"A chance to rattle some cages and see what shakes loose." He laughed. "Sounds like a load of fun."

She shook her head. "Don't you take anything seriously?"

"Life's too short, Houdini. That serious stuff will give you ulcers, gray hair and wrinkles."

"And a family, stability and security."

"No such thing." A shadow of raw pain etched Gabe's face. "The sooner you learn that, the better off you'll be. Look out for number one. That's the only way you'll make it in this world.''

Her heart fisted, sharing his pain. She fought the urge to clasp his hand and offer comfort. ''That sounds like a lonely way to live.''

''It does the job.'' He smiled, but his eyes had lost their usual shine. ''Let's finish up. I'm anxious to get back under you again.''

Annoyed by his continual baiting, but more annoyed with herself for caring about him so much, she stabbed a tomato slice with unnecessary force. He wanted under her? Fine, she'd put him under her.

They returned to the office in silence. As Tessa entered the lobby, Darcy Griffin, one of her tellers, called out, ''A man is holding for you on line two.''

She hurried to her desk. ''Tessa Beaumont speaking.''

A click echoed in her ear. The line went dead. Frowning, she held out the receiver and stared at it.

''Problem?'' Gabe spoke up behind her.

''A customer probably got tired of waiting. I'm sure they'll call back.'' She gave him a saccharine smile. ''Since you're so anxious to work under me, I'll get you started immediately.''

For the rest of the afternoon, Tessa assigned Gabe every menial, despised job in the office. To his credit, he performed each awful chore cheerfully, without a single complaint.

At five o'clock, she exited the vault. Not sure why, she stopped. The eerie feeling of being watched crept over her. She glanced around. A well-dressed businessman and a tall, dark-haired teenage boy were the only customers. Everything else was quiet. Shrugging off the heebie-jeebies, she entered her office, where she'd sent Gabe to examine each of Darcy's nearly four hundred transaction slips for a nine-dollar discrepancy.

''How's it going? Enjoying working under me?'' she trilled.

He glanced up, flashing his lightning grin. His eyes twinkled. ''Ah, sweetheart, you know how I love it when you're masterful with me.''

She pretended to ignore the suggestive comment, and the resulting wash of heat. Gad, he was impossible! "It's closing time."

An hour later, all the tellers had balanced out and left. Tessa set the timer on the vault, turned on the main alarm and then exited, locking the front door behind her. Gabe waited up the block in the yellow Pinto. He didn't want anyone to see them leave together. Dodging the evening commuters on the crowded sidewalk, she hurried along. Once she passed Gabe's car, he would follow her around the corner so she could slip inside.

Once again, a stranger's intent gaze crawled over her. She stopped to peer into a store window, watching passersby in the reflection. Nothing odd, only the usual crowd of tired people hurrying home after a long workday. She continued on, catching a glimpse of Gabe's angry scowl in the side mirror as she scurried past. Her nerves jittered. She'd never seen him angry. Was someone following her after all?

Safely around the corner, she stopped in front of the courthouse. Gabe pulled up and she climbed into the Pinto.

"Of all the idiot—" His low voice shook with controlled fury. Nostrils flaring, he clamped his lips shut and stared out the windshield for several heartbeats. "Somebody out there wants to punch your ticket, and you stop to look at *shoes?*" He jerked his head in her direction, his cold gaze drilling into her.

"I wasn't. I thought..." Uncertain, she trailed off.

"That you needed a matching purse?" he snapped. "I told you exactly what to do. You'll damn well do it, or else."

This was a different Gabe, one she didn't recognize. She should tell him what she suspected. But she didn't have anything concrete, only a creepy feeling. She'd been under a lot of pressure, and stress triggered anxiety.

When Tessa didn't answer him, Gabe rammed the Pinto into gear and stomped on the gas. His heart was pounding like a jackhammer, cold rage churned in a greasy ball in his gut, and his chest was so tight he could barely breathe. What the hell was wrong with him? He never lost it. Ever.

He flicked a glance at the mute woman in the passenger seat. When she'd stopped to look in the store window and presented her back like a neon target, the possibility of anything happening to her had made him grip the steering wheel so hard he'd nearly broken it.

She wasn't in any real danger; he didn't think the counterfeiters would risk undue attention by whacking her in public. If he had any doubts, he wouldn't allow her out.

So what was his problem?

He'd never let work, or anything else, get under his skin. His picture was in the dictionary under calm, cool and collected. His usual MO was to shrug and stroll on. Emotional involvement of any kind had no place in his life.

But here he sat, shaking like a raw recruit in his first firefight.

Control kept him sane, kept him alive. But his control was slipping.

And Mr. Calm, Cool and Collected was scared spitless.

Chapter 7

The next morning, Tessa flicked an uneasy glance at Gabe as he parked the Pinto in front of the courthouse. The heavy gray clouds glowering on the horizon mirrored his unusually sober face.

Dressed in a powder-blue polyester leisure suit and hot pink shirt, he returned her puzzled stare with narrowed, inscrutable green eyes. "Don't stop for any reason today. If the world comes to an end, you keep walking. You're not offering your brains for target practice on my watch, is that clear?"

A chill skittered up her spine, and she shivered, gulping down a lump of fear. Had he seen something yesterday after all?

Gabe jerked his gaze away and rammed on the nerdy glasses. "Get going." The rough edge to his satin voice told her she only imagined the tenderness in his expression.

As she scurried around the corner, the weight of someone's attention prickled along the back of her neck, making her feel like a hunted animal. Prey. Safely inside the bank, she heaved a sigh of relief and flipped on the lights. It had to be tension. She was one big raw nerve. A minute later, she let Gabe in the door, more reassured by his presence than she had a right to be.

His alert gaze probed the corners and roved over each cubicle. "Nobody else here yet?"

"I arrive early to review the schedule, check memos, and answer the phone if anyone calls in sick. Trask stops by around ten, then has meetings the rest of the day."

"What about his administrative assistant?"

"Lorna usually slips into her chair at nine, but the other employees arrive at eight-thirty, and expect me to be here. The executives on Trask's floor trickle in then as well."

"Perfect time to search his office."

She chewed her lip. "I don't have a key."

His five-hundred-watt grin flashed, banishing the storm clouds from his face. "Who needs a key?"

Her stomach churning, she followed him as he bounded up the stairs to the fourth floor and strolled down the gold-carpeted hallway to Trask's office as if he owned the place.

He tucked his glasses in his jacket pocket before bending to study the doorknob. He extracted a leather case from inside his blue jacket, and chose a slim metal tool. His competent, graceful fingers slid the pick into the keyhole. He jiggled the knob and popped the lock with a twist of his wrist.

"You've done that before."

"Who me? I've never been to Trask's office."

She shot a nervous glance down the hallway. "Keep your day job, Mr. Bond," she whispered. "You'll never make it as a comedian. Let's get this covert operation over with."

He swung the door wide with a flourish. "After you."

The butterflies in her stomach morphed into jumbo jets as she entered the dark room and crept past Lorna's desk to the inner office. She tested the brass knob. "This is locked, too."

Gabe again made short work of the lock, and she tiptoed into Trask's huge office behind him. The thick gold carpet swallowed up the sound of their footsteps. He eased the door shut. "Open the blinds, I don't want to use the light." His low voice vibrated through the darkness, jolting her charged nerves like lightning dancing along a high-voltage wire.

The breath she didn't realize she was holding exploded out of her in a silent rush, and she commanded her frozen feet to walk to the bank of windows on the far wall. She groped for the wand that slatted open the ivory vertical blinds.

He let out a low whistle. "That's quite a view."

Sometime in the last few minutes, the glowering sky had split, and sheets of rain poured down. The Willamette River bisected the city, dark water churning under five bridges starkly silhouetted against the gray horizon. Lighted windows from surrounding multistory office buildings strained to break the gloom.

She glanced at her watch. "We've got less than twenty minutes."

"Okay, you check the file cabinets for the vault logs."

"But I can get legitimate copies by submitting a request."

Gabe shook his head. "We don't want to alert the perps." In seconds, he picked open the file cabinet. "I'll search Trask's computer for the endorsement codes. We need to know who processed the checks we intercepted."

"The computer is password protected and has a security program."

His smile as broad as a kid at the circus, he slid into Trask's plush leather chair and leaned back. Linking his hands in front of him, he cracked his knuckles. "Want me to approve your promotion and give you a raise while I'm at it?"

"Why do I bother?" She wiped her sweaty palms on her black wool skirt. "You act as if you're at a cocktail party. Doesn't this scare you at all?"

"Tessie, my sweet, you've got to learn to enjoy life and not sweat the small stuff."

"We're breaking into federal bank records," she muttered, heading for the file cabinet. "Hardly *small stuff.*"

The computer hummed on. She heard Gabe's fingers dancing over the keys as she sorted through folders inside the oak drawers. She quickly located the file. "I found them."

He glanced up from the screen. "Copy machine?"

"Down the hall and around the corner."

"Great. Make copies of the last six months, longer if you've got time. Meet me here when you're done. We'll replace the files and get back downstairs in time for coffee."

"Coffee." Her tight, dry throat couldn't swallow anything if her life depended on it. She again wiped her damp palms on her skirt before peering into the hall. The empty corridor loomed before her. Leaving the door open a crack, she scurried down the hall and around the corner to the copy room.

She managed to make copies going back almost six months, and was rearranging the logs when the elevator's low hum shattered the thick silence. Her heart thundered into a gallop, and she shot a frantic glance at her watch. Eight-ten, too early for anyone to arrive on these floors. Maybe the passenger would go further up. A loud ping announced a disembarking passenger. *Oh, no!* If anyone noticed Trask's partially opened door...

Think! Cover Gabe's butt! She rushed around the corner and down the hall. Lorna stepped out of the elevator, sorting keys in one hand, juggling a briefcase and a paper cup of espresso in the other. Of all the days for Trask's admin to break habit and show up early!

Tessa's chest constricted. She slid the incriminating folder behind her and shoved it up under her jacket. "Hello." Her greeting emerged slightly shaky.

Lorna's head snapped up. "Hi, Tessa. What are you doing here at this hour?" Keys at the ready, she stepped around Tessa.

Stall! Something! Anything! "I, um, the employee banquet. Do we have anything special planned to—to show Mr. Trask how much we appreciate his inspiration?"

The tall brunette lurched to a halt, and turned to face her, looking puzzled. "Okaaay. I planned to catch up on paperwork before Trask's vacation, but I can spare a minute. Come on in."

Tessa deliberately slowed her rapid breaths. *Don't panic. Speak normally.* "Let's go to the cafeteria and discuss it over coffee."

Lorna held up the espresso. "I have coffee." She turned her back on Tessa, making a beeline toward Trask's office.

Now what? Tessa's desperate gaze darted in every direction, finally locking on a bright red box. *FIRE. Pull in case of emergency.* This was definitely an emergency. She reached up and pulled the lever.

Bells, buzzers and whistles blared. The hallway chimed like

Times Square on New Year's Eve. Lorna screeched and jumped, dumping espresso all over her briefcase.

Tessa hurried toward her. "Quick, we better evacuate." She grabbed the stunned brunette, propelling her toward the stairwell. "Not the elevator, they shut down during a fire."

"You're so calm," Lorna panted as they hustled down the stairs.

Tessa shoved the slipping file folder more firmly up the back of her jacket. "I've become used to dealing with emergency situations lately." The other woman frowned in puzzlement, and Tessa shrugged. "Never mind. Long story."

Outside, she glimpsed Gabe standing in the drenching rain with the other staff. He gave her a bucktoothed grin and discreet thumbs-up. A relieved sigh whispered out of her. That had been way too close for comfort.

The fire drill turned out to be the least chaotic incident of the day. By the time the firemen cleared the shaken employees to reenter, cranky customers had lined up around the block. They streamed into the lobby in a neverending rush, and Tessa ran from one end of the branch to the other, trying to keep distracted tellers working, and soothing wet, irritated clients.

Surprisingly, Gabe turned out to be a huge help. He slid into his teller role as though he'd been born to it, processing twice the transactions of even the most experienced employees.

Blessed five o'clock finally arrived. She locked the door and rested her forehead on the cool, misty glass.

"Miss Beaumont?"

"Yes?" She turned and saw Darcy frowning at her.

"The kiosk ATM is on the fritz again. The security panel is red-lighted."

Tessa stared out at the rain, pelting muddy puddles on the sidewalk. "Of course it is. I'll go check it, thank you." Heaving a weary sigh, she trudged into her office to fetch her raincoat.

"Where do you think you're going?"

Gabe's low question spun her around, one arm tangled in the sleeve of her coat. "The drive-through ATM is jammed again."

His brows slammed together. "You don't go anywhere without me."

"It's been so hectic, I honestly forgot."

He helped her into her raincoat, the brief brush of his fingers on her neck making her pulse jump.

"That it has. Okay, show me how to un-jam the ATM."

"How about blowing it sky-high?" she muttered.

"I'm pretty good with explosives. I could—"

"Don't you dare!" she snapped. "I was only kidding."

"I know, boss." His teasing grin brightened the gloomy day. "So was I."

Her shoulders slumped, heavy with fatigue. "Sorry. I'm beat."

"No problem. Let's double-team the beast, shall we?"

After twenty minutes kneeling on the soaked pavement prying a jammed twenty out of the slot—and one hard kick—the ATM was running again.

Followed by Gabe, Tessa trailed back inside. Water streamed off her coat and plopped onto the carpet. "Everyone else is finished. You'd better dry off and balance your cash drawer. I'll let the others out."

Tessa ushered out the employees and relocked the door, then hurried to the rest room. She hung her raincoat on the back of the door and quickly stripped off the damp suit jacket, soggy pumps and thigh-high stockings. She filled the sink with sudsy water. The heavenly warmth soothed her chilled skin as she washed her feet and legs before drying them with paper towels. Releasing the gold clip at her nape, she blotted her hair. The wild mass spilled in damp curls past her shoulders. After rinsing out her stockings, she hung them and the jacket near the heater vent and arranged her pumps to one side. Maybe they'd dry by the time she finished the paperwork.

The textured gold carpet grazed the soles of her feet as she tiptoed down the hall and scooted into her office. She settled into her chair and tucked her bare toes safely under the desk. A weary sigh trickled out as she grabbed a form off the mountain in the inbox. A repair report from the ATM company.

"Hey, boss, I'm done. How about you?" Gabe leaned on the door frame, untouched by their miserable chore. His tacky polyester suit had shed water as efficiently as armor, and only a hint of dampness glistened in his short, dark hair.

"Not even close. Go find a chair in the lobby and relax."

He glanced at his watch. "It's after eighteen hundred. I know for a fact you skipped both breaks and your lunch today."

"So did you, even though I told you to go."

"What's good for the boss is good enough for me." He strolled into the room. Propping one hip on the corner of her desk as if he belonged there, he plunked his nerd glasses in her inbox, then removed his fake buckteeth. Thank goodness he didn't put *those* in her inbox, but stowed them in his baby-blue jacket.

His gaze swept over her, and his eyes darkened. "You should always wear your hair loose." A slow, sensual smile curved his lips. He reached out and snagged a stray curl, winding the lock of hair around his finger. "Very quick thinking on that fire alarm this morning. I think I'll keep you on the team."

She frowned at him until he dropped his hand. "I plan to resign from the team as soon as possible. I hope you got everything you needed. My blood pressure can't handle another spy mission upstairs."

"Aww, come on. Didn't you have a little fun?" He grinned. "There's nothing like a good old-fashioned adrenaline rush for a great high. And that was merely an itty-bitty tingle."

Tessa slumped, resting her forehead in her hands. "Go amuse yourself for a couple of hours, Mr. Adventure. I have work to finish." Her hands slid around to rub the back of her aching neck. "I know," she jerked open her desk drawer, and handed him Trask's vault log file. "Return this upstairs."

He dropped the folder on her desk. "And leave you all alone? Nuh-uh. Besides, you know what they say." He moved to her side, sinking down on the carpet cross-legged. "All work and no play makes Tessie cranky." He pushed her chair back and grasped one bare ankle in his strong hand.

She gasped at the contact. "What are you doing?"

"You think you can sneak in here with nekkid feet unnoticed?" Heat crept up her neck, and he barked out a laugh. He lifted her foot into his lap and massaged her sore, tired muscles. "You're exhausted, and so tense, you could open a can of cola with your buns."

"Charmingly eloquent as always." She tried to yank her foot from his grip, but he held firm. "Stop that!"

His nimble fingers gently kneaded an extrasensitive spot. Her tight muscles softened like a Hershey bar in July. Warm, soothing contentment spread through her foot to her leg, and flowed up her spine. She moaned and went limp.

"Hmm. Are you sure you want me to stop?" His thumbs rubbed her instep in tiny circles, exerting exquisite pressure.

Her eyes drifted closed, and she melted into the chair. "I don't like you, Mr. Bond," she murmured.

"I know, sweetheart." He chuckled. "Don't blame you. I'm despicable."

Adrift in a warm glow of pleasure, she slowly nodded. "And an oversexed gorilla."

"Duly noted."

As he continued his soothing strokes, her tension evaporated, and she floated away in a peaceful daze.

"Ms. Beaumont!" Trask's booming voice echoed from the lobby.

She jerked upright. Her panicked gaze shot to Gabe. "My boss!" she whispered. "If he sees you, me, like this—"

Gabe touched a finger to his lips. "My lips are sealed." He tossed her a mischievous grin before scooting under her desk. He pulled her chair into place as Trask entered the office.

She took a deep breath and pasted on a smile. "Good evening. This is a surprise."

Her boss dropped into the seat opposite her and slapped a stack of papers onto the desktop. "With my vacation coming up, I want the employee reviews done early."

She glanced down at the papers, and a cold chill skittered over her skin. Like a neon arrow of guilt, the vault log file she'd stolen from his office loomed on the desktop in plain view. Holding her breath, she nudged the folder to one side with her elbow and slipped the ATM report on top.

He picked up the first page in his stack. "The kiosk ATM?"

Under the desk, the tip of one callused finger tickled the sole of her right foot. Her toes curled. "Still causing headaches on a regular basis."

"The down time on the last repair?"

She looked at the repair invoice covering the incriminating file, praying he wouldn't ask to see it. "Two hours."

Warm fingers stroked her foot before sliding up her calf. A quiver rippled through her body. She bit her lower lip.

Trask made a notation in the folder. "Obviously, the service rep isn't tweaking the correct part."

"No. He doesn't seem to get the point no matter how many times I've shown him the exact problem spot."

Gabe's palm glided up her calf and over her knee toward the tender inside of her thigh. Her stomach lurched.

Trask frowned at her from across the desk. "And the cash supply from the main vault? Are you getting what you need?"

Fighting the insane desire to urge Gabe's hand upward, she instead clamped her shaking knees together, trapping his fingers between them. "Um, yes. I'm g-getting plenty." She snatched up a pen and frantically began to jot illegible notes.

"About the new teller..."

Gabe tugged his hand from between her knees. Spine stiff, she waited for his next trick, torn between hoping he'd stop and wishing he wouldn't.

Her boss consulted the second memo. "Mr. Bond? How is he performing?"

No movement came from under the desk. Gabe's little game must be over. She leaned back slightly in the chair. "He's—"

Suddenly, hot, moist breath, followed by soft lips, tingled over her left kneecap. Her pulse fluttered into a stampede.

"I'm going to strangle him," she muttered between clenched teeth.

"I beg your pardon?"

"I said, he's got a handle on things."

"His transaction rate is twice that of our fastest teller."

Warm lips nibbled her calf. She gripped the pen until her knuckles turned white. "Oh, he's definitely fast."

"Would you like to add more responsibilities to Mr. Bond's training?"

She wanted to throw Mr. Bond down on the floor and ravish him. She must be losing her mind. Tessa swallowed a moan. She sucked in a deep, shuddery breath before daring to continue. "He seems to be taking the initiative himself. I just hope he doesn't get in over his head."

"Are you feeling all right? You're rather flushed."

"Now that you mention it, I do seem to have picked up an unpleasant parasite I can't shake loose," she hissed, launching a discreet, but hard kick. Her foot connected with what felt like ribs. A soft grunt echoed from under the desk, and she coughed loudly to cover the sound. "But however annoying, it will not prevent me from doing my job. Please continue."

"Yes, quite. Perhaps you should see a doctor about that. Now, about the search for a new vault teller. Have you found anyone who meets our needs?"

Those soft lips roved down the sensitive skin of her ankle and along the top of her foot. Liquid heat streamed through her veins, pooling low and heavy in her abdomen. She gripped her pen with both hands. "My needs are not being met at all," she groaned.

"Ms. Beaumont, are you sure you're up to this? Perhaps we'd better continue at another time."

Gabe pressed his lips to the sole of her foot and the warm flick of his tongue sent hot and cold ripples up her spine. Her nipples contracted into hard, painful peaks. Her hands clenched, snapping the pen in half. Ink sprayed out, spattering her blouse, the desktop, and Mr. Trask's beige suit with dripping blue blotches.

Swiping at the front of his suit, Trask leapt up like he'd been jolted with a cattle prod. "Obviously, you are not well at all. I'd better take care of this before the stain sets. I'll speak to you tomorrow." He stormed out.

Too weak to care, she flopped back, her chair rolling away from the desk.

Gabe emerged, his expression stunned. "Tessa, I, ah, hell." He thrust his fingers through his hair.

Dazed, she stared at him. Anger snapped her upright. "How dare you? You promised you wouldn't touch me again."

"I know." He swallowed, then finally, he spoke. "I'm sorry."

Furious with him, but more furious with herself, she gripped the armrests until her hands ached. Even now, she craved more. How humiliating. What did that say about her? She was behaving like someone totally unacquainted with morals.

Like Vivienne.

The realization made her want to throw up. "You, Mr. Colton, are the most loathsome, contemptible, irresponsible—"

He managed a weak, shaky laugh. "I won't argue with you there, sweetheart."

She clamped her lips shut before disgracing herself any further by bursting into tears.

Because she wasn't listing his faults.

She was describing her own.

Late into the night, Gabe lay awake staring into the darkness. He clenched his jaw, trying to ignore the desire that still pulsed, thick and heavy in his blood. What had started as an impulsive prank had turned into a double-edged blade and speared him in the guts. He'd only meant to tease Tessa a little. But when the pulse in her ankle had galloped under his hands and her silky skin had trembled at his touch, he'd lost his head. Gone too far.

No doubt about it, the lady had been turned on. And so had he. He'd gloried in her response. Far more than he wanted to acknowledge. He'd committed a serious tactical error and let the situation escalate out of his control. Damn it, he'd *never* lost control with a woman before. His relationships with women had always been fun and playful, nothing more than a good-time romp.

However, he didn't feel at all casual about Tessa.

There was a light inside her, sweet warmth that beckoned to him from the darkness. The burning need to make love to her grew stronger every day. His need, his vulnerability filled him with fear. Because it wasn't just physical. The two of them shared an emotional pull both continued to deny. A smart man would make a hasty retreat before he got his wings singed.

He rolled over and viciously punched his pillow. From now

on, his policy was strictly hands-off. Before he did something really stupid.

Like get attached to her.

That road led straight to perdition. Gabe had been there once, and once was enough to tear his heart to shreds, to shatter his trust. It had taken years to claw his way out of a lonely, agonizingly mute prison. He almost hadn't made it back.

He'd be damned if he was going to make a return trip.

He had nothing left for anyone to take away. And he sure as hell had nothing to give.

Chapter 8

The next evening, Tessa stood in front of the mirror in Gabe's guest room, applying makeup in preparation for the banquet. The bruise on her forehead had faded to a shadow. She blotted concealer on it, and dabbed another layer on the purple rings under her eyes. Covering the ugly physical evidence of her sleepless night was easy. Too bad they didn't make a concealer for consciences.

Self-disgust and anger festered inside her like poison. She'd come so close to betraying Dale. She cared for him as a friend and partner. He was everything she wanted: solid, steady and loyal. Gabe was a temporary pesky fly in the ointment, and she was determined to ignore the temptation.

He'd actually been subdued since the under-the-desk incident. Perhaps he'd realized he'd crossed over the line. Heck, he'd traveled clear to another continent. However, she wouldn't hold her breath believing his sudden attack of good behavior would last long. Holding her breath until Gabe grew a conscience? Ha! Death by asphyxiation sounded unpleasant in the extreme.

Speaking of Mr. Adventure, he'd decided to attend the party as "Cousin Val," instead of Gabe Bond, hoping he could find out more information pretending to be her cousin than he could as an employee of the bank. She leaned forward to sweep another coat of dark brown mascara on her lashes. The man was acquiring so many aliases, she'd soon need a scorecard.

A knock sounded on the door. ''Tessa? You ready?''

That was another thing. He'd called her by name for a full twenty-four hours. No honey, baby, sweetheart, Houdini, or even boss. This afternoon at the office in front of several employees, he'd respectfully addressed her as Miss Beaumont. The shock had rendered her speechless for sixty long seconds.

''Two minutes,'' she called out. After slicking on neutral lipstick, she stood back to examine her image. Her dress had been purchased at Mel's urging, mocha lace over satin with sheer lace sleeves and a straight, floor-length skirt that disguised her hips. She patted her upswept curls self-consciously. Though she'd never achieve beauty like Vivienne's, she looked good. Grabbing her cashmere shawl, she tossed it over one arm.

In the hall, she paused to watch Gabe prowl the living room. Gabe in a tuxedo was nothing short of magnificent. The jacket clung lovingly to his broad shoulders and narrow waist. Those lean, muscled legs looked even longer in tailored slacks. The pristine shirt rivaled his gleaming smile and emphasized his bronzed tan. And the black suit brought out the dark sheen in his hair and deepened his incredible green eyes.

Tessa groaned inwardly. Obsessing over him again. Not good. She wrestled her wayward thoughts into submission and forced herself to stroll nonchalantly toward him.

His head snapped up at her entrance, his face expressionless.

''Dale will meet us there. I said you were nervous and wanted to arrive with me.'' The lie had stuck in her throat, but as usual, Dale had affably agreed.

Gabe draped her soft wool shawl over her shoulders with efficient, impersonal hands before escorting her outside. ''Remember to stay in my sight at all times. I'll be watching Trask and his sons. Those three have main vault access.''

He opened the car door and Tessa slid into the Jaguar. She pressed her hands to her abdomen. ''I hate suspecting my co-workers of such horrible crimes. It makes my stomach hurt.''

His mouth tightened. "Betrayal is ugly." Her throat constricted at the pain in his eyes. He looked like he had firsthand knowledge. She'd seen hints of the darkness that lurked under his lighthearted manner. Was he haunted by his life-or-death job? Or something more personal?

Either way, he wouldn't tell her. Whatever burdens he carried, he seemed determined to shoulder them alone. Her heart aching, she watched him stroll around the front of the Jag with his deceptively graceful walk. "Are you all right?" she asked as he started the engine.

His strangely flat gaze roved over her face before returning to the road. "I'm fine. Watch out for yourself."

His warning rang in her ears with double meaning. She was on the verge of starting a new life, the life she'd always wanted. She couldn't afford to ruin it by getting personally involved with him. "I'm learning."

He didn't respond. Instead, he slid a CD into the player. Mick Jagger serenaded them all the way to the Chantal Ballroom. *You can't always get what you want.* Profound words.

Gabe stopped the Jag in front of the valet parking sign. He climbed out and handed his valet key to the attendant. Squaring his shoulders, he consciously focused his thoughts. Showtime.

Behind them, Trask stepped out of a new Porsche, followed by a tall redhead who could pass for playmate of the month.

Gabe whistled. "A Porsche. Bank managers must make pretty good wages these days. Or—"

"Mr. Trask?" Tessa whispered? "Do you think he's the one?"

"We'll definitely keep an eye on him." At least until Gabe's boss faxed all the suspects' tax returns. Gabe's request had been delayed by an IRS computer glitch and the usual end of the fiscal-year jam. Even the highest government clearance couldn't force the IRS into efficiency.

He placed his hand on the small of Tessa's back and escorted her into the foyer. At the coat check, she handed over her wrap. As she bent her head the chandelier's muted glow caressed the velvety nape of her neck.

His heart pounded like a kid sneaking a peek at his first girlie magazine. Damn it, he should feel zilch when he looked at her. She was strictly business. The desire burning through his veins mocked his resolve. Confused, he shook his head. Why did his traitorous body continue to defy his brain?

Dale detached himself from a group of conversing guests and strode up to them, bending toward Tessa's cheek.

"Dale!" Tessa threw her arms around his neck and turned so Dale's lips met hers, thwarting the innocuous peck on the cheek he'd been aiming for.

"Hello, pretty lady." The big man appeared puzzled, but gently returned her kiss. "Ready to dance the night away?"

Gabe barely held in a snarl. The putz didn't deserve her.

"Nice to see you again, Val." Dale's gaze bored into Gabe's a second too long for comfort. The giant's eyes narrowed.

Maybe the Jolly Green Giant wasn't as dense as he appeared. Gabe lowered his lids. How much had his expression given away? Double damn! He was screwing up a scenario a rookie could manage. *Get to work.* "Don't you look marvelous," he simpered, toying with his bow tie. Not far from the truth, he grudgingly admitted. Accounting must be more profitable than Gabe had been led to believe. Or maybe mamma had picked out Dale's designer tux. The snide thought cheered him slightly.

"Our table is in here." Dale took Tessa's elbow and led them through the foyer into a large dining and dancing area.

Just like in the country club, Gabe beat Dale by a second to hold Tessa's chair, earning another curious glance from the big man. To hell with it. He indulged in a nanosecond of satisfaction. "Tessa, do you want something from the bar?"

She patted Dale's hand. "Dale can get it. He knows what I like."

Gabe slanted her an intimate, knowing look. "I promise I can deliver something that will satisfy you."

Her cheeks pinkened, and he clenched his fists under the table. Two minutes and he'd broken his vow. First his body went AWOL, now his brain.

With agile grace, Dale rose to his feet. "I don't mind. Val, what can I get you?"

How about handing over your fiancée, Bubba? "I take care of myself," Gabe snapped, dropping into a chair. "Thanks anyway," he belatedly amended.

Dale melted into the crowd.

"What is your problem?" Tessa hissed. "I thought you were a pro at this cloak-and-dagger stuff."

"I have a headache," he lied. Unfortunately, the throbbing ache originated much farther south than his temples. He'd lost his freaking mind. Everything he knew, everything he stood for, had suddenly come into question. Never before had he had a problem maintaining detachment and control. Never before had his depend-on-himself-at-all-costs attitude seemed shallow and lonely. And he had never before allowed a woman to twist him into knots of self-doubt, and threaten his carefully guarded equilibrium.

"I'm sorry." Her sympathetic gaze caressed his face. "Do you need ibuprofen? I have some in my bag."

"Sure." He had a feeling he'd need serious pain meds before the night was over. He accepted two pills and chewed them dry, swallowing his self-doubt with the bitter powder.

Work, focus on work. Concentrating on the job had always been his salvation. His buffer against dangerous emotional involvement. "Is the senior Mr. Richards around?"

"Yes, he's over by the bandstand with his wife."

Relief coursed through him, and he forcibly snapped his focus into place. "Time to introduce him to cousin Val."

As they wove through the crowd, he mentally reviewed the dossier on Donald Richards. The fifty-eight-year-old bank president had a second wife half his age, and a baby son. His marriage had occurred at the same time the phony checks started showing up.

The short, bald man turned to greet them. "Miss Beaumont."

Tessa nervously cleared her throat. "Hello, Mr. Richards. I'd like to introduce my cousin, Valentine Colton."

Donald shook his hand, then gestured to the woman beside him. "My wife, Kiki."

The bodacious blonde was poured into a clingy silver dress cut down to South America. A diamond necklace that would choke a boa constrictor glittered around her neck. Gabe offered her a smile as he took her hand.

She returned his smile with a scorching *I'd like to eat you up* look that would have normally inspired an automatic reaction.

His body didn't even stir.

Unfamiliar, suffocating panic jammed his throat. He enjoyed women, enjoyed sex, but he'd always kept things light and playful. He'd never succumbed to one woman and let her fill his mind so completely he couldn't respond to another. But he'd just subconsciously made a mental comparison, and Kiki didn't even come close to Tessa. Cold fear crawled up his spine.

Beside him, Tessa stiffened. "I see Dale returning with our drinks. It was nice to see you again."

Ruthlessly burying his dread, Gabe tucked his hand under her elbow to guide her through the crowd. He had a job to do, and it didn't matter one damn bit how off-balance he felt. He reached deep inside for the cool control that always sustained him. "What is it with these bankers and their hot babes? I thought only ballplayers scored such knockout chicks. There's got to be something to numbers crunching I'm missing."

"A sudden, miraculous cure for your headache?" Tessa muttered.

"Jealous?"

"Not in this lifetime, Super Ego."

Her scathing reply didn't ring true. She *was* jealous. In a small, idiotic corner of his brain, he couldn't help feeling pleased. Damn, he *was* losing it.

He lightly squeezed her elbow in reassurance. "I wasn't making comparisons. My point is, these are high-maintenance women. Designer clothes, diamonds, hundred-dollar hairdos and fancy cars add up. Let's face it, they aren't hanging around with Trask and Richards for their looks."

"Maybe they're compatible, did you take that into account?"

"Yeah, Trask has such a warm, fun personality. And Richards—I'm quivering with excitement after talking to him."

"You're impossible," she huffed. "Because a person doesn't bungee jump off the Empire State Building at high noon does not make them boring."

With that proclamation, they arrived at their table. Dale rose, but again didn't challenge him for the privilege of seating Tessa. She scooted closer to the hulk and covered his hand with her own where it rested on the tablecloth.

Gabe stalked to the bar for a Coke. He stayed on the wagon when he worked, but that didn't stop him from craving a shot of tequila. He ground his teeth. Couldn't Tessie see Dale was all wrong for her? The dolt didn't even recognize the spirit under her cool facade. She needed a man who would set her free, let her soar. Gabe had managed to do just that. Every time he touched her, they both went up in flames.

But she deserved better. He couldn't stay. Couldn't be that man.

The fact that he wanted to be sent his internal alarm hurtling to defcon one. He navigated the mobbed dance floor, gripping his icy Coke with white-knuckled fingers. *Detach, Colton.*

He and Peter Richards arrived at the table simultaneously. Clearly nervous, Tessa introduced Gabe to Peter as her cousin Val. She needn't have worried. Peter barely noticed Gabe as they shook hands, unaware that "Cousin Val" and his new employee "Gabe Bond" were one and the same.

Peter released Gabe's hand and smiled at Tessa, but the courtesy looked forced. "Tessa, would you care to dance?"

"Yes, thank you." She sighed softly, seemingly resigned to her fiancé's non-reaction to her dancing with another man.

And with good reason. His expression pleasant, Dale sipped his wine. Gabe watched the couple circling in time to the music. Peter's face appeared haggard as he bent stiffly toward Tessa, engaging her in intense conversation.

Gabe waited until the dance was nearly over to approach them. "Mind if I cut in?"

Tessa frowned, but Peter turned her over without a word.

Careful to hold her at a respectable distance, Gabe took her in his arms. A new song began, a slow ballad. He tried to ignore the tug in his heart at the scent of her familiar sweet cloud of warm vanilla. "What was that all about?"

"Peter's upset because Neil and Donald got into an another

argument. Neil can't stand Kiki, and vice versa. He and Donald have been on the outs ever since the marriage.''

The crowded dance floor made maneuvering difficult. He drew her close, lying to himself that it was only to avoid a collision. She felt like she belonged in his arms. He squelched his longing. ''Did he say what caused the argument?''

She sighed. ''They have huge differences about how to run the company. Donald is conservative, while Neil dreams big. Neil's willing to take risks to expand, no matter how costly.''

''Sounds promising. I'm going to see what I can find out.'' Reluctantly, he returned her to Dale. ''Stay put,'' he murmured in her ear. ''And don't do anything I wouldn't.''

''A short list, Mr. Bond.''

Grinning at her retort, he exited the ballroom and sauntered down the plush burgundy carpeted corridor. He arrived in time to see a man he recognized from intel photos as Neil slam out of a private room. Neil furiously brushed past Gabe and stalked out the exit. So much for eavesdropping.

Gabe reentered the ballroom. Looking for Tessa, he homed in on their empty table, then scanned the couples on the dance floor without success. His jaw clenched on a rush of emotion he refused to acknowledge as anxiety. She was supposed to stay in sight. Finally, he caught a glimpse of her and Dale walking out a pair of double doors, onto the brick terrace.

He discreetly followed. For her own safety, he needed to keep her in sight. Dale wouldn't be able to deal with an aggressive magazine salesman, much less a real threat. To afford them privacy, yet still keep an eye on Tessa, he ducked behind a large potted plant.

The couple strolled to a bench in the corner. They sat facing the fountain in the center of the deserted patio. Tessa scooted closer to Dale and rested her hand on his thigh. ''I'm glad no one is out here. We don't get much time alone.''

''No, we don't. But after the wedding that will change.'' Her fiancé picked up her hand and cradled her fingers tenderly in his, but edged his body away slightly.

Gabe drew his brows together. Hmm. Interesting reaction.

Tessa reached up and stroked her fingertips along Dale's wide jaw. Her hand slid behind his neck. Then she urged his head down and kissed him full on the mouth.

Sucker-punched, Gabe's guts cramped. The air slammed out of his lungs, and he squeezed his eyes shut. His fists convulsed around the plant, the rough bark cutting into his palms. He sucked in a painful breath, wrestling with the urge to rush over and yank her out of the other man's arms.

It wasn't his concern.

Not his problem.

None of his business at all.

Then why did it hurt so damn much?

He repeated the mantra ten times before he dared open his eyes.

Dale was kissing her back, but his posture was ramrod-straight. He didn't appear at all comfortable with the intimacy.

Very interesting reaction.

Tessa pulled back and stared up at her fiancé. Even from where he crouched, Gabe could see her pain and confusion. Though he didn't want the other man to desire her, at the same time he wanted to smash Dale's face in for hurting her. Torn by his battling emotions, he gripped the plant harder, struggling to regain his equilibrium.

"Dale, do you," Tessa asked in a shaky voice. "Find me...desirable?"

Gabe held his breath, waiting for the answer.

Dale's Adam's apple jerked convulsively. "Of course I do, but this really isn't a good time or place—"

"It's never the time or place." Tessa jumped up and paced in front of the fountain. "I know I'm not exactly a femme fatale, but you did ask me to be your wife. You must be attracted to me, and yet you've never—we've never—"

Dale stood. Gently, he turned her to face him. "When the time comes, I promise I'll be everything you need in a husband. You'll never want for anything." He enveloped her in a chaste hug. "We should get back inside and join your co-workers."

She huffed out a sigh and nodded. Dale led her back into the ballroom.

So, they weren't lovers. That was the most interesting of all.

What was wrong with the Gomer? If Tessa were his woman, Gabe would never let her out of his arms.

His heart thundered painfully against his ribs. She wasn't his, and never would be. His temples echoed the pounding of his heart as they throbbed in a clamoring duet. Good thing he'd taken those aspirin. Too bad they didn't do anything to ease the empty, burning ache in his chest.

Tessa rolled over in bed, hugging the pillow. A bleary glance at the clock showed nearly 3:00 a.m. Her second sleepless night in a row. Both times over men. Last night, she'd worried about her passionate response to Gabe. Now she lay here fretting about Dale's lack of response to her. And hers to him. She'd felt nothing when she'd kissed him. Maybe she was one of those people who didn't feel strong emotions. She never had.

But that wasn't entirely true. Because lately, she'd experienced plenty of incredible feelings.

With Gabe.

Since they'd met, she'd run the gamut from terror to exhilaration. She'd never felt more vital and alive.

She sat up, combing her fingers through her tangled hair. This useless train of thought had to be derailed. *Now.* Dale was a good man. She cared about him, and he cared about her. They'd be happy together. And she would have the stability she'd always dreamed of. Tessa swallowed, her dry tongue sticking to the roof of her mouth. She desperately needed a drink of water.

She belted her sapphire blue robe over her matching silk nightshirt. In the dark, she tiptoed to the bathroom and fumbled for the stack of paper cups beside the sink. The first cool sip slid down her parched throat, bringing instant relief, and she gulped the rest.

A moan caught her attention. She cocked her head, listening in the blackness. Gabe? She sprinted down the hall.

"No!" he cried out.

She swung open the door. Moonlight streamed through a gap in the curtains, illuminating the center of the room, where Gabe thrashed on the bed.

"Please. Please, no," he begged. "Don't."

She hurried to his side, and bent over the writhing man. "Gabe?" Her fingertips touched his warm cheek.

His strong hands grabbed her upper arms. The room spun as she whirled through space. In an instant, she was thrown on her back onto the mattress. His hard weight pressed her body down, held her immobile. His hand clamped over her mouth. His forearm squeezed her throat.

Panic screamed through her. Her vision darkened around the edges as she struggled to breathe. She kicked and squirmed, clawing at the steely arm across her throat, her muffled cries smothered to tiny squeaks.

Suddenly Gabe jerked. His loud gasp echoed in the silent room. "Tessa?" He snatched his hands away. "Oh, God," his sleep-roughened voice rasped into her ear. "Are you all right?"

Trembling all over, she gulped in huge draughts of air.

"Talk to me, honey." His shaking hands cradled her face, soothing, stroking. "Are you okay? Did I hurt you?"

She swallowed. "I'm fine. You were having a nightmare—"

"Yeah." He was shaking so hard the bed vibrated beneath them. "That happens." He buried his face in her neck.

She wrapped her arms around him, holding him close. "It's all right," she soothed.

Still trembling, he clenched his fists in her hair, clinging to her like a security blanket. "Don't leave me," he whispered brokenly.

Her heart turned over. "I'm here." She rubbed his damp, taut-muscled back. "Who hurt you so badly, Gabe?"

He quivered in her embrace, clearly fighting for control. Finally after what seemed like an eternity, his shaking eased and he lifted his head. The agony in his eyes stabbed into her soul. "I'm—I'm okay."

He closed his eyes for a heartbeat. When his thick lashes floated up again, only a raw shadow of pain remained, the rest shoved back into the secret part of him he hid so well. "I'm sorry. It's survival training. Reflex. Don't ever touch me without waking me first." He choked out a ragged laugh that held more torment than humor. "That's what happens when you sneak in here in the middle of the night. Next time you want into my bed, just ask.''

She was in Gabe's bed. Tessa's hammering pulse kicked up another notch. Her robe had opened in the struggle and her bare legs were intimately entwined with his slightly rough, muscled thighs. His scent bombarded her, warm and fresh and blatantly male. Her stomach clenched. Flames licked through her, burning out of control.

Gabe had sworn he wouldn't kiss her again unless she asked. She stared into his eyes. If she asked now, how would he react? Would he tense, like Dale? Would he laugh?

Or would he cover her mouth with his. Devour her. Slide his lips down her neck, then move lower to quench the fire raging inside her.

As though he read her thoughts, Gabe's pupils dilated. His hungry gaze scorched her face, the feeling as hot and compelling as if his fingertips had stroked her skin. His heart thundered against her own. But he didn't move. He waited, exactly as he'd promised, his taut weight immobile on top of her.

All she had to do was ask.

She drew a shuddering breath. "Gabe?"

"Yeah, honey?" His raw, husky growl shivered up her spine.

She gulped. "Do you think you could get off me now?"

He whispered a curse and scrambled off her like she had the plague.

Gathering her robe closed, she fled to her room.

She slammed her bedroom door and fell against the panel, sickened to her soul, her chest hollow and aching. She didn't know if she despised herself more for nearly betraying Dale...

Or because she hadn't had the guts to stay with Gabe.

Chapter 9

The dark, rich smell of coffee enticed Tessa awake. The clock on the nightstand read 10:00 a.m. She hadn't slept this late since her bout with the flu last winter. She combed her fingers through her curls before she shrugged on her robe, belting the sapphire silk tightly on her way to the kitchen.

Dressed in a body-hugging gray T-shirt and faded jeans, Gabe sat at the small dining-room table with the Sunday paper spread in front of him. Faint blue smudges marred the skin beneath his eyes. He took a sip of coffee. "Mornin'." He didn't meet her gaze, focusing somewhere near her chin.

"Good morning." She crossed to the coffeemaker and poured a generous helping of the steaming, fragrant brew before taking a chair opposite him. "About last night—"

He stiffened. A muscle twitched in his cheek, his distress radiating across the table. Obviously, he didn't want to talk about his nightmare. This morning, the light that normally shone from him had dimmed, revealing the shadows under the surface. Shadows he tried so hard to hide.

She relented. None of her business, anyway. "Never mind. I

have a list of errands to complete before the rehearsal this afternoon.''

He dropped his head forward and rubbed the bridge of his nose. ''Okay.''

''If you don't want to come with me—''

''No.'' He straightened. ''You're not going alone. I'm ready when you are.''

After a quick shower, she clipped back her hair, donned brown tweed slacks and a rust-colored knit twin-set, then chose a beige suit and matching pumps to change into at the church.

Wearing a gray wool sport jacket over his T-shirt and jeans, Gabe entered the front door as she stepped into the living room. He still wouldn't meet her gaze. ''Car is clean.''

A horrible suspicion made her stomach lurch. ''You mean— do you suspect a bomb?'' she whispered.

''A precaution.'' He thrust his fingers through his hair, making the short, raven strands stand on end. ''Nobody knows our location, but I don't take your safety for granted. I won't let anybody hurt you, so relax.'' He opened the door. ''Let's go. We're driving Miss Tessa in the 'Vette today.''

Tense and anxious, she couldn't help but watch the side mirror as he drove into the city.

''Earth to Tessa. I asked what our first stop should be.''

Belatedly, she realized he'd spoken to her. Twice. She opened her day planner. ''I need to run by the bank and check on the ATM. Then Mario's Bakery, right around the corner.''

''They pay you to service that machine on your day off?''

''No, but I want to. I feel a responsibility to make sure things at the bank function smoothly.''

He grimaced. ''Responsibility. Such ugly language so early in the morning.''

''Why do you pretend like you don't care about anything? I know better.''

His lean, capable hands convulsed on the wheel, the knuckles white. ''What you see is what you get.'' His mouth quirked in a humorless smile. ''Like I said before, a rolling stone gathers no chains.''

And no foundations, no support. No love. She absorbed his

grief like a physical blow. Her heart contracted. In reality, the good-time guy was a solitary, lonely man.

He parked at the curb. "The bank, *ma belle*. You going inside?"

"No, I'll try a withdrawal." She felt Gabe's intent gaze focused on her as she walked to the machine. The ATM spit out forty dollars without a fuss, so she pocketed her card and hustled back. As she reached the car, the hairs on the back of her neck prickled. She paused with her fingers on the door handle. If she didn't know better... Her gaze darted to the left.

Gabe appeared beside her before she finished the thought. He shielded her body with his as he flung open the door and shoved her inside. Hand inside his jacket, his gaze swept the deserted sidewalk before leaning down to ask, "What?"

"Nothing." She sucked in a shaky breath. "I've felt jittery since I realized you searched for a bomb this morning."

His gaze scanned the block again before he returned to the driver's seat. "We're going home."

"No! The rehearsal is this afternoon, and since Frederick flaked out, I've got to confirm the details and pay the balances today." She put her hand on his forearm, tempered steel under the soft wool. "It's anxiety. Everything is fine."

His jaw tightened. Finally, he pulled away his arm to start the car. "The bakery is right around the corner?"

"Yes." A relieved sigh whispered out of her.

Inside Mario's, the warm, yeasty smell of fresh-baked bread tantalized her nostrils. Mario looked up from behind the glass counter, gifting her with a beaming smile. "Miss Beaumont. You have come to confirm?" He opened his order book.

"Yes. Chocolate cake with peach blush roses."

His bushy gray brows furrowed. "But your mama-in-law ordered the all-white poppyseed with white *fleur de lis*."

She might have known. Good thing she'd decided to double-check everything and pay the remaining balances in person. "I would prefer to stick to my original order. The chocolate, please." No matter what Lucille thought, Tessa wasn't about to let the other woman control her. And if push came to shove, who would Dale support, her or his mother? She tuned out the little warning voice that said "Lucille" and crossed *bakery* off her list.

Mario wrote on his tablet. "All right. Now, Lucille, she wanted a plain white bow on the top."

She studied a display of tiny figurines. Tearing her gaze from a raven-haired groom embracing an auburn bride, she shook her head. "Bride and groom. Blond groom, auburn bride."

Beside her, Gabe inhaled sharply. He stalked to the window, fidgeting with the buttons on his jacket while she paid.

Their next stop was Petal Pusher Florals. Gabe held open the glass door and silently followed her past tiers of rainbow-colored blooms. The perfumed bouquets sweetened the autumn air with warm memories of summer.

A crystal vase overflowing with apricot roses caught her attention. "Mmm. My favorites." Unable to resist, she reached out a fingertip to stroke the velvety peach petals before leaning down and burying her nose in the tea-scented softness.

Gabe choked. She jerked her gaze up and saw him running a finger around the collar of his T-shirt. "What's the matter?"

Scowling, he pivoted, nearly knocking over a pot of yellow mums. Ramrod-stiff, he stared at a purple-and-white sympathy arrangement. "Nada."

She sighed. Though blessed with abnormal patience, even Dale hated shopping. For fly-at-warp-speed Gabe, this must be torture.

The florist arrived bearing Tessa's wedding folder. Tessa nixed Lucille's purple-and-white orchids and requested apricot roses instead. If it resulted in a showdown at the church, so be it. No matter what, nothing was going to stop her dream of security and having a family.

Tessa consulted her list. "Wedding gown. Bernard's Bridals is two blocks over and one down."

When Gabe didn't move, she prompted him. "Hello?"

He blinked, shaking his head. "Two blocks over and one down," he parroted. Even though he was right beside her, his mind seemed miles away.

They entered the bridal store, where he dropped into a chair outside the fitting room. Leaning back, he stretched out long, hard-muscled legs, his arms crossed over his chest. While she waited for the clerk, Tessa wandered over to a nearby evening-wear display.

"Here you are, Miss Beaumont." The clerk returned, bearing her Victorian lace gown. "Oh, and Mrs. Winters selected something special for you last week. I brought it along for your approval." The clerk held up a filmy pink negligee, so sheer Tessa could see through the fabric to the store beyond.

The clerk draped the nightgown against Tessa. "Lucille is right. This hot little number will turn any man from teddy bear to tiger. Your husband won't be able to keep his hands off you."

All the blood drained from Tessa's face. Light-headed and queasy, she groped for the dress rack to steady herself.

A strangled cough burst out of Gabe. He surged to his feet. "I'll be outside." He rushed out of the shop like his pants were on fire.

The clerk zipped her dress into a garment bag. Tessa declined the provocative negligee and joined Gabe. He was pacing the sidewalk. Though the temperature hovered near a pleasant sixty degrees, sweat beaded his forehead and upper lip.

"Are you all right?"

"Why wouldn't I be?" he snapped, wiping his face on his sleeve. "All this froufrou girly sh...crap is getting on my nerves, that's all."

This man had robbed her bank with cool control, played chicken with speeding police cars and calmly dispatched a gun-toting giant. But he was falling apart while running errands?

Enlightenment belatedly dawned. "I'd forgotten. When you kidnapped me, you mentioned marriage being akin to prison. Your phobia must be nearly as bad as mine to the ocean."

"Uncomfortable, yeah," he muttered. "But I've never unraveled before."

She looked at his grim face, then her watch. Only an hour until the rehearsal. "Let's grab some sandwiches and head for the park. We can eat and relax before the rehearsal."

"Don't change your plans on my account," he growled. "I'm a big boy, I can hack it."

"I'm a little frazzled and could use some fresh air myself.

It's a beautiful day." She slipped her arm through his. "Daffy's Deli is right up the street. They make a killer pastrami sub."

He covered her hand with his, giving her fingers a squeeze. "Careful. I might start to think you actually like me."

She liked him all right. More than she wanted to admit. She squelched the disturbing thought as she stashed her wedding gown in the car. They strolled down the block, arm in arm. "Stay out from under my desk and we'll get along fine."

He stopped so suddenly, she stumbled, and he had to catch her. He pointed at a boutique window. "That's perfect for you."

Tessa stared at a mannequin wearing an amber crepe sheath and matching jacket. "Too bright and too short." And the form-fitting cut would reveal way too much of the body underneath.

He snorted. "Give me a break. The skirt hits two inches above the knee." He tugged her hand. "That aged whiskey color exactly matches your eyes. Try it on."

"No." But she wanted to. The dress was beautiful.

He wiggled his impudent brows. "It's on me. A wedding gift." He pointed at the mannequin's feet. "Including footwear. Aren't those Italian?"

She groaned inwardly. Buttery brown leather pumps, exquisitely crafted. How could any sane woman resist those shoes?

"And a purse, too. You're on your way to your wedding rehearsal. Don't you want to knock 'em dead?"

Lucille would disapprove. But maybe the snappy outfit would inspire a spark of interest in her fiancé's eyes. "You *should* be a used-car salesman. I have a perfectly good suit in the car, but who can resist this temptation?"

"If only you found me that irresistible all the time." He chuckled.

Truth be told, the longer she knew him, the harder he was to resist. In every way. Their gazes met. Held. As if he'd read her mind, heat flared in his eyes. A short, awkward silence ticked by until she jerked her gaze back to the dress. What was the matter with her? She had a wonderful man waiting at the church. She banished her idiotic imagination and determinedly marched through the boutique door.

Twenty minutes later, she strode up the sidewalk wearing the gold sheath, accessorized by brown Florentine leather pumps and a matching purse. Brand-new topaz earrings set in lacy gold filigree dangled from her ears.

Gabe smiled. "Did I mention that you look fantastic?"

She felt wonderful, too. To be perfectly honest, in the few weeks since Gabe had burst into her life, she'd had more fun than in her entire steady, well-planned existence. An answering smile lifted her lips. "Merely six times. But thank you. Again."

"No sweat. My pleasure. Now the only thing that will make me happier is chow. My stomach thinks my throat's been cut."

Luckily, the deli wasn't busy, and within fifteen minutes they arrived at Laurelwood Park with sandwiches, coffee and chocolate éclairs tucked in a white paper bag.

Tessa chose a table near the pond, and Gabe slid onto the bench across from her. She handed him his coffee and sandwich.

He bit a giant chunk out of the sub, and his face lit up. "Mmm, you're right, these are great."

"I told you." A smile tugged at her lips as she pointed at a gaggle of squawking ducks charging across the pond. "Let's save our crusts for those guys. They look hungrier than you."

One corner of his mouth quirked. "Okay, but they're not getting my éclair. It looks melt-on-your-tongue soft and sweet." His eyes sparkled with a familiar roguish glint for the first time in far too long. "Exactly the way I like it."

Warmth tingled over her. One look from him and she nearly incinerated. Dale had never affected her that way. Guilty heat flooded her cheeks. Dale had stood by her for two years. Soon, Gabe would be nothing but a memory. "You must be recovered from shopping. You're back to your normal obnoxious self."

Gabe wiggled his eyebrows. In the midst of the teasing action, he tensed, and his alert gaze darted over her shoulder.

His unexpected, taut wariness jolted her. "What?" She whirled, looking behind her.

"It's okay. Eat."

Just like at the ATM, a creepy feeling put her on edge. She tried to shake it off. Gabe's watchdog attitude must be getting to her. Either that, or these odd pre-wedding jitters.

When they'd finished their meal, she stood. A walk in the brisk autumn air might help. "Let's walk around the pond."

They strolled the path, stopping to toss their crusts into the water and laugh at the ducks who rushed to squabble over the crumbs. As they rounded the trail at the far end, Tessa noticed Gabe sneak a glance over her shoulder. Again. Sudden chills wracked her with a shiver. "Maybe we better head for St. Michael's."

Without any warning, he grasped her arm and steered her toward an oak tree. He pushed her against the broad trunk. Planting both hands on either side of her head, he leaned down. "Shh." He bent closer. "Look at me and smile, like we're having a cozy chat. Don't look to either side."

She went ice-cold. Her heart kicked into high gear. "What's happening?"

"Maintenance shed twenty feet to your left. There's a guy behind the corner, watching you. I think he's been following us." His gaze held hers and she stared into the cool, alert depths. He was about to conduct business again.

She started to shake.

"The tree is between you and him. Stay put. Unless bullets start flying. In that case, hit the ground."

"Bullets?" She grasped his arm. "Gabe, no!"

"This is my job, honey." His warm fingers tenderly brushed her cheek. "On three. One. Two." His body tensed.

"Maybe you should find a new line of work," she quavered.

The megawatt grin she hadn't seen for days gleamed. "Ah, but the fringe benefits can't be beat. Three!" He pushed off the tree trunk and exploded into action.

She couldn't help it; she had to watch. The rough bark dug into her palms as she peered from behind the trunk.

He sprinted around the building. A yelp and a thud rang out. Gabe grunted, and then reappeared carrying a man by the lapels of his denim jacket. Gabe slammed him against the wall and pressed his forearm across the other man's throat. "FBI. Who are you?" he demanded, his voice low and dangerous.

The mute captive stared at him with terror-widened eyes.

"I asked you a question," Gabe growled. "Don't make me ask again." He raised his hand threateningly.

"Wait!" Tessa raced across the grass to his side.

He threw a furious glance in her direction. "I told you to stay put!"

She grabbed his upraised arm. "Don't hurt him."

"I am not going to discuss interrogation techniques with you. Get your butt back to cover. *Now!*"

"Gabe, he's only a boy." She squeezed his forearm, the rigid muscles unyielding beneath the wool sport jacket.

"Yeah, so?" But the steel bands under her hand eased slightly. His gaze raked over his prisoner. "What are you, eighteen, nineteen?"

"F-fourteen. I'll b-be fifteen next month."

"Big for your age, aren't you? Why are you following Miss Beaumont?"

The teen gulped. His tall body shook in Gabe's grasp.

Tessa studied the boy. "Haven't I seen you at the bank?"

He shuddered. "Y-yeah. The other day."

"That's right. I noticed you in line. Is that why you were watching me, because you recognize me from the bank?"

His head bobbed nervously.

"Let him go, Gabe."

Gabe's gaze burned over the kid again. "What's your name?"

"C-Colin. Colin O'Shea."

Gabe lifted him against the wall. "ID?"

The kid nodded vigorously. "Student ID. B-back pocket."

"Reach one hand around very slowly. Then hold it up."

Gabe silently stared at the ID for a full sixty seconds. "If I were you, I'd quit sneaking around and spying on people. And if you have the slightest thought about hurting this lady…" His arm flexed across the teen's throat and Colin's brown eyes widened farther. "Let's say the idea won't be the best you ever had. But it might be the last."

She tugged on Gabe's sleeve. "You're scaring him."

"I intend to scare him." He drilled his captive with another stare. "You read my message loud and clear?"

"Yeah." He gulped again. "Yes, sir."

Gabe released him, and Colin shot across the grass as if the hounds of hell chased at his heels.

She crossed her arms over her chest to still their trembling. "Was it necessary to scare that boy to death?"

He thrust his fingers through his hair. "Have you seen the news lately? *Boys* regularly commit robbery, rape and murder. That kid is big, easy to mistake for an adult. He's lucky he didn't follow somebody who shot first and asked questions later."

"Yes, I saw the way you asked questions."

"You think I should have sat him down over a cup of tea and politely inquired about his intentions? Would that be before or after he blasted a bullet through the back of your head?"

She flinched, and he sighed. "I wouldn't have hit him. Basic alpha psychology. Establish dominance, get your suspect cowering and they cooperate." He gripped her shoulders, squeezed gently. "Remember Gregson? The stakes are too high. I can't afford not to play hardball."

"Remind me not to become one of your playmates."

His wicked grin shone for the second time in fifteen minutes, and she had a sudden crazy urge to press her lips to the cleft in his chin.

"Playing hardball with you would be an entirely different game, Houdini."

A flush warmed her from toenails to forehead.

He laughed and stroked his finger under her chin before consulting his watch. "I'd better get you to rehearsal or Steel Lucille will make sure I can't play ball with *anyone.*"

The thought of him with another woman made her queasy. As they crossed the park, her head reeled in confusion. Why should she care? He was a free agent. And she'd soon be a married woman. "The female population of the world would go into mourning, I'm sure."

"Haven't you ever heard of the Goodwill Games? A guy's gotta do what he can to facilitate international relations."

"And they claim patriotism is dead."

He pressed his right hand over his heart. "I regret I have but one libido to give for my country."

"If you start singing "The Star Spangled Banner," I swear, I'll shove you in the pond."

His husky chuckle made her stomach flip. "I'm not much of a singer, but I could show you some fireworks."

"Give it a rest, Cousin Val."

Inside the car, she heaved a relieved sigh. So she hadn't imagined someone following her. Clients had approached her to say hello before. Except Colin hadn't exactly approached her. Perhaps he was shy. After Gabe's macho stunt, the poor kid would probably never dare meet anyone's eye in public.

The clock on the dash read 4:00 p.m. sharp when Gabe dropped her off at the front door of St. Michael's and went to park the car. She started up the steps.

"Tess!" Mel called out. "Wait up." Her friend bounded up the stairs. "Holy crud! Did you run into the makeover fairy?" She embraced Tessa. "You look hot!"

She grinned. "Thanks. Hot is exactly what I was going for."

They waited for Gabe, and the trio strolled into the church.

Phillip, Dale's best friend since college and best man, was there. They chatted in the vestibule until Dale and Lucille arrived fifteen minutes late, highly unusual for the punctual pair.

"Hello, Tessa, dear." Lucille's eyes narrowed. "That shade is—"

"Gorgeously perfect," Mel butted in. "The honey gold matches her eyes. And those shoes are to die for!" Mel turned toward Dale. "Doesn't she look like a hottie in this dress, Dale?"

Tessa could have sworn Gabe winked at Mel.

"She looks great. But then she always does." Dale smiled, but no heat warmed his cool blue eyes. "Sorry we're late. Are you ready?"

So much for sparks. Obviously, her fiancé didn't share Gabe's enthusiasm. Maybe she should have worn the negligee. Lucille would have keeled over on the spot. But knowing Dale, he'd probably exhibit the same subdued reaction. What was she doing committing herself to a man with no passion? And a marriage that was certain to be the same? Bombarded by last-minute doubts, Tessa stopped for a drink of water at the fountain in the vestibule.

Reverend Williams met them at the altar. The tall, gray-haired man smiled. "Everyone's here, let's begin." His gaze settled on Gabe. "Have we met?"

Tessa turned. "This is my, uh, c-cousin, Val. Val, Reverend Williams." Eek. Lying in church. To a man of the cloth, no less. She cringed inwardly, waiting for a lightning bolt to strike.

The reverend shook Gabe's hand. "You're giving away the bride?"

Gabe blanched. "No way!" He edged into a pew toward the rear of the sanctuary.

After a puzzled frown, Reverend Williams recovered his concentration and positioned the wedding party. Patiently, he walked them through the vows.

Out of the corner of her eye, Tessa watched Gabe fidget. The more nervous he grew, the more uneasy she felt.

Reverend Williams intoned, "To love and to cherish, from this day forward, till death do you part."

Gabe slipped out. Moments later, he returned, his face grim. Her stomach churned.

"Tessa?"

She jerked to attention. "I beg your pardon, Reverend?"

He chuckled. "Brides. So distracted." He consulted his book. "I'll say to Dale, 'Do you take this woman to be your lawfully wedded wife?' And Dale, you'll reply..."

"I do," Dale said, quiet but firm.

The minister turned to Tessa. "And then I'll ask you, Tessa, do you take this man to be your lawfully wedded husband?"

The Reverend's question blazed through her mind.

Tessa glanced over her shoulder at Gabe, a muscle working in his cheek. Then she studied Dale, standing stiffly beside her. Pledging the rest of her life to this man felt wrong. She gulped down the surge of apprehension, the insane urge to blurt out *no way,* and opened her mouth to respond.

Chapter 10

"I—" Tessa could not force the words out. She looked up at Dale and saw surprise blooming in his blue eyes. "Ah, just a second. We have to talk. Privately."

Lucille surged to her feet. "What do you think you're doing?"

"Mother." Dale pivoted. "Tessa was speaking to me."

Lucille pinned Tessa with an icy glare. "Don't do anything you'll live to regret, young lady."

"That's enough." Dale held up his hand. "Don't speak to Tessa like that."

Shock blanked out Lucille's face. She blinked. "After all my hard work, all the money I've spent, she's getting cold feet. And you're *defending* her?"

Dale turned to Tessa. "Give me a couple minutes to calm her down, then we'll talk."

Tessa stared at her fiancé in amazement. Wow, he'd suddenly sprouted a backbone. Perhaps dealing with the immediate problem first would be best. If Lucille launched a rampage to rival Godzilla in downtown Tokyo, they'd never be able to talk without interruption. Heaven knew she didn't want to put this off any longer. "Yes, of course."

"Mother, let's discuss this in the vestibule."

"I'm not going anywhere. This concerns me, too."

Mel stepped out from her maid-of-honor position behind Tessa and confronted Lucille. "This is between Tessa and Dale." The petite women stared one another down, two gunslingers at high noon. "You seem very upset. I'll bet Reverend Williams has a sofa where you can recuperate." Mel grasped Lucille's arm. "C'mon Dale, let's help your mother to the Reverend's office."

"Miss Parrish, take your hands off me!"

Mel patted Lucille's shoulder. "Now, now. How about a cup of coffee, a glass of water, or maybe a nice eye of newt?"

Dale grasped Lucille's other arm and the duo hustled the protesting matriarch down the aisle. Reverend Williams trotted at their heels like a worried sheepdog.

As they reached the doors, Lucille dug her Gucci pumps into the carpet. "This is a time for the family to circle the wagons."

Mel again patted the distraught woman. "You can tell me all about your girlhood when we get to the office." Mel tossed a wry look over her shoulder, and Tessa gave her friend a tremulous smile. Hurricane Mel to the rescue.

Tessa didn't dare look at Gabe. What must he think of her? She'd insisted on forging ahead with her plans, no matter the inconvenience to him. Worse, he'd been forced to baby-sit her while she ran all over town arranging this momentous event. Now, at the last possible minute, she was pulling the plug.

Needing time to collect herself, she fled to the ladies room. She sank onto a padded white vinyl bench and buried her face in her hands. She'd nearly let her yearning for a family override her common sense and made the worst mistake of her life.

The door creaked. The cushions beside her dipped. Warm fingers kneaded her neck.

She leaned into the comforting touch. "Back so soon? Thanks, Mel."

"You're welcome," Gabe's deep voice replied.

Tessa's head snapped up. Confused, she stared into his concerned green eyes. "I thought you were Mel."

"Nah, she's busy committing a mercy killing. Not that I blame her." Continuing to rub her neck, he touched her cheek with the other hand. "You went toe-to-toe with the dragon, Houdini." His expression turned enigmatic. "In more ways than one. And stood your ground."

She leaned into his touch. "I didn't expect this."

"Remember, honey, what doesn't kill you makes you stronger." His talented hand soothed the tight, aching muscles at her nape. "As my foster mom used to say, 'life is wonderful if you don't weaken.'"

"You're chock-full of happy little proverbs." In spite of her inner turmoil, she smiled at his attempt to help.

"You're doing the right thing, Tessie."

Her troubled glance traveled over the gold-and-cream decor. She sure hoped so. "That doesn't make it any easier."

He grinned. "If the right thing was easy, more people would do it."

"True. But I don't want to hurt anybody."

"Look at it this way, you're saving both of you a hell of a lot of pain in the long run."

"I'm sorry I put you through so much trouble."

"And I've never caused you any trouble?" His grin broadened. "I'd say we're finally even."

The door flew open. Mel rushed in, spotted Gabe and lurched to a stop. "Last time I looked, this was the *ladies'* room. And last time I looked, you most definitely are in the wrong plumbing department."

"Mel, honey, you may be vertically challenged, but you could bulldoze a hungry grizzly bear into retreat." Gabe's easy chuckle spilled out, warming Tessa and taking the edge off her anxiety. "Unlike Lucille, I'm smart enough to know when I'm outgunned."

Mel grinned at him. "And don't you forget it."

Her nerves jitterbugging, Tessa looked at her friend. "Is Dale ready?"

"Not yet. Lucille is pitching a royal hissy fit, and he and the reverend are still reining her in. They nixed my suggestion of a muzzle. He said to tell you it shouldn't be too much longer.''

Gabe smiled. ''So she's still alive and kicking, huh? You're slipping, Trixie Tornado.'' He gently stroked Tessa's neck one last time. ''I'm outta here. Holler if you need anything.''

''I'm feeling better. Let's all wait in the sanctuary.''

They returned to the sanctuary, where only Phillip, the somber best man, remained. The trio joined him on the front pew. Heavy silence hung over the empty room.

She stared at the stained glass windows. Blood red and stark cobalt blue. *C'mon, Dale, hurry up.* She was looking forward to the looming discussion about as much as gum surgery, but wanted the ordeal over with.

Mel glanced at her watch. ''That man had better not keep you hanging.''

She'd like to confide her change of heart to her friend, but she owed it to Dale to tell him first. She and Mel would have plenty of time later to hash over her decision.

Finally, the sanctuary doors opened, and she swiveled. Dale trudged up the aisle. The dread mixed with sympathy in his expression reminded her of the doctor who had delivered the news that her father had died. She went rigid.

He leaned down, his voice low. ''Sorry about the wait. Ready when you are.''

Mel squeezed her hand, and Tessa rose on shaky legs. As she passed Gabe, his eyes flashed a silent message of encouragement. She held his gaze, drawing strength from the jade depths, then raised her chin and marched down the dark blue carpet.

Dale escorted her to the pink-and-white bride's dressing room, and sat beside her on a pale pink moire love seat. ''I'm listening.''

Her hands were trembling, and Tessa pressed them together. This was going to be harder than she thought. Facing reality always was. ''Since the robbery, my life has changed in so many ways. I've begun to see things in a new light, see clearly for the first time. I'm not the same woman.''

She studied his strong, solid features. They'd had some good times. She was going to miss him. ''You're a wonderful man, but we're just not right together. I'm so sorry, Dale, I can't marry you.''

He looked away from her and studied the ribboned bouquets dotting the wallpaper. In light of her decision, the overtly bridal decor seemed like a cruel taunt. A long span of heartbeats ticked past. Oh, dear, she hoped she hadn't crushed him. For a man, he was pretty sensitive.

Finally, he spoke. ''Perhaps...perhaps, in light of recent developments, that's for the best.''

Well, that was certainly much easier than she'd expected. Too easy. She didn't want to hurt him, didn't want him to cause a scene, but geez, a slight objection wouldn't have been out of line. Or questions about her reasons. ''Recent developments?''

He hesitated. ''The reason why I was late today is because I got a phone call from a boy named Colin O'Shea.''

''Colin O'Shea?'' It took her a few seconds. ''That's the boy who followed me in the park. You know him?''

''Yes. Five years ago, I gave him violin lessons at the community center. The minute he picked up the bow, I knew he had the special something that distinguishes good from genius.''

''He was your student five years ago, and still keeps in touch? Why on earth was he following me around?''

He scrubbed a hand over his solemn face. ''He was more than a student. I gave him free private instruction, which is how I met his mother, Maureen. She was funny and easy to talk to, and we became close. I grew to love Colin like he was my own.'' A tender smile softened his face.

She'd never seen him exhibit this much emotion. In their two years together, he'd never smiled at her like that. She couldn't help it. A niggle of jealousy stung her. His confession struck an all-too-familiar chord. She'd always come dead last in her mother's life—behind her brother, acting, and the man-of-the-moment. ''I think I'm beginning to understand. And Maureen?''

''Yes. I eventually fell in love with her, as well.'' Unaware of her inner tumult, he continued. ''At first, being attracted to a woman eight years my senior threw me, but eventually, it ceased to matter. I proposed to Maureen.'' Looking into the past, his unfocused blue eyes glowed with warmth and vitality.

Bewilderment picked up her scattered thoughts and whirled them through her mind like a stray funnel cloud. He'd proposed to another woman before her? Dale had never mentioned his past, and she'd never asked. "What happened?"

"I knew Mother would react badly, but I hoped..." He sighed. "I decided to marry Maureen anyway. Then Dad got lung cancer. We suffered eight months of hell, and when he died, Mother fell apart. After the funeral, Maureen broke down and confessed she couldn't handle the age difference after all. I tried everything to change her mind, but she wouldn't listen." Pain bracketed his mouth as he fell silent.

Tessa had plenty of experience with rejection. "I know how much that must have hurt."

"I was devastated. Not only had I lost the love of my life, but also Colin. I'm sure he thought I abandoned him. I quit caring about everything and started sleepwalking through life." He shook his head. "Six months later, Mother met you at the children's charity. She convinced me to ask you out."

She went cold. "You dated me to please your mother?"

"At first, yeah." He gave her an embarrassed smile. "But then we meshed, and I genuinely began to care for you. I hold you in such high regard, and we have a lot in common. You're the best friend I've got. Lots of successful marriages have been built on less."

She sucked in a shaky breath. "But your heart is elsewhere."

He fisted his hands in his lap. "I haven't seen or talked to Maureen in three years. But after I spoke to Colin today, I called her, and got her to spill the truth. Apparently, Mother had a 'discussion' with her at Dad's funeral. I knew Maureen had had a hysterectomy years ago, but I didn't care. Colin was enough for me. But Mother convinced her that carrying on the Winter name was important to both of us, especially with Dad gone. Mother offered to pay Colin's way through Juilliard if Maureen moved to New York. Can you believe that?" Bitter laughter burst from him. "Maureen refused. But she didn't want to cause a family rift, so she ended our relationship."

He leapt up to pace the small room, his rugged good looks incongruously masculine in the feminine environment. "She sacrificed her happiness for mine. If I'd only known, I would have walked away from everything for her.'' He turned to face Tessa. "I tried so hard to love you, Tessa. And I do love you, but like you said before, just not in the right way. I know now it's because I've never been able to forget Maureen.''

Her stomach clenched on a sickening rush of realization. For two years, they'd both been trying to force their relationship into something it could never be. How unbearably sad, for both of them. The only thing sadder would be if they kept up the charade. She swallowed hard. Even if she'd known what to say, the aching lump in her throat blocked the words.

Thrusting his fingers through his hair, Dale dropped back onto the love seat. "Colin never lost hope. When he saw our wedding announcement, he started following you. He hoped if he explained, you'd step aside, and he could reunite his mom and me.'' He threw her a sharp glance. "He told me what happened in the park.''

She found her voice. "Gabe wouldn't have hurt him.''

"Val, Gabe, whatever his name is, he's not your cousin, is he? And if he's gay, I'll eat my violin case, buckles and all.''

Her face warmed.

"I thought so. I saw the way he looks at you.''

The image of sparkling green eyes warm with promise invaded her thoughts. "We merely have...a business arrangement. He's leaving town.'' She frowned. "And none too soon.''

"I almost ruined four lives with my inability to act. If you have feelings for him, don't wait until it's too late. Not everyone gets a second chance.''

How did she feel about Gabe? The memory of lying under him in his bed burned through her whirling thoughts. She'd come *this close* to turning her back on everything she believed in last night. Tessa stared into the full-length mirror across the room and saw herself sitting there with Dale by her side. So right. And yet all wrong. If Gabe hadn't blasted into her life, she would have been standing in front of that mirror next week wearing her wedding gown.

Icicles of fear stabbed into her. No-commitment, freewheeling Gabe was the opposite of her ideal man. And he had a marriage phobia, to boot. Self-preservation demanded she remain indifferent. She may have been short-sighted in the past, but she was no masochist.

Dale held her gaze, his eyes tender. "Will you be all right?"

She gave him a wobbly smile. "I'll be fine." As long as she didn't make the mistake of wanting something she could never have. She slid off her diamond solitaire and held it out to him. "I hope we can still be friends."

"I'd like that. And I'd like you to keep the ring as a memento."

She gently placed it in his palm and folded his fingers around it. "I don't need it to remind me. I'll never forget what we shared. Good times." Tears pressed behind her eyes, and she blinked them back. Though their relationship wasn't meant to be, letting go of him, letting go of all her hopes and dreams was so hard. "Like that concert we gave in Schubert Hall where the conductor's toupee kept slipping, and every time we looked at one another we almost couldn't stop giggling long enough to play."

"Good times." His own smile crooked, he tucked the ring in his pocket. "I'm sorry, Tessa. I've known for a long time that things weren't right between us, but unlike you, I didn't have the guts to say so. You wouldn't be out of line to call me a few choice names. Or slap me upside the head."

She forced out a chuckle. "Not my style, and you know it. Mel, on the other hand, just might take you up on that offer." She stood on legs that trembled. "I guess that's it, then."

"Right. Let's go face our friends, and the Dragon Lady."

She shook her head, her mouth wry. "You might have to buy bigger shirts to accommodate that new backbone of yours."

Dale smiled sheepishly. "She may be my mother, but I'm not blind. I allowed her to lead both of us around by the nose."

She rested her hand on his broad forearm. "Some of the responsibility rests on my shoulders. I should have tossed out the nose ring long ago."

He studied her thoughtfully. "You *have* changed since the bank robbery. I hope you find happiness, Tessa. You deserve it."

The choking lump in her throat returned with a vengeance. She cleared it away. "Thank you. Well...ready to get this over with?"

He placed his big hand on the small of her back and they walked to the sanctuary. Dale stepped in front of the altar. "I appreciate everyone's patience. We need to speak to you."

Mel, Phillip, and Lucille, who had apparently regained her chilly composure during their absence, gathered around them.

Tessa glanced at Gabe. He returned her look, a question in his eyes. She motioned for him to join the group. Holding her gaze reassuringly, he walked to her side.

Dale glanced at Gabe briefly, then her, before continuing. "Tessa and I have decided to call off the wedding."

Lucille's mouth opened and closed like a beached trout, but only a small squeak emerged.

Dale continued. "I'll refund everyone for expenses incurred, and I apologize. Tessa will explain to Melody and her...cousin." He turned to his best man. "I'll call you."

Two spots of hot color surged into Lucille's cheeks. She clutched her chest. "My heart," she moaned.

Dale flicked a resigned glance at the tiny woman. "Forget it, Mother. You've exploited that ploy for three years, and I'm not buying the act anymore. Go home. I'll join you shortly."

"But, Dale, darling—"

He held up his hand. "Nothing you say or do is going to change my decision. If you can't accept that, you're the one who will lose out, far more than you think. You'll spend the rest of your life alone, with nothing but your arrogance for company. Is that what you want?"

Lucille's shoulders slumped. Without another word, she turned and trudged down the aisle, a defeated dragon with her fire quenched.

With nothing more to be said, the solemn group trailed out behind her.

Dale walked Tessa to the door, together for the last time. Fighting a hard-won battle against tears, she turned to him. "The best of everything, Dale. For you, Maureen and Colin."

He placed a soft kiss on her cheek. "You're a real class act. Goodbye, Tessa."

The tears threatened to burst free. "Goodbye," she replied, relieved when her voice quavered only slightly.

A light caress brushed across the small of her back. She turned. Gabe was directly behind her. Brows lowered, his worried gaze searched her face. "Are you okay?" he murmured.

No. Her dreams lay in shattered pieces at her feet. She clung to a thin edge of control, barely holding back the emotional storm. Not trusting her voice, she nodded.

"I'll get the 'Vette. Hang in there." Gabe disappeared around the corner of the church.

Tessa waited on the front steps with Mel. With a last apologetic glance, Dale strode toward his car.

Blinking rapidly, Tessa bit the inside of her lip and tasted blood. She yearned for a real family. But under the circumstances, her marriage would have been as hollow and unsatisfying as her relationship with Vivienne and Jules. She wanted a deep, emotional commitment, a true soul mate.

Even though her aching heart now knew Dale wouldn't have been that soul mate, hurt and loneliness twisted like a knife in her chest as she watched him walk away.

Chapter 11

Gabe's knuckles whitened on the steering wheel as he followed Melody's dilapidated red Volkswagen. He'd broken the rules big time by directing Melody to the house and letting Tessa ride with her. But a girl needed her best friend at a time like this. He wouldn't be any help. He *couldn't* be any help. He didn't know how to give Tessa the comfort she needed. And for both their sakes, he had to keep his distance.

When they arrived, he deliberately avoided looking at her. He could still see her standing on the church steps, pale and trembling, her spine straight, her chin high. Another up-close and personal glance at her brave misery and he'd be a goner. "I'll leave you two alone." He fled to his room. Cold wind rattled the windows, but failed to drown out soft sobs from the kitchen. Oh, no, not tears. Gabe rubbed his breastbone, trying to banish the piercing ache. *Damn it!* He had the awful suspicion Tessa's tears could bring him to his knees.

Torn between the desire to go to her and self-preservation, he shoved a CD in the player and jammed on headphones. Kicking off his shoes, he flopped down on the bed. She didn't deserve a guy like him. No way was he sticking around. Letting her depend on him, and then taking off was cruel. She'd become involved with one wrong man, and Gabe was witnessing the consequences. He refused to be the next man to break her heart. He knew far too well how much damage abandonment caused.

When the CD finished, he had another ready. Four CDs later, he tugged the headphones off his ringing ears. Thick silence surrounded him. He tiptoed to the threshold, easing the door open a crack. The house was dark.

He hadn't had any dinner and he was starving. Without turning on the light, he cat-footed to the kitchen. He'd memorized the floor plan the first night and could navigate blindfolded. Opening the fridge, he grabbed an apple. As he swung the door shut, an empty carton of chocolate-chip ice cream and a bottle of chocolate syrup on the counter caught his eye. Melody must have made an emergency run. He shook his head. What was the deal with chicks and chocolate?

He started to return to his room, and stopped short. Out in the dark, Tessa stood gazing into the backyard, huddled against the deck rail. She wasn't wearing a coat. Her arms were wrapped around herself, and she was shaking. She must be cold, or still upset, or both. His throat constricted.

It wasn't his concern.

He hurried to the living room to peek out the drapes. Melody's car was gone.

Not his problem.

Fists clenched, he marched down the hallway to his room.

None of his business at all.

He stripped, and then tugged on a pair of black sweat shorts. Normally, he slept in the raw, but since Tessa had moved in, he'd started wearing sweat shorts. If she needed him, he didn't want to get caught swinging in the breeze.

After a quick trip to brush his teeth, he climbed under the covers and squeezed his eyes shut, determined to forget about Tessie and go to sleep if it killed him.

In living Technicolor, the image of her alone on the deck, shivering and forlorn, projected on his closed eyelids. Even though common sense said she'd probably stopped crying hours ago, her soft sobs echoed in his ears. He spat out a curse and snapped on the lamp to rifle through his CDs. Something mellow to help him relax. His hand stopped on a Righteous Brothers CD. Man, he hadn't listened to that one for ages. He wrenched up the volume to ten. Snapping off the light, he flopped back into bed and shut his eyes again.

He lasted through the first song.

Two minutes and fifteen seconds.

You're heading for big-time heartbreak, Bubba. In spite of the warning screaming through him, he flung off the covers and climbed out of bed. His bare feet sank into the thick carpet, silencing his steps. His throat tight, he stood with his hand gripping the patio door, wrestling with himself. *You might as well stick your head in the garbage disposal, you chump. It'll hurt less in the long run.* Heaving a resigned sigh, he slid open the door.

The frigid night air snatched the breath from his lungs, and his toes curled on the cold wooden boards as he walked toward Tessa's shaking body. She was still huddled in the same spot. "Tessie?" He rested his hands on her shoulders. Her icy, quivering skin chilled his palms through the soft silk.

She flinched and went rigid. "G-go away," she whispered through chattering teeth.

Gabe burned with the desire to rip out Dale's eyeballs and feed them to him. He battled down his anger. She didn't need that right now. "It's cold. Come inside."

"L-leave me a-alone. I h-have a lot of th-thinking to do."

Ignoring her feeble resistance, he turned her around and pulled her into his embrace. "You're hurting." And he was hurting right along with her. Somewhere along the line, his objectivity had been blasted all to hell.

Not good.

Her icy, shaking hands shoved against his bare shoulders. "I don't n-need your p-pity."

"How about comfort. Compassion." He stroked her cool, silky curls. "Friendship?"

She made a soft, vulnerable sound that punched him right in the gut. Her arms slid around his waist, and she rested her cold cheek on his chest.

He drew her trembling body closer. "You're freezing. How long have you been out here?"

"D-don't know." She barely stammered the words. "A-after M-Mel left."

Fear grabbed him by the throat. She was borderline hypothermic. He had to get her warm, in a hurry. "What are you trying to do, turn yourself into a human Popsicle?" He scooped her up, ignoring her startled squeak as he strode across the deck. He stepped down into the bubbling hot tub.

Her arms constricted in a stranglehold around his neck. "Wh-what are y-you doing?"

"Warming you up." He settled her on the bench, shoulder deep, and sat beside her. She continued to cling to him.

"Does the deep water scare you?"

Her face flushed in the moonlight and she jerked away. "No." Sighing, she slid down until her chin touched the fizzing water. Thick steam drifted upward, cradling them in an intimate cocoon of white vapor.

Relieved to see color return to her pale face, he smiled. "Better now?"

"Much."

"You'd be a lot more comfortable with your dress off."

She jerked upright. "My new dress! And my shoes!"

"Sorry. I'll replace them. I had to get you warm in a hurry. You should get out of those wet clothes. You'll warm up faster."

"I don't think so."

"Why not? You've got skivvies on. Your underwear is as good as a bathing suit." He shifted to the bench opposite her. "I can't see you in the dark, and I'll sit way over here."

"Well...these soggy clothes *are* uncomfortable." She nibbled her lower lip. "I...guess."

He fixed his gaze on the diamond arch of stars in the black velvet sky and tried to turn his mind away from Tessa splashing and wriggling out of her clothes across from him. He heard drops of water rain down, her shoes thud, and then a slap of wet fabric. The Righteous Brothers serenaded them through his bedroom window. *You've Lost That Lovin' Feelin'*. Not quite.

The exact opposite in fact. He'd wanted her to feel comfortable and relaxed, but he was paying with his peace of mind. Why, oh, why did he suddenly think this was a very bad idea?

"Mmm. This *is* nice."

Against his better judgement, he lowered his gaze. Her luminous eyes shone in the moonlight, a lingering edge of pain darkening the amber depths. His equilibrium shattered. He sucked in a breath of cold, crystal-clear air tinged with pungent wood smoke, desperately trying to relocate his center of gravity. Crickets chirped from the shadows, mocking his feeble attempt.

She swirled her arms through the bubbling water. "I feel weightless, like I could float."

He closed his eyes and leaned his head back, letting the tingling warmth caress his skin and loosen his taut muscles. He'd always been more at peace in the water than anywhere else. "Zero gravity. I've always loved this feeling. You should try scuba diving in the Caribbean, where you can see the tropical fish and coral clear as day. Incredible."

He relaxed, letting his arms float. "Unchained Melody" began to play in the background. Drifting on the surface, he breathed in the tranquility.

Tessa's soft whisper broke into the silence. "Kiss me."

He sank like a rock. Hot water closed over his head and surged up his nose. He jerked upright, spitting water. "What?" he choked.

"You said you wouldn't kiss me again until I asked you to. I'm asking."

His stomach clenched. He wanted to. Too much. Which was why he couldn't. He shook his head. "I don't think—"

"Please." Her voice trembled. "Please, Gabe."

Her soft plea arrowed into his chest and wound around his heart. She was seeking reassurance after the debacle at her wedding rehearsal. Understandable. He could put his own feelings aside and give her that much, couldn't he? What felt like forever, in reality only took two steps to close the distance between them. He stopped inches from her.

She reached up and touched his face, her fingertips tracing the droplets of moisture trailing down his cheek.

In slow motion, his hands glided through the water and grasped her shoulders, warm and silky beneath his palms. "Are you sure?"

She melted into his embrace, sliding her arms around his neck. He breathed in her tantalizing vanilla scent, and his pulse hammered erratically. She raised her face. He gazed into the soft, golden pools of her eyes. Open trust glimmered in the wide depths, sweet and welcoming. An invitation he couldn't refuse if his life depended on it.

Gabe groaned. He was toast. Completely fried.

He lowered his mouth to hers, brushing her lips in a gentle, feather-soft kiss. A quiet sigh whispered out between her lips. Their breaths mingled as she leaned into the kiss, opening to him. He glided his tongue inside, savoring the taste of rich chocolate and sweet Tessie.

All traces of shy, uncertain Tessa disappeared. She met him thrust for thrust, exploring his mouth with a boldness that made him gasp for breath. She glided her fingertips over his cheek and along his jaw, down his neck. His fragile control splintered. He plunged his fingers into her hair, pulling her closer, deepening the kiss. Her heartbeat thundered against his chest, her nipples teasing him through the thin wet bra.

His pulse roaring in his ears, he slid his hands under the water to cup her breasts, rotating his palms in slow circles over the slick fabric. She shivered and moaned into his mouth. Her hot, water-slicked body pressed against him and she began to tremble.

He drew back to nibble her earlobes. Licking water droplets off her soft skin, he kissed a sweet path down her neck. He grasped her waist and lifted her upper body out of the bubbles. Her pebbled nipples beckoned through the transparent satin bra. Bending down, he drew one into his mouth and suckled her through the wet fabric.

Her back arched, her breathing fast and ragged. Her fingers dug into his shoulders. "Make love to me."

His mind's eye saw him strip off the tiny scraps of wet satin, slide into her welcoming warmth and take her hard and fast against the wall. Then an attack of conscience slapped him upside the head, squelching his passion as effectively as a bucket of ice cubes. What the hell was he doing? He gritted his teeth, sucked in a sharp, chilly breath of air and gently eased away.

She stared up at him, bewilderment clouding her expression. "Honey, we can't do this."

"Don't you want to?" She sounded dazed.

"Yeah, I do." *Damn, Colton, you mucked that up.* He'd wanted to comfort her, and had hurt her instead. Furious with himself, he thrust his trembling fingers through his hair. "But what I want doesn't matter. You're confused and vulnerable. I can't take you to bed."

A flush crept up her neck, darkened her cheeks. She planted both hands on his chest and shoved. He backed up, giving her space.

"I told you I didn't want your pity. You can count this as your good deed for the day, Mr. Boy Scout wannabe."

He touched her cheek, but she jerked away, her eyes tormented. His throat closed up, making it tough to speak. "I kissed you because I wanted to, not because I felt sorry for you."

"Right." Her voice tightened. "You love to tease and play. Until things get serious. You never really wanted me. Everything you've done from day one, kissing me, touching me, was all a joke. Nothing but a game." She lunged for the steps.

He caught her arm and turned her to face him. "This is *not* a game, Tessa. We're not on the same page here. I refuse to take advantage of you when you're hurting. You'd wake up tomorrow with major regrets, and hate me. Worse, you'd hate yourself."

"Amazing. You even manage to sound sincere."

Gabe's jaw tightened. "What is that supposed to mean?"

"Exactly what it sounds like. I'm not the type of woman men can love. Not the type they desire. I know it, and you know it."

The ache in his groin begged to disagree. Without stopping to think, he grabbed her hand and pressed her palm to his shorts. "Then how come I'm hard enough to rivet steel crossbeams?"

She gulped and yanked her hand away, backing to the wall.

Oh, smooth move, Bubba. He sucked in another deep breath. "That was crude and out of line. I'm sorry."

Eyes wide, she stared up at him. "So you find me attractive?"

He snorted. "Do you see anybody else in this tub?" He gave her a shaky grin. "Damn, Houdini, you're tough on a guy's ego. You've been under me twice before, you must have noticed my, uh, interest. A great deal of interest."

She shook her head. "Interest, huh?" A slow smile spread across her lips, until she grinned from ear to ear. "And I wasn't even trying. Imagine."

Laughter bubbled in his chest. "God help me if you ever decide to try. I might not survive."

She moved close to him again and looked up, her teeth worrying her lower lip. "I owe you an apology. You're right. Even though calling off the wedding is for the best, I am upset and tried to push you into making love to me for all the wrong reasons. Thank you for stopping."

His glance roamed over the wet, warm, and willing woman only a hand's reach away. Two years ago, the president had pinned a Congressional Medal of Honor on his uniform for *conspicuous gallantry and intrepidity at the risk of life above and beyond the call of duty,* in a war-torn hell half a world away. Gabe hadn't felt as if he'd deserved the honor then. But he'd accept ten medals for what he'd managed two minutes ago.

"You handled a tough situation today with guts and class. You can be proud of yourself." He cupped her chin in his hand. "You deserve a man who recognizes how special you are. And who will put you first in his life. You deserve the best."

She smiled up at him. "You are a nice guy."

He managed a laugh, but it rang hollow. If only she knew. "Don't bet your life on it, honey. Or your virtue."

Her smile broadened. "I just did."

A very long, very cold shower and another aching, sleepless night loomed in his immediate future.

That's what he got for pretending to be a nice guy.

Chapter 12

As they climbed into the Pinto to drive to work the next morning, Tessa avoided looking Gabe in the eye. The way she'd thrown herself at him in the hot tub last night... She groaned.

Her cheeks heated at the memory of Gabe's impressive arousal pulsing under her palm. Dale had always been physically restrained, in fact so had she. Now she knew the lack of fire was because they shared nothing more than friendship. Tessa frowned. Then why did she have such an explosive response to Gabe? She'd always believed her heart would have to be involved for her body to respond.

Horror prickled over her skin. Did that mean she cared for him? She knew men were different; they could react merely to the female body. Maybe women and men were more alike than she'd realized. Maybe the chemistry between her and Gabe was merely lust.

She prayed it *was* only lust. Because if she thought her dreams were smashed to pieces now, falling in love with Gabe would blow her life to smithereens. She'd hand him her heart and he'd retreat, leaving her with an empty, bleeding hole in her chest.

"Music?" Gabe's question interrupted her gloomy thoughts.

She opened his CD case and pulled out a double volume. "Hey! Elvis wasn't here before."

"I bought it yesterday when you were trying on the dress." He grinned. "I noticed you have a fondness for The King."

Warmed by his thoughtfulness, she slipped the CD into the player and Elvis's smooth, deep voice flowed out like warm honey.

"You a fan of that pelvis action?"

"That's *not* why I like him," she huffed.

"Enlighten me."

Why not? It was better than sitting here worrying. "I've loved music all my life. My first memory is sitting on my dad's lap while he pounded out Elvis tunes on his beat-up, secondhand piano." She smiled as warm memories blanketed her. "He'd explain the keys and the notes. The very first song Dad taught me to play was 'Love Me Tender.' I was four."

He whistled. "You could play that young?"

"I have a gift called perfect pitch. I can hear a song and duplicate it." She uttered a hollow laugh. "My ability drove my mother crazy. She always wanted musical talent in order to boost her acting career, but she has a tin ear."

"Your mom's an actress? Would I know her?"

"You watch the soaps? Vivienne has been on *Light Of The World* for fifteen years." She shrugged. "You're probably more familiar with my brother, Jules Martin."

His brows rose a fraction. "The Wimbledon champion three years running? That Jules Martin?"

"That's the one. He and Vivienne use professional names. I kept Dad's."

"I take it you're not close to your family."

"She sent me to boarding school when I was six, after the near-drowning. I saw her once a year on parents' day, with a publicity photographer in tow. When the photographs appeared I'd always been replaced by a child model. Vivienne said it was to protect me. But—" She shook her head. "Never mind."

He glanced at her, his expression tender. "No, tell me."

Maybe the cold, hard truth would jolt them back to reality and stop this ridiculous attraction simmering between them. "I was a terribly ugly child. If my wide mouth and odd-colored eyes weren't bad enough, I wore railroad track braces. Once puberty kicked in, I had stringy hair and a face like a pepperoni pizza. And I was fat. Vivienne is a lovely woman, and extremely image-conscious.''

He swore. "She sounds coldhearted and selfish. For the record, you happen to be a very beautiful woman.''

"That's nice of you, but I've accepted the truth. I didn't inherit any of my mother's attributes. I look more like my dad.''

"Maybe that's the problem.''

"What do you mean?''

"Your mom may have projected ambivalent feelings about him onto you. Or sick as it sounds, some women view all other women, even their daughters, as competition. You and your dad were pretty tight. Maybe she was jealous.''

Intrigued by his insight, she paused, considering. "That never occurred to me. But your theory explains a lot. I haven't even seen Vivienne since I graduated. Whenever I try to call, her publicist says she isn't available.''

"Vivienne lost the most. She missed out on knowing you. Consider yourself well-rid of her.'' He touched her shoulder reassuringly. "Compared to that, I had it easy. No mother at all is better than a cold, unfeeling bitch.''

The memory of his first, tender kiss in the boat shimmered in her thoughts. She balled her tingling hand into a fist. "You mentioned a foster mom. What happened to your parents?''

A muscle jumped in his cheek. "Never mind. Where's your dad?''

"He's—he died when I was five.''

His warm, compassionate gaze held hers for a moment before he returned his attention to the road. "Sorry, honey. I didn't mean to bring up painful memories.''

"I love remembering him. He was wonderful. The year before he died, Vivienne bought him a new piano. It wasn't fancy by any means, but Dad was ecstatic. He polished it every day. I wanted to show how much I loved him, so I found a permanent marker, crawled under the keyboard and traced my hand. Then I drew a heart beside my handprint, right above where the bench slides in. I figured he'd see it when he polished, and think of me.''

His lips quirked. "I'll bet that thrilled him."

"He was at work, waiting tables while he tried to get his music career started, so Vivienne saw my handiwork first. She was furious. She spanked me with a wooden spoon and sent me to my room without dinner. I sobbed myself to sleep."

Gabe's stormy green eyes flashed. "What happened when your father found out?"

"He carried me to the piano and played 'Love Me Tender,' then asked why I'd done it. When I explained, his eyes filled with tears, and I was scared I'd upset him, but you know what he did? He wrote our initials inside the heart and traced his hand on the other side of it. Dad said whenever he looked at our handprints, he'd remember how much his little girl meant to him." Her eyes brimmed with moisture, and she blinked rapidly.

"Not long afterward, Mom divorced him to live with an actor. Back then, mothers got custody, whether they deserved it or not. Six months later, Dad died. The doctor said it was pneumonia, but Dad's heart was broken. He'd lost the will to live. He died because Vivienne couldn't control her libido."

Gabe muttered something that sounded like, "That explains a lot."

"What?"

"Nothing."

She forced her voice to remain steady. "He left me the piano, but Vivienne gave it to charity. I haven't been able to play 'Love Me Tender' since. But nothing can steal my memories. When I'm upset or scared, I hum an Elvis tune, and I feel Dad beside me."

She looked at Gabe's rigid profile as he stared out the windshield, then his white-knuckled hands clutching the wheel. "I apologize, I shouldn't have rattled on like that."

"It's okay." His voice sounded husky. "I appreciate you sharing your childhood."

"Well, I've bared my sordid past. What about you?"

He frowned. "No time to get into that now, here's the courthouse. I'll follow you to the bank, like always."

She walked up the block. Gabe invariably retreated when she got too personal. His childhood must have been a nightmare, too. Someone had hurt him. Badly. Her steps faltered. Was that it, literally? Did memory of abuse make him cry out in the night, and cause the hidden pain in his eyes? Her heart turned over. No wonder he had a problem with trust.

Her thoughts whirling, she unlocked the door and punched in the alarm code.

Less than a minute later, Gabe arrived. His eyes narrowed behind the thick glasses of his disguise. "Why are you looking at me like that?"

"Like what?"

He scowled. "Like I'm a shivering stray puppy you want to pat on the head."

She lowered her lashes, hiding her turbulent emotions from his too-discerning gaze. "Mr. Bond, I think your vivid imagination is running amok again. Let's get to work."

Still scowling, he ambled down the hall. She entered her office and sat at her desk to sort memos, but her mind wasn't on the task. How could she help Gabe? *Could* she help him? Was there a way to heal the wounds he tried so hard to hide? She looked up as he entered carrying a steaming mug.

"Howdy ma'am, brought you a cup of Earl Grey." He perched on the corner of her desk and handed her the mug.

She smiled. "Trying to kiss up to the boss?"

He beamed a naughty grin. "Nah. If I wanted to do that, I'd get under the desk."

Molten lava flooded her veins, and she jerked her gaze away from his sparkling eyes. A lesson well learned. She couldn't afford to get involved, even on a "just friends" basis. Things too easily got out of hand between them. She'd better keep her distance, let him do his job and leave.

Seeking a distraction, her attention snagged on a pile of ink-spattered papers. "Speaking of that incident, you either owe Trask a new suit or a cleaning bill. I'm surprised he didn't fire me." She shook her head. "Blue ink all over his beige suit. What a mess." She stared at the papers, frowning. "Something..." She concentrated on the dried silvery-blue puddles. "Blue ink."

"Yeah? So, it's blue."

Tessa looked up at him. "'Black pens only' is one of Trask's unbreakable rules. Black ink looks more professional and photocopies better." She touched the dried ink. "And this isn't even regular blue, it's a silvery-blue. Where did I get that pen?" She tapped her chin, trying to remember. "I know! The day I showed you the vault. I logged out and stuck the pen in my pocket. I didn't register the color because I was...distracted."

Gabe leaned forward. "And the significance would be?"

"Since we constantly have a pen in our hand, one of the bad habits we bankers have is subconsciously picking them up wherever we go. Only Carla and I had vault access, and this ink is a very distinctive shade of blue. It's a long shot, but if we can trace the pen—"

He leapt up. "I like the way your mind works. Where's the pen?"

"I threw it away." She peered inside her wastebasket. "Uh-oh. The janitorial staff emptied the trash last night."

"Where do they take the garbage?"

"Documents are shredded, paper is recycled and the trash—" She groaned. "We are *not* digging through the Dumpster."

He grinned. "Do you have anything better planned?"

"Yes, work. What if somebody sees us? Besides, it will be like looking for a needle in a very unsanitary haystack."

"Where's your spirit of adventure?" He removed the mug from her clenched hand and set it on the desk.

"At home, with my hazmat suit." She shuddered. "You can fly solo on this one, Secret Agent Man. I refuse to rifle through a Dumpster."

Gabe was staring at her mug. "Maybe you won't have to." He moved the cup aside, and then lifted her inbox. "Look." He held up a jagged half of a pen.

"I missed a piece." With a smile she rolled her gaze heavenward. "Thank you," she breathed.

He squinted at the printing on the side. "—ue Moon Club?"

"The Blue Moon Club is a jazz and blues place downtown."

"If Carla *was* involved with the counterfeiters, and she frequented the Blue Moon Club, it bears checking out. Immediately."

"I can't leave right now, I'll get fired!"

He punched numbers into the phone. "I assume Trask has voice mail?" His voice spiked high and nasal. "This is Dr. Franklin's office. Miss Beaumont was treated in urgent care yesterday for laryngitis. She requires bed rest and won't be at work for several days." He hung up, and then phoned himself in sick as "Gabe Bond." "All set."

"But who's going to run the office?"

"I'm not sitting on this until the trail gets any colder." He held the door open. "Maybe after Trask does your job for a while, he'll appreciate you more."

"After this fiasco, I won't have a job." Reluctantly, she followed him to the car.

Gabe made a five-minute stop at a gas station to change from his nerd disguise into a black rayon T-shirt, pleated slacks and black sport jacket he produced from a gym bag in the trunk. He climbed inside the car, still finger-combing his damp hair.

Her glance locked on his lean, graceful fingers stroking the shiny raven strands. Musician's hands that had caressed her body, evoking a symphony of hot, shimmery pleasure. Goose bumps prickled on her skin, and her stomach flip-flopped. She sucked in a breath. Her eyes lifted to his.

He stared at her for a long space of heartbeats. His eyes darkened, reflecting back her own raw, aching need. Then he lowered his lashes. "Do I have spinach stuck between my teeth or what?"

She gulped, jerking her gaze away. There he went, backpedaling fast and furiously. She'd be smart to do the same.

He started the car. "Tell me about the Blue Moon Club."

Not only did Gabe dodge personal questions, he ran from emotion. But he had a huge capacity for caring when he let himself. She'd experienced his tenderness firsthand. It must be tough for such a naturally outgoing man to keep his feelings under tight rein all the time. He had to have a very compelling reason. A reason he didn't want to divulge. Or couldn't divulge.

"Hey, where are you?"

In your arms. She forced her mind back to business. "Sorry, just thinking. I've heard the club is nice, though it's in a rough part of town. Somebody bought the building two years ago and renovated."

Morning traffic began to thin as he negotiated a series of one-way streets. "I see what you mean about the neighborhood." He made another turn, and pointed to a two-story building painted the same silvery blue as the ink pen. A neon sign in front read Blue Moon Club.

He circled the block. "No one around. They probably don't open until evening. I'd say a little recon is safe."

He parked the Pinto two blocks from the club. They strolled past the entrance. "Nobody's home."

"No," she whispered. She studied the neon pink help wanted flyers posted in the front window. "Everything is dark."

"Why are you whispering?" He shot her a grin.

"Probably the laryngitis," she snapped in her normal voice.

His low chuckle spilled out. "I wonder what's around back?"

She followed him down a deserted alley strewn with garbage. Two battered gray Dumpsters emanating a sour stench loomed side by side against grimy brick walls, lending a sinister cast. A shiver trailed up her spine and she moved closer to Gabe.

Though he couldn't have seen her shiver, he reached back and grabbed her hand. "Here's your chance. Sure you don't want to go Dumpster diving?"

The spooky feeling retreated, and she smiled. "I'll pass."

He stopped in front of a metal door and peered into a thick, wire-reinforced window. "Everything is dark." His glance ricocheted left, then right before he tried the knob.

"What are you doing? Breaking into Trask's office was one thing, but—"

"You can go back to whispering now. This would be more effective if you didn't announce our presence to the entire neighborhood."

"What if somebody is in there?"

"I'll have to shoot them, I guess." He took in her appalled

expression and laughed. "Relax, honey, I was kidding. The place is deserted."

"Can I help you?" A gravelly male voice rasped behind them.

She whirled. Instinctively she stepped in front of Gabe, blocking the stranger's view. In back of her, she felt Gabe's careful movement. Drawing his gun? Her pulse thudded loudly in her ears.

"I said, can I help you?" the man repeated. He was a few inches shorter than Gabe, but had at least a twenty-pound advantage. Rock-hard biceps bulged under the sleeves of his white T-shirt. His red-blond hair was buzzcut. A jagged white scar bisected his right eyebrow, and his nose sported a distinct bump, as though it had been broken. Probably more than once. He regarded them with the cold stare of a wary Rottweiler.

"We were just leaving," Gabe replied. His fingers squeezed her shoulder. When he stepped in front of her and started forward, she was relieved to see both his hands were empty.

The Rottweiler blocked their escape. "Why are you nosing around?"

Gabe's body went rigid. "Look, Bubba—"

Her mind spun. No telling what Gabe would do if this man wouldn't let them past. "It's about the job," she heard herself blurt out.

"Job?" the stranger growled.

She willed her voice not to quiver. "Your flyers in the front window said you need a singer. I'm here to audition." She waved a hand at Gabe who had turned and was staring at her like she'd grown another head. "This is my...manager. No one answered the front door, so we came around back."

The man's steel gray gaze bored into her. Holding her breath, she stood unmoving beneath his scrutiny. Finally, he spoke. "Come in." He moved forward, extracting a key from his pocket.

With Gabe behind her, she followed muscle man down a long dark corridor.

"I hope you know what you're doing, because we're between the devil and the deep blue sea," Gabe hissed into her ear.

"I hope so, too," she whispered.

Tessa's whispered reply sent adrenaline stinging through Gabe's veins. But instead of a heady, exhilarating rush, anxiety tightened his muscles. He'd let his awareness slip and trapped them in a no-win scenario. If these were the perps he'd been tracking, they'd be suspicious and jumpy. Likely to act first and ask questions later. From the silent, battle-ready way this guy moved, he had martial arts experience and was well-trained, probably ex-military.

Gabe mentally played-out his options. If it went down ugly, Tessa could get hurt. Then again, even if he took the guy out now, she could still get hurt. Not to mention he'd burn his cover *and* tip off the crooks. Damn!

His fingers gripped the Glock tucked into his waistband. He hesitated. In the short time he'd known her, Houdini had demonstrated a remarkable ability to think on her feet. He'd have to be an idiot to pass up an opportunity to get inside. As they progressed deeper into the bowels of the building, he wrestled with himself. *Now or never, Colton, make your move.*

His gut said trust her. He released the gun and let his hand drop to his side. *Okay, gut, you'd better not be wrong.*

The man they were following opened a padded door and switched on the lights. He led them into a silver-blue room with close to a hundred round chrome tables circled by black chairs. A chrome and black bar filled one side.

"I'm Leo Drumm, manager." His steely gaze flicked over Gabe before fixing on Tessa. "What's your name and what do you sing?"

Gabe could see her trembling, but she answered steadily. "Patrice...Aron. One *A*. And I can sing anything you want."

Gabe bit back a grin. His instinct was still batting a thousand.

Leo gestured at a black baby grand piano on the stage. "I wasn't expecting anybody this early. I don't have an accompanist. Go ahead and sing *a cappella.*"

"I play." She walked to the stage, and sat at the piano.

"Grab a chair, Mr. Manager." Leo waved his hand.

He slipped into his Cousin Val demeanor. "The name's Valentine, Val to you." He sauntered toward the front table.

Leo rolled his eyes. He flipped a chair around and sat with his arms folded across the back edge. "She better be good."

Man, he sure hoped so. "She is."

Tessa glanced at him, her eyes wide. He sent her a silent message. *You can do it, honey.* Her breasts rose and fell under her brown suit as she drew a shuddery breath. Then she gracefully splayed her fingers and music began to spill out. He recognized the tune as she began to sing. "I Can't Help Falling In Love With You."

Sucker-punched, Gabe sat frozen in his chair. She wasn't good. Her husky, sensuous voice traveled way beyond good. Clear into fantastic. Time suspended as her seductive melody floated out and wrapped around him, weaving right down into his soul. He forgot to breathe.

Fingers snapped under his nose and he jolted, realizing he was sitting in the sudden silence like a poleaxed steer.

Leo drilled him with a curious look. "You okay, pal?"

Unable to locate his voice, Gabe nodded.

Drumm stood. "Lose The King, and you got the job," he called to Tessa. "You start tomorrow night. And do something about those old-lady clothes. If you work here, you gotta be sexy."

Gabe sucked oxygen into his air-starved lungs. Any sexier and he was a dead man. He signed the contract Leo produced, and he and Tessa left.

She held her silence until they reached the car. She flounced into the passenger seat. "I can't believe you agreed I'd start tomorrow night! I'm supposed to have laryngitis! What if someone from work sees me?"

Gabe strode around the car. He slid into the driver's seat. "They won't. You're using your middle name and a phony surname. That reminds me, I need to get you ID and a social security card for Patrice Aron." He twisted the key in the ignition. "With different clothes and your hair down, nobody from the bank is going to recognize the sultry siren on stage."

She crossed her arms over her chest. "I am not going to dress like some sidewalk strutter—" She frowned. "How did you know Patrice was my middle name?"

Still reeling from the lethal punch of her singing, he'd slipped up again. It was getting to be a bad habit, one that could turn deadly if he wasn't careful. He should have known she would catch him, his sharp cookie never missed a trick. He lifted a shoulder. "You mentioned it, I guess."

"No I didn't." Her eyes narrowed. "You checked up on me." A flush darkened her cheeks. "I shouldn't have wasted my breath confiding in you. You probably know what my blood type is."

O positive, but he wasn't about to admit it. He sighed. "I order dossiers on everyone in every case." He clasped her hand, but she snatched it away. "Your report was bare bones. Priors, warrants, credit history, only enough to tell me you're not involved in anything illegal. The investigator didn't list any information about Jules and Vivienne, or your dad for that matter. Your mother covered her tracks on that one like a pro."

"You violated my privacy." Her voice was tight.

"Nothing personal. Just smart business."

"It's always business with you. The only reason you trusted me is because of the report." Her voice wavered and she ripped her gaze from his face, jerking her head toward the window.

He trusted her far more than he wanted to admit. Far more than he felt comfortable with. Far more than he'd ever trusted anyone.

Enough to threaten his safety.

That trust made him vulnerable, and he couldn't afford the resulting pain. "In my line of work, one small detail can mean the difference between living or dying." He slammed on the brakes and wrenched the car to the curb, then twisted to face her. Dry-eyed, she turned back to stare at him.

He heaved a sigh of relief. *No tears.* "You're intelligent and talented and one hell of a terrific lady. I knew in my gut from minute one you were on the up-and-up. But our relationship *is* business. And that's *all.*"

Mute and blank-faced, she stared at him, and he soldiered on. "Yeah, we've got intense sexual heat zinging between us, but nothing will come of it. I'm not the kind of man you deserve.

So we'll solve the case, lock up the bad guys and then go our separate ways."

He gentled his voice. "Tessie, do you understand?"

She regarded him with a thoughtful, speculative gaze. "I believe I do."

Instead of bringing relief, her quiet agreement intensified his discomfort. Maybe she understood way more than he wanted her to. He looked away from her discerning topaz eyes, ground the gears on the Pinto, and pulled back out into traffic. "Where do we get you some sexy duds?"

"That depends. This is case related, so is Uncle Sammy picking up the bill?"

At her jaunty tone, his unease evaporated and he grinned in relief. "As long as I get to choose."

"Sorry, red spandex minis aren't my style."

A picture of her in that exact garment sprang to mind and thick, hot blood flooded his groin. His hands clenched on the wheel. Ruthlessly, he squelched his desire. "Spoilsport."

She smiled. "I know how you feel about shopping."

"Don't worry, there won't be a wedding dress in sight. Sexy is right up my alley. And I'm going to replace the dress and shoes you wore into the hot tub last night."

Gabe shifted gears and the car roared past a blue minivan. Tessa studied his set jaw and white-knuckled grip on the wheel. His words were casual, but his body language told a whole different tale. Her intuition rang off the scale. He'd spouted a sincere speech loaded with common sense, but the man was on the run. Underneath the swashbuckling attitude and lightning-bolt smiles, he was scared.

Of her.

Now she needed to figure out why.

And what she was going to do about it.

Chapter 13

They arrived at the Blue Moon at ten the next morning so Tessa could rehearse. Gabe sat at a table in the back, reading a folder of papers. Every so often, she'd catch him staring at her, wary bewilderment clouding his eyes. When he caught her looking, he'd drop his gaze. What was that all about?

Right after her short lunch break, he approached the stage. "The liquor delivery just arrived," he murmured. "While Drumm checks the shipment, I'll search his office. Keep your eyes open, and if he heads that way, stall him."

"How am I supposed to do that?"

He grinned. "I have faith in you. You'll think of something." He sauntered through the doorway to the hall. The delicious sight of his perfect behind cupped by well-loved denims almost banished the anxiety his words had caused. Almost.

Four songs later, she cast an anxious glance at the clock, and then the empty club. How much longer would he be gone?

The door opened, and she whirled in relief. But instead of Gabe, Leo entered, carrying a large carton labeled *Dewars*. Bottles rattled inside the box as he lumbered across the room.

Vic, a huge burly man with a buzz cut, stuck his head in the door and called, "Boss, Vinnie says it'll be twelve grand."

Leo stopped midmotion. "It was only ten last Tuesday."

Vic's big square head disappeared for a few seconds, then reappeared again. "He says you're dreamin'. It was twelve."

"Damn it, I've got the invoice in my office. I'll shove it up his skinny ferret—" Leo shifted the box and bottles rattled again. "I'll be right there."

Oh, no! Leo was going to his office! She flicked another desperate glance at the doorway. No sign of Gabe. She gulped. Leo passed the stage, and she hesitantly called out, "Mr. Drumm?"

He halted, turning to glare at her with cold gray eyes.

"Uh, would you mind taking a look at the song lineup?"

He stared at her, then at the box in his hands before looking at her again. "You blind, deaf or both?"

"But it will only take a minute, and I really—"

"You artsy types are a such pain in the ass. Figure it out yourself." He plodded toward the bar.

In a minute, he'd reach the bar, put away the box and go after the invoice, possibly catching Gabe in the act. Should she jump down and bodily stop him? She stumbled forward, almost tripping over a cordless microphone lying at her feet.

Drastic situations called for drastic measures.

Coughing to disguise the noise, she nudged the mic with her shoe, and it rolled off the stage, landing in front of Leo.

His vision blocked by the box, he stepped right on it. The cylinder spun, increasing his momentum, and his feet scrabbled for traction before flying out from under him. He hit the ground with a thud. The box flew up, then crashed to the floor. Pungent, amber whiskey flooded the shiny oak surface. The sound of smashing glass echoed around the room. Then heavy silence descended.

If she weren't so scared, she would have chuckled at the stunned disbelief on his face.

He clambered to his feet. Shook off his pants. Shuffling to the microphone, he stared down at it. Slowly, he looked up, directly at her.

"Oops," she offered quietly. "How did that get there?"

"Oops?" he repeated. "Oops? Six hundred bucks' worth of Scotch is eating the varnish off my five-thousand-dollar dance floor, and all you can say is 'oops'?" he roared. His upper lip curled. "I'd fire you, but it'll take you months to pay me off." He stabbed his finger at the rapidly spreading mess. "Get down here and clean this up, you stupid bitch," he bellowed. *"Now!"*

Her heart pounding, she started for the steps.

"Hold it," Gabe snapped from behind her.

She whirled. He strode through the doorway toward Drumm wearing an expression she'd never seen on him before. Cold fury turned his face to stone.

Stopping inches from Leo, he spoke so low she could barely hear. "I'm her manager." His carefully measured tone made the soft admonition sound deadly. "If you've got a problem, talk to me." He leaned closer, until the men were nose-to-nose. "And if you ever yell at her like that again, or call her anything other than Miss Aron, I'll take you apart."

Drumm bristled and curled his fists, ready to do battle. Something in Gabe's eyes stopped him, because after a wary glance, Leo stepped back. "I don't need this," he growled. "If not for the dough she owes me, you'd both be outta here."

"Go about your business." Menace edged Gabe's silky voice. "I'll see that this is cleaned up and you get everything coming to you."

Drumm muttered under his breath, but he turned and stormed toward his office.

Gabe looked up at her. His iron features relaxed into the man she knew. He sauntered to the stage and held up his hands. She let him lift her to the floor. He brushed a lock of hair back from her face. "You okay?"

Aside from Mel, nobody had ever stood up for her before. She kind of liked having a champion. *Don't get too used to it.* Her knight in tarnished armor wasn't sticking around. Suddenly shaky, she nodded. "I'm fine."

He cupped her cheek. "Great job, sweetheart." His sensual lips curved into a grin. "But I said stall him, not kill him."

His impish humor banished her distress. She grinned back. "It seemed like a good idea at the time."

Gabe's shoulders shook. "Man, his legs churned like Wile E. Coyote going over a cliff."

Only Gabe could turn an ugly confrontation into something humorous. Giggles bubbled into her throat and she swallowed. "Don't start. If Leo catches us laughing, he'll have a fit."

"You're absolutely right. Mmeep, mmeep," he intoned in a perfect imitation of The Road Runner.

She bit her lip, trying unsuccessfully to squelch her laughter. "Stop it. He could have been hurt, you know."

"Yeah, he'll probably have to sit on an ice pack for a week." He laughed. "Not to mention being marinated in Scotch until he's going to have to fight off every lush in the county. When he's not too busy picking glass out of his—"

"Gabe," she groaned, holding her stomach.

"Okay, okay, I'll behave."

"That'll be that day." But she didn't really want him to change. She liked him just the way he was, naughty, irrepressible and brimming with mischief.

He gave her a gentle push. "Go on. I've got a mess here."

"I'll help you."

"Nope, there's broken glass all over. Go sing."

As she turned away, he grasped her arm. "Remind me later to show you what I found in Leo's office."

Whatever he'd found, she hoped it was worth infuriating Leo. She practiced her set, and Gabe mopped up the Scotch and glass before returning to his table.

Tessa finished rehearsing, and rearranged her sheet music. The tap of high heels on the wood floor made her glance up.

The beautiful blond hostess slinked into a chair next to Gabe. Her man-killer body was poured into a turquoise spandex dress that barely covered her...assets. And those assets certainly didn't have a deficit. Her portfolio was designed to accrue Gabe's interest. The blonde touched his arm, leaned closer so her ample breasts brushed his chest and whispered in his ear. He threw back his head and laughed. Blondie responded by cuddling closer.

Hot jealousy arrowed through Tessa's chest. Breathing hurt.

She turned away to stuff sheet music into a folder. No reason to feel upset. She didn't have a claim on the vermin.

Gripping the folder so hard it was a miracle the paper didn't disintegrate, she stomped down the hall to her dressing room. She slammed the door, wrenched the bolt home. The physical release felt good. She was tired of behaving like a lady. What had being a lady gotten her? A safe, flawless, humdrum life.

She dropped into a chair in front of her dressing table and shoved aside a jar of cold cream. Her palm itched with the temptation to fling it at the wall. Instead, she slapped the music down on the table's black veneer surface. Not nearly as satisfying, but one couldn't change lifetime habits overnight.

A knock sounded on the door.

"Who is it?"

"Bond, Gabe Bond."

Her fingers flexed in a stranglehold. "Mr. Bond doesn't politely knock. He barges in like an oversexed gorilla."

His chuckle echoed through the door. "I'm good, but even I can't get through a locked door."

"I've seen you. Use one of your picks."

He chuckled again. "Picks don't work on bolts. But I *could* kick in the door, if that particular fantasy rings your chimes."

"You'd love that, wouldn't you?" She stalked across the room, flung back the bolt, and yanked open the door. "It's probably number three on your list of titillating fun."

His brows furrowed. "I was teasing. What's eating you?"

You were canoodling with a bimbo, you cretin. She couldn't say *that.* Her fragile composure snapped. "Just how much is one woman supposed to take? I've had it! I've been robbed and kidnapped. Twice! A marriage I've been counting on for two years just went down the toilet. I'm risking my career by stealing files from my boss and playing hooky as a nightclub singer, only to get bellowed at and cussed out by some lowlife while saving your fanny! My life is in ruins!"

Her voice rose. "And if that weren't enough, I'm joined at the hip with the most irritating man I've ever known," she was yelling now, "and I'd like to wring his grinning, adrenaline-loving neck!"

"No need to shout," he said mildly. I can hear you fine."

"I never shout," she hollered. "Shouting is not dignified! Shouting is not necessary! Shouting is bad for your blood pressure!"

His mouth kicked up at the corners. "But it sure feels good, doesn't it?"

Her temperature shot up ten degrees. "Don't you *dare* laugh at me, you rodent! This is all your fault! My life was perfect until you showed up!"

"I'm not laughing." His expression carefully blank, he innocently widened his eyes. But amusement shimmered in the jeweled green depths. "Perfect, was it?"

"I really don't like you," she gritted.

His lips twitched and he pressed them together. "You've mentioned that. I told you, I don't blame you."

"Will you stop agreeing with me!" she yelled.

"Okay. I mean no. Or is that yes?"

Tessa's hands clenched into fists, and she growled at him.

Losing the battle for self-control, he threw back his head and roared with laughter. "Damn, sweet thing, you are gorgeous when you're mad."

Her temper exploded. She snatched up the cold cream and threw the jar at his head.

He blinked, ducked. The jar missed by a mile and smashed on the door frame behind him.

For a brief, satisfying moment, she reveled in his startled expression. Ha! How'd you like *that* surprise, Mr. Adventure! Almost instantly, cold dismay doused her anger. She gasped. "I could have hurt you! I don't know what came over me. I'm sorry."

He brushed blobs of cold cream and stray glass chunks off his jacket, as his steady gaze studied her face. After a moment, one dark brow arched. His lightning grin flashed. "Feel better?"

She shook her head. "I feel like a two-year-old. I don't know what's the matter with me, I've *never* lost control."

"That's exactly what's wrong, honey. Everybody needs to blow off steam now and then. With everything you've been through, I'm surprised it took you this long. Don't apologize for acting human.'' He grinned again and glanced over his shoulder. ''Lucky for me, you've got lousy aim.''

She sank into the chair, her head in her hands. ''I need a few minutes.''

''Sure. I'll wait in the hall.'' He opened the door, turned back. ''I meant what I said. You're beautiful, Tessie.'' The door gently closed behind him.

She stared into the mirror. *Beautiful?* A stranger with wild hair, flushed cheeks and flashing eyes stared back at her. ''Who are you?'' she whispered. The woman didn't answer.

She closed her eyes, forcing her rioting emotions back into their steel cage. She couldn't afford to fall apart now. In six hours, she had to go onstage.

Tessa watched the minute-hand of the chrome clock on the dressing room wall twitch to seven fifty-five. She gulped as the butterflies in her stomach started bungee jumping.

Valiantly trying to keep from throwing up, she tugged at her neckline for the third time. Why, oh why, had she agreed to this? She wasn't some sexy blues singer.

A fist pounded on the door, and she nearly jumped onto the vanity top. ''Ten minutes, Miss Aron!'' a man's voice shouted.

She pressed her sweaty palms over her churning stomach and groaned. She only sang at home, where no one else could hear. She had a decent voice, but could she carry this off? Leo liked her, but what if the audience didn't? What if Leo discovered she was a fraud and sicced the gigantic Vic on Gabe?

The door swung open and she whirled.

Gabe breezed in. ''You decent?''

''Fine time to ask, *after* you invade the place.''

With a flourish, he pulled a dozen apricot roses from behind his back. *''Pour vous, ma belle.''*

A lump lodged in her throat. He'd remembered her favorite roses. ''You shouldn't have.''

''I believe roses are traditional for opening night. I know I'm supposed to give them to you afterward, and they're usually red, but—'' He smiled. ''I was never one to stand on tradition. I thought flowers might settle your nerves.''

"Thank you. But I doubt anything will help. Unless you have an elephant tranquilizer handy?" Her hands shook as she laid the perfumed bouquet on the dressing table. "Yesterday morning, I was sitting at my desk like always, then we were in the alley, and next thing you know, I've got the bright idea to audition for Leo. I'm not sure I can do it."

He gripped her hands. "Buck up, Houdini. You'll knock 'em dead." His warm gaze caressed her. "You look incredible."

She glanced down at her full-length midnight-blue velvet dress. The close fit and scoop neckline had been her only concession to Leo's demand that she dress sexy. If Drumm didn't like her gown, too bad. "Blue velvet isn't quite in the same league as red spandex, but I suppose it will do."

He reached up and fingered a lock of hair at her temple. "And your hair is pretty, even if you did ignore my suggestion."

She had refused to wear her hair loose and wavy. Instead, she'd piled the thick mass on top of her head and left random tendrils trailing down her temples and neck. The soft classical style complemented her gown. "Thank you."

She risked another apprehensive glance at the clock. "I—I'd better go." Her stomach pitched again, and she groaned.

"Don't lose it now." Gabe pulled her into his arms. "You've got a lot more going for you than you realize. Believe in yourself, honey. You only have to get through one song tonight."

She rested her cheek against his chest. His strong, steady heartbeat thudded under her ear. "I'm trying. But I'm not even sure I know who I am anymore."

"You'll do great." His arms tightened in a hug. "Break a leg." After a reassuring wink, he left.

Tessa wobbled down the hallway to the backstage entrance feeling like she was about to face a firing squad. She clutched the sparkling silver curtains, waiting for her cue. "One song," she whispered. Since she'd only been hired the day before, Leo had allowed her to start slowly, with a single song this evening. The way she was shaking, she'd be lucky to get through it.

The musicians hit a crescendo. When the music stopped, the alto sax player spoke into his mic. "Ladies and gentlemen, the

Blue Moon Club is proud to present our newest talent, Patrice Aron.''

Polite applause rang out. She ordered her quivering legs to walk through the curtains, and stood center stage. She couldn't see past the first two rows, but felt a million eyes staring back at her. Her face flushed hot. Her body turned ice-cold and her lips went numb. Her throat constricted. She began to hyperventilate. *I can't do this!*

Then she saw Gabe at the front table, practically sitting at her feet. His warm, encouraging gaze caught and held her. *You can do it, Houdini,* he mouthed. Awareness of everything but him faded. She could almost feel his embrace. Her breathing calmed, and her thundering heart slowed to normal.

The pianist played her intro. Gabe's wide grin gleamed, and he gave her a thumbs-up. Suddenly, she felt capable of anything. Holding his gaze, she began to sing the wrenching words of unrequited love.

Gabe's eyes darkened to emerald, his gaze clinging to hers as fiercely as his hands had clung to her hair after his nightmare.

She started the second verse. Staring into his smoky eyes, a flash of realization exploded inside her. Profound and bittersweet, the pain jerked her heart to a stop.

She loved him.

Her voice faltered, and alarm flickered through Gabe's eyes. She stared into the concerned green depths, the well from which she drew comfort, and at the same time the source of her agony. For long moments that felt like an eternity, she struggled for control.

Then by sheer will, she pulled herself together. She began the finale, singing for him, and him alone. Scalding tears welled behind her eyelids. She sang on, pouring out her heart with her music, knowing she could never tell him any other way. *I can't make you love me, if you don't. I can't make your heart feel something that it won't.*

The music slowed, finally ended. Oblivious to the applause, she stood, lost in Gabe's gaze. Hot, silent tears she could no longer hold back spilled over and ran down her cheeks. Her head high, she pivoted and strode offstage.

She ran down the long, dark corridor, straight for the dressing room. Slamming the door behind her, she threw the bolt. She leaned against the door, gasping for breath.

She loved Gabe.

Oh, Lord, how could it have happened? Every self-protective instinct she possessed cried out in horror. Anything but love. Anyone but Gabe.

He was everything she feared. A rolling stone, allergic to commitment, unwilling to open up, be intimate. He jokingly avoided even the simplest questions. Hadn't she learned anything from the fiasco with Dale? Hadn't she experienced enough gut-wrenching rejection?

A knock on the wood panel behind her snapped her up, spine straight. "Tessie?" Gabe called. "You okay?"

She willed the tears from her voice. "I'm fine."

"You got pretty shook up. But the audience loved you. Next time won't be so bad." The doorknob rattled. "Let me in."

"I'm changing." *Was she ever.*

"Okay, I'll be right here if you need me."

Bright, panicked spots danced in front of her eyes. No he wouldn't. Because if Gabe found out how she felt about him, he'd run so far so fast, she'd never catch up.

Calm down. He never had to find out. Two could play emotional hide-and-seek. She dashed the moisture from her eyes, set her jaw and changed her clothes.

So what if her hands trembled as she unbolted the door and exited the dressing room? Only she knew.

Arms crossed, Gabe leaned against the wall in the corridor, facing her. His worried gaze shot to her face. "You're still pale. You went so white onstage, I thought you were gonna keel over."

The concern in his low, deep voice made her heart race. She focused on the cleft in his chin. "I've never fainted in my life. I got hit with a little stage fright, that's all."

Uncrossing his arms, he moved nearer. "Is that why you started to cry?"

She edged away. If he touched her, her brittle control would shatter. Out of the corner of her eye she caught his puzzled scrutiny. "Probably."

"It didn't affect your voice. You did good, damn good. You can be proud."

"Thank you. I'm beginning to realize I'm capable of doing things I never thought possible. Rise to the challenge."

A slow grin slid across his lips. "I keep trying to tell you that, honey. Maybe by the time I'm done, you'll believe me."

And maybe by the time he was done, her heart would be hanging in bloody, tattered pieces. She banished the dreadful image and raised her chin. "What's our next move?"

He nodded, warm admiration in his gaze. "You are definitely a class act."

Right. She would make sure he left town with that impression intact.

Even if it killed her.

Chapter 14

After a miserable night, Tessa rose early. She showered, and then dressed in her gray wool suit. She'd wrestled down the demons of self-doubt during the dark, sleepless hours. And won. Today marked a new beginning. Striding out to the living room, she set her purse and briefcase on the arm of the sofa. She'd finished two cups of coffee by the time Gabe wandered into the kitchen barefoot, wearing snug, faded jeans and a dark green T-shirt that accentuated the sparkle in his eyes.

Squelching the awareness zinging through her nerve endings, she scuttled to his room while he was busy pouring coffee. She quietly pocketed his car keys off the dresser.

He glanced up as she joined him at the table. "You look like somebody dragged you through a knothole backwards."

"Thank you. That's one of the nicest things anyone has said to me first thing in the morning."

"Sorry. That was my way of asking what's on your mind." His eyes narrowed. "How come you're all dressed up?"

"I'm going to work." She glanced at her watch. "Right now."

"No way. The doctor told you to take three days off."

She slammed down her mug and coffee sloshed onto the table. "There *is* no doctor. You made him up, remember? I'm beginning to have serious doubts about your ability to differentiate your fantasies from reality."

"Somebody got up on the wrong side of the bed." He grinned, his good nature unruffled. "You were at the club until after one, and as far as the bank is concerned you've got another day off. It's the safest choice for now."

Not bothering to answer, she stalked to the hall closet and shrugged on her coat. Snatching up her purse and briefcase, she swept outside. She made it to the driveway and had the car door open before he caught up with her.

He slammed the door shut and pinned her against the car with his body. "What the hell?" Bewildered, he stared at her.

She glared back at him. Enforced confinement with him had chafed her already frazzled nerves raw. After her jolting realization last night, she had to get away for a while. "I'm reclaiming my life."

"You won't have a life if you don't chill out. You're staying home."

"Nothing has happened since Gregson's body was found. During the time you've been dogging my every step, you've apprehended one heartbroken teenager. You're overreacting." She shoved at his chest. "I'm going to work and you can't stop me." If she buried herself in work, she might be able to forget him for a while, feel something close to normal again.

He didn't budge. "What are you going to do, get out the motion sickness pills?" His lips quirked in amusement.

The smug smile clinched it. She stomped down hard on his bare foot.

"Ow!" He shook his foot.

She wrenched open the door, flung herself into the seat and slammed the door shut. She reached for the lock just as he yanked the door back open.

"Hey," he muttered. "That hurt!"

"I meant for it to hurt."

"I can't let you do this." He grabbed her by the arm and hauled her out of the car.

Work was the only sane, stable thing she had left. She wasn't losing her job on top of everything else. She struggled as he hustled her up the driveway. "Let go of me!" She smacked his shoulder with her briefcase.

He pulled her against his hard body, restricting her movement. "Will you cut that out?" he growled into her ear. "I don't want to accidentally hurt you. But I am not turning you loose."

Hurricane Gabe had stolen everything, including her heart. He was *not* taking her independence, too. She kicked him in the shin. "Yes, you are."

"Damn, Tessa!" He flinched, but hung on. He inhaled sharply, then swooped her up and carried her inside.

She tried to wriggle free. "Put me down!"

"Can't afford to. I've only got one good leg left." He carried her down the hallway and into his bedroom.

"What are you doing? I'm going to be late!"

"Sorry, sweetheart." He dropped her on the bed. Holding her down with one hand, he rummaged in the nightstand drawer.

In the blink of an eye, both her wrists were handcuffed to the wooden headboard. "Valentine Gabriel Colton!" she yelled. "Unlock these this instant!"

"No can do." He stood back and crossed his arms. "Let's see you get out of *that,* Houdini."

"Motion sickness pills be hanged, next time I'll feed you rat poison!" Gasping for breath, she yanked furiously on the cuffs, ignoring the metal's cold bite into her tender skin.

He leaned down to grasp both her arms, holding her immobile. "Don't struggle. You'll hurt yourself."

She stopped wrenching on the handcuffs, but her anger raged like a living thing, seething and burning inside. How dare he!

"Calm down," he soothed. "Let's discuss this rationally."

She gritted her teeth. "Easy for you to say, you're not the one being held prisoner."

"Talk about a fantasy."

In spite of her rage, his suggestive chuckle, and the resulting images her traitorous mind conjured up sent desire hurtling through her. Which made her even madder. How could she possibly be attracted to such an infuriating man? "Pervert."

He laughed. "I have a beautiful, sexy woman handcuffed to my bed." He leaned over her. "Helpless and at my mercy."

She was through playing games. "Not quite." She slammed her knee into his stomach.

He groaned, doubling over.

"Count yourself fortunate I didn't aim a few inches lower, or The Spy Who Loved Me would be out of commission."

Wheezing, he fell into a chair. "I believe I just made the *numero uno* mistake my martial arts instructors warned against." His laugh turned into a moan. He pressed his hand to his stomach. "Never underestimate your opponent." He sobered. "But I'm not your enemy, Tessie. I'm on your side, remember?"

At his soft words, pictures scrolled through her mind. Gabe rescuing her from Gregson. Gabe shielding her with his body in the park. Gabe standing protectively between her and Leo.

Remorse drowned her fury. She closed her eyes, let her head fall back against the wooden headboard. "I'm sorry."

He crossed to the bed, sank down beside her and gently stroked her cheek. "If I let you go, will you stay put?"

The fight drained out of her. She was normally calm and reasonable. Even under the worst provocation, she never lost her temper. What was it about Gabe that brought out her most primal emotions? Passionate, frightening emotions she needed to keep under tight rein. "Yes."

He used a tiny key to unlock the cuffs, then grasped her hands and turned them palms up. "Did I hurt you?"

She looked at the blue bruises shadowing her ivory skin. "I hurt myself." Not only with the handcuffs. She'd hurt herself by allowing Lucille to manipulate her, by settling for second best with Dale, and most of all by striving uselessly all these years for Vivienne and Jules's approval.

No more, she vowed.

Holding her gaze, he raised her arm and pressed a soft kiss on the tender inside of her wrist. Then he kissed the other wrist.

Her stomach lurched. Gasping, she snatched her hands away. "Don't!"

He stood, somehow understanding her inner turbulence, her

need for distance. "You're having a tough time of it. How can I help?"

She longed for normalcy, for a haven from the emotional and physical upheaval of the past weeks. "Take me home. I miss my piano, my plants and Andrew, Lloyd and Webber. I want to make sure everything is okay. I've put up with all your nonsense, and nothing has happened. I deserve one concession."

He sighed. "All right. But only for a short visit. And I'll have to check it out first." He drilled her with a hard stare. "No funny business. Meet me in the living room in ten minutes." He strode to the dresser on the far wall.

She paused at the threshold, turned back. "Gabe?"

Holding a pair of white athletic socks, he looked around. "Yeah?"

"Remember, paybacks are hell. And now I owe *you* one. A great big one." She quietly closed the door.

His shout of laughter rang down the hall.

She changed into brown tweed slacks and a taupe sweater before heading out to the living room.

Gabe was waiting by the door, holding a manila folder. He shrugged on a black leather jacket. As they walked to the Corvette, he limped, groaning theatrically.

She knew a play for sympathy when she saw one. "Don't think you can manhandle me and get away with it."

"I'll never tap dance again. You don't fight fair, Houdini." His sensual lips curled into a teasing smile. "I like that in a woman."

She'd stomped his foot, kicked him in the shin, slugged him with her briefcase, and kneed him in the stomach, yet he stood here smiling and joking. Amazed and chagrined, she bit her lip. "I'm sorry about getting physical with you. I guess I reached the last of my rope and slid right off the frayed end."

"You can get physical with me anytime." His smile widened into a grin as he offered her his car keys. "You seemed pretty anxious to drive this baby. Speed is a great stress reliever."

Would this man ever stop surprising her? She accepted the keys with a delighted smile. "I've never driven a stick shift."

"How did you plan to drive it to the office?"

She shrugged. "How hard can it be?"

He rolled his eyes before climbing into the passenger seat. "Ladies and gentlemen, it's going to be a bumpy ride."

She managed to reach the middle of the first busy intersection, where she ground metal against metal trying to find second gear. The engine died. Gabe didn't even flinch.

She restarted the car, but killed it again. Following Gabe's patient instructions, she finally got it restarted, but it hopped like a spastic frog before cruising forward. She took a deep breath and maneuvered back into traffic. Cringing, she risked an apprehensive glance at him. "Sorry."

He lounged in his seat, relaxed and at ease. He lifted a shoulder. "It's only a car."

"Most guys would be having a brain hemorrhage about now."

"I'm not most guys."

Now there was the understatement of the millennium.

He chuckled. "Besides, I *like* to live dangerously."

His laid-back acceptance gave her confidence. Delighting in the growl of the engine and the immense power under her command, she loosened her death grip on the wheel and pressed harder on the gas. The responsive car instantly shot forward. A thrill zinged through her, inspiring a big grin. By the time she pulled up in front of the music store, she was not only having fun, but could competently handle the Corvette.

Gabe started to speak, and she held up her hand. "Stay in the car, lean on the horn, yadda, yadda. This cloak-and-dagger stuff isn't necessary any longer, but far be it from me to shatter your illusions." Sighing, she handed over her keys.

In less than five minutes, he returned. "Looks okay."

The elevator whisked them upward. She opened the door, breathing in the familiar lemon polish scent mingled with her plants' earthy smell. Gabe's cleaning service had done a great job. The place was spotless.

"Twenty minutes," he warned.

"I want to polish my piano and water my plants. And get additional clothes. I hadn't planned on being gone this long."

"Before you morph into Suzy Homemaker, how about I show

you what I found in Leo's office?'' He held up the file. ''Then I can read you the IRS reports while you do that other stuff.''

In the tumultuous aftermath of realizing she loved him, she'd forgotten all about whatever he'd discovered at the club. She sat beside him on her pale yellow sofa, and he passed her a photocopied memo from the folder. She squinted at the words scribbled in a bold scrawl. ''This is a description of Sav-Mart payroll checks, including the bank routing and account numbers. Where did you get this?''

''Leo's desk. I used his personal copy machine, conveniently located in his office.'' He smirked. ''I also downloaded an incriminating disk of check styles, and a check-printing program off his hard drive. Some checks match those I snatched in the robbery. And I bugged the office and phone.''

''Don't you need a warrant for that? How did you get a judge's signature so quickly, and without letting anybody know you're working on this?''

He laughed. ''A couple of federal judges owe me big-time favors.''

She shook her head. He'd told her he colored outside the lines. Outrageously true. Heavens, at times the man veered clear off the page. ''If I let myself think about the unlimited resources at your dubious command, I wouldn't sleep at night.''

''If you're lying awake with nothing to do, feel free to call on me, sweetheart.''

She pretended to ignore the sexy suggestion, but her breath hitched in her throat. ''Is this enough to convict him?''

''No. He could still pin the crime on anyone who works at the club. And remember, we strongly suspect law enforcement is involved. If dirty cops are out there, I want them. The maggots have slipped away from us too often, and I plan to catch them red-handed. No way will they weasel out of this one.''

She traipsed to the kitchen for cleaning supplies. ''Tell me the rest.'' She went to her baby grand, poured lemon oil on a rag and began to massage the shiny golden oak.

''I sent for IRS reports on our suspects. Financial records are very revealing. But due to the fiscal year-end rush and a computer screw-up, the reports didn't arrive until yesterday.''

She arched her brows. "What, no string pulling?"

"Honey, even I can't budge the IRS. But wait until you hear this." He laughed. "Your Mr. Trask is the proud inventor and owner of the *Ab Annihilator* and the *Bun Buster.*"

Her jaw dropped and her hand froze on the piano. "The exercise gizmos that redheaded actress advertises on TV?"

"He uses a corporate name, but we traced the patent to him. Guess he doesn't want his influential banker buddies to know he's in the hard body business. He's got half a million dinero, and his balance is on a steady uphill climb. Totally legit."

"Why would he continue to work at the bank?"

"From what I saw, he doesn't work very hard." He shrugged. "For some people, there's no such thing as enough money. Maybe he's into the power, or prestige in the community, or maybe he needs the medical benefits. I doubt he'd risk his rising fortune by involvement with counterfeiters."

Tessa knelt to polish the piano legs. "Wow. You work with people for years and never really know them."

"That brings up our next candidate. Donald Richards, president of Oregon Pacific Bank. Richards has a mansion in an exclusive part of town, two grown sons, a toddler, and a new, very young wife with expensive taste." He laughed again. "However, the wife appears to be keeping him, rather than the other way round. Does the name Katherine Starr ring a bell?"

She dropped her rag. "The author of *Hollywood Affairs, Beyond Hollywood Affairs* and *Lovers and Liars?*"

"Kiki Richards aka Katherine Starr. With seven bestsellers to her credit, she's racked up a cool two million in the last couple years."

"Next you're going to tell me Peter is starring in a soap opera disguised as his own sister or something."

He frowned. "Nope. This is where it gets sticky. Peter looks clean. Nothing there. Neil looks clean, too."

She wandered back to the kitchen. She filled a pitcher with water and sprinkled the plants in the mini-greenhouse window over the sink. "Good. Then what's the problem?"

"I didn't say they *were* clean. They *look* clean. Big difference. I have my suspicions. Two years ago Neil's daughter was diagnosed with an expensive heart problem.''

"Peter mentioned that. That's what insurance is for.''

"It only goes so far. Neil's house is mortgaged and nearly one-third of his income was spent on medical expenses.''

She paused with the pitcher over a Boston fern. "You think Neil got involved in crime to pay for his daughter's care?''

"Parents will go to extreme lengths for their children.''

"Why wouldn't he ask his father? Even though Kiki and Neil can't stand each other, I can't imagine she'd turn down Donald's grandchild.''

"Not much of Kiki's income is liquid. Most of it is tied up in investments, and a large chunk is in trust for the baby. I don't know about the family dynamics, but even if she wanted to, she probably couldn't come up with this much dough.'' With a sigh, he closed the folder. "Here's the clincher. Do you know what Neil's wife does for a living?''

"Peter doesn't talk about his sister-in-law much.''

"The missus is a police detective. She has access to ongoing investigations. And she was promoted two years ago. Right when the counterfeits started turning up.''

Tessa watered the plants lined along the white countertop. "Might be coincidence. I can't believe either Neil or Peter would be involved in such an awful crime against their father's bank. It still could be someone else.''

"Who else has vault access? Face it, one of them is guilty. While I'm not ruling out Peter, I think Neil's our guy. Now that we've narrowed our suspects to two, the next step is to lay down the trap. We'll need to—''

"Gabe?''

"Bug the offices, their houses—''

"Gabe!'' She stood frozen, staring at the plant under her up-held pitcher. "Look.'' She pointed a shaking finger at her Sensitivity Plant. Her wilted Sensitivity Plant. "I didn't touch it,'' she whispered. "Someone was in here.''

He rocketed off the couch to her side. "Are you positive?''

"Even though *Mimosa pudica* recovers, repeated stress causes the plant to die. I'm very careful never to touch it.''

He swore. "Get down." He snatched the pitcher from her, gripped her upper arms, and sat her on the kitchen floor with her back to the counter. "Stay put while I come up with a plan to get you out of here."

Someone had been in her apartment. Again. The thought of another violation sickened her. She lowered her head, covering her face with shaking hands. Just when she'd begun to believe this whole ugly mess would go away and she could get on with her life.

The door bell pealed. She jerked her head up, her mouth automatically opening to call out.

"Quiet!" A gun appeared in Gabe's hand so fast she didn't even see him move. He stood to one side of the door, his gun held at the ready.

"I hardly think criminals would ring the door bell," she hissed in a whisper. "It's probably Mel. She's been worried about me since the robbery. Don't go off half-cocked and shoot one of my friends."

He peered out the peephole. "It's Peter. Judging by his face, he's not on a social call."

"Peter's a friend and co-worker. He's been here before."

"My gut says different." He glided silently toward the bathroom. "I'll cover you from inside. See what Peter wants."

She swallowed. "All right."

"Don't worry, sweetheart. I can shoot the eye out of a mosquito. If this guy even looks at you cross-eyed, he's dead."

"Thanks for the reassuring words, but I repeat, please don't shoot my friend." She rose on trembling legs.

The door bell chimed again. Peter called out, "Tess?"

"Coming." When Gabe was out of sight, she opened the door.

Peter stepped inside, his face pinched, his eyes red. He looked like he'd been crying.

Tessa gestured at the sofa. "You look like you need to sit down. What's wrong?"

He sank onto the cushions. "I've come from the morgue," he blurted out. "Carla's dead."

Tessa reeled. "What?" she gasped.

''They found her this morning. The coroner said it was a drug overdose.'' He scrubbed his face with shaking hands. ''It's all my fault. God help me, I can't do this anymore.''

She tried to speak twice before words emerged. ''What happened?''

''Carla never used drugs a day in her life. They killed her.'' His anguished hazel eyes bored into hers. ''They're going to kill you, too. I can't let that happen.''

Her heart leapt into her throat. Carla murdered? This nightmare kept spiraling, growing worse. If only she *were* dreaming. ''What exactly are you talking about?'' But she was afraid she knew.

''I saw you at the Blue Moon. I went hoping to find Carla. She's been gone for days. I knew something terrible had happened.'' His voice broke. ''They approached you after the robbery, didn't they? After you'd seen the checks. I can imagine what they offered you to keep quiet. Get out, Tessa. Now, before it's too late. Do whatever you have to.''

Nausea churned in her stomach. ''You—you're involved with Leo Drumm?''

''Not voluntarily.'' He gave her a pleading look. ''I know how easy they make it sound, how tempting the money is. But it isn't worth it.''

Hazy and sick, a selfish part of her wished the traitor *had* turned out to be Neil instead of her friend Peter. ''How deeply involved are you?''

He jumped up and began to pace. ''It started with gambling.'' He groaned. ''I kept losing, but I *knew* a lucky score was right around the corner. Before long, I'd lost everything.''

''Oh, Peter. I never realized.''

''I hid my duplicity well, didn't I? I had a gambling problem in college. Dad paid a fortune to cover my debts, and for treatment at a private clinic. He made it clear he would never bail me out again. I was desperate. Desperate enough to go to a loan shark.''

''Leo?''

''He bought off my creditors. At forty percent interest. I lost that money, too, then owed him nearly double. Leo offered a deal. If I supplied payroll checks from the bank, he'd let me live." Peter shook his head. "Carla and I had been lovers for a year. Please understand, I didn't see any other option."

Still reeling at the extent of his lies, and the deadly consequences, she wrapped her arms around herself. "So you got Carla involved."

"Leo needed two of us on the inside." He groaned again. "I stole the checks from processing over a period of time. You're well aware that like most banks, we don't return checks, only statements. The processed checks are sent to storage. Nobody keeps track after that, unless a customer requests a copy. Even in the unlikely event a client requested that particular check out of thousands..." he shrugged. "Banks are notorious for misplacing paperwork. We'd send them a copy from the microfiche, end of problem. I talked Carla into helping me."

Tessa hugged herself tighter as realization dawned. "Carla used the ATM for the drop, didn't she? The constant repair calls were a front. The 'repair service' picked up the checks, right?"

Peter's eyes widened. "How do you know that?"

"It makes perfect sense. It's the only way you could smuggle the checks off the premises without suspicion or risk. And it explains the 'unfixable' problem with that particular machine, and the constant service calls."

"You're right. I'd slip the checks into a money bag for Carla to retrieve during the cash count. She'd hide the checks inside the ATM when she filled the machine with cash. Drumm's guy who worked the repair service, the same contractor Leo used for his club, would transfer them to the ATM at the Blue Moon." Peter halted outside the bathroom door and cocked his head.

Had Gabe made a noise? The last thing they needed was a confrontation. She hurried over to Peter. "But the day I took Carla's place blew your scheme."

Raking his fingers through his sandy hair, Peter stumbled into the kitchen. "Carla tried to contact me, but was too late. You found the checks." He slumped against the counter. "Drumm told Carla to phone in her resignation, that he'd take care of her. Then she disappeared. He told me he'd hidden her until everything blew over. I had my doubts, but I wanted to believe she was okay. I hung around Leo's club hoping for some word. When I saw you there, I knew they'd gotten to you.'' Peter began to tremble violently.

Torn between anger and sympathy, she marched to the sink and filled a glass with water. She handed the water to her friend. A friend who had turned out to be a man she didn't know at all. ''How could you let this go so far?''

''I never dreamed it would turn deadly. It's too late for me, but not for you. I'm going to the police. I can't bear another death on my conscience. I've never trusted Leo. Hell, I would have been an even bigger fool if I had. I stashed evidence in my safe-deposit box at the bank. If I die, the court can open the box.'' He transferred the water to his left hand, fumbled a safe-deposit box key from his pocket. His fingers shook as he held it out. ''This is an extra key. Even if they put me in witness protection, I doubt I'll live to testify. If something happens to me, turn it in anonymously.''

She reached for the key. ''Peter, I—''

Gabe stepped out of hiding. ''Don't go to the police. I can help you.''

Chapter 15

Peter blanched dead white. He whirled. The glass crashed to the floor.

Gabe held up his hands. "Remember me, Tessa's cousin Val? I can help you. I guarantee you won't get killed, or serve time. I have connections. Tell him, Tessa."

She nodded. "He'll do what he says. You can trust him."

Peter shook his head. "I don't know...."

"Look, you were going to the cops anyway." Gabe's voice was pitched low, soothing. "You said yourself you might end up in prison, or dead. What have you got to lose?"

"Who are you? Who do you work for?"

"That's not important. I can get your butt out of the sling. Who would you rather do business with, me or Leo?"

Tessa gripped Peter's arm. "I'd put my life in his hands without hesitation. You can trust him. My word of honor."

Peter gulped in a shuddery breath. "What do you want me to do?"

"What evidence have you got?" Gabe asked.

"Photocopies of the checks I passed to Leo, the dates and amounts, and some of his phonies. That and my testimony will sink him for counterfeiting. If you can link Carla's death to him, you'll have him on murder.''

Gabe glanced at his watch. ''We've barely got time to get to the bank before it closes for the weekend.'' He grabbed the notepad and pen beside the telephone and scribbled an address and some numbers. ''Once we get the evidence, go to this safe house. Here are the codes for the door lock and alarm system. I'll follow you from a discreet distance and make sure you get there in one piece. You won't see me, but I'll be there. Stay put until you hear from me. I also wrote down my private cell number.''

Peter tucked the paper inside his jacket. ''I'm supposed to meet Leo sometime in the next few days. He's been on my back to replace Carla and get the operation moving again.'' He closed his eyes. ''Poor Carla, she didn't deserve to die.'' His eyes flew open, dark with distress. ''Should I stall him?''

''He doesn't suspect you're getting ready to turn on him?''

''If he did, I'd already be dead.''

''If you can't get out of the meeting without arousing his suspicion, agree to it. I might bag him before then, anyway. I'll call you in twenty-four hours. Until then, sit tight.'' Gabe glanced at his watch again. ''I'm not waiting until Monday to do this. We haven't got time for anything fancy, so this is how it will go down. Peter, I want you to access your safe-deposit box and get the goods. Is your box in the branch vault?''

''No, I have a private box downstairs in the main vault.''

''I don't want you to have direct contact with Tessa, just in case. Take the evidence to your office and put it in an interoffice envelope. Have it sent immediately to her office. Tessa will stop in after being sick to pick up her mail. That's all you need to know. She and I will discuss the rest on the way over. Go ahead. We'll follow.''

Casting a last anxious, apologetic look at her, Peter left.

First Lucille, then Dale, now Peter. Apparently, her ability to judge people's character was badly flawed. Who was next? Her stomach clenched. Gabe? Would he also turn into a stranger and let her down?

They walked silently downstairs to the car. Gabe swung open

the passenger door. "You don't mind if I drive this time?" Though his tone was light, his trademark grin was noticeably absent.

He slid into the driver's seat. "We'll be in a public place. Even if Leo suspected Peter, he'd have to be the biggest idiot on the planet to pull something. And he hasn't kept his operation afloat by acting stupid. This has almost zero risk, or I wouldn't let you do it."

"I'm not afraid," she lied. She was terrified. But Carla's murder had strengthened her resolve to help catch the criminals responsible.

"I said *almost* zero. There's a small chance something could go wrong." He deftly maneuvered the car through snarled rush hour traffic. "So listen up. You say, hi, collect the package, then casually leave. I'll cover you from outside. If it goes to hell, hit the sidewalk. If anything happens to me, get inside, lock the doors and call this number." He recited a phone number and made her repeat it twice. "Say, 'Falcon Three,' tell them your location and that you need an extraction, code red-five. They'll rescue you and retrieve the evidence."

"Translation? I don't happen to speak spy."

"You don't have to understand. Just do it."

Gabe's pep talk eliminated her fear. For herself. Instead, her imagination conjured up gory images of the terrible "something" that could befall him. Her blood chilled. She rubbed her icy hands together. "Nothing—" her teeth chattered and she clamped them together "—will happen." She silently repeated the mantra. By the time they arrived at the bank, she almost had herself convinced.

Gabe stopped the car halfway up the block, but left the engine idling. He studied her, his expression grim. "Ready?"

She managed a jerky nod, and he squeezed her shoulder. "Okay, sweetheart, it's gonna be a walk in the park. But stay on your toes."

She steeled her nerves and exited the car. Clutching her briefcase, she willed herself to casually walk to the bank, push open the glass doors and stroll inside.

The office hummed with preclosing Friday rush. A dozen customers impatiently waited in line, and four account representatives had clients at their desks.

Darcy waved from behind a window. "Are you feeling better?"

She forced a smile and friendly nod. Inside her office, a foot-high stack of papers towered precariously on her desk. The phone rang, and she jumped. She snatched up the receiver, praying that it wouldn't be Peter calling with bad news. "Hello?" she said cautiously.

"It's about time!" Edwin Trask's voice bellowed over the line. "Do you know what I've been through the last three days?"

Since she handled the job every day, she was pretty sure she did. "I have a general idea."

He harrumphed. "This doesn't look good on your record. You've been taking entirely too much time off lately. I'm glad you're back. Now I won't have to come down and oversee closing."

She gripped the receiver tighter. "I'm afraid you will. I'm still not feeling a hundred percent. I merely came in to pick up my mail and paperwork and then I'm leaving again."

"It sounds like you don't want that promotion."

"Yes, I do. But my health comes first." She raised her chin. "I've been considering revamping my diet and exercise. I've had time to watch TV while I've been ill and those ads for the *Ab Annihilator* and the *Bun Buster* look enticing. Whoever developed the concept is a genius. Perhaps we could contact the owner to sponsor an employee fitness program."

Thirty seconds of silence ticked by. She pictured Trask's mustache twitching like a centipede in the throes of a convulsion, and smiled.

Finally he spoke very quietly. "Ah, taking care of yourself until you feel completely well is wise. I'll arrive shortly to close out the office."

Her smile broadened into a grin as she hung up. She'd learned a thing or two from Mr. Bond.

She glanced at the clock. Five minutes until closing. Surely Peter should have sent the evidence by now. She piled the backlog of papers inside her briefcase. Her anxious gaze darted around the lobby. Most of the customers had left. Staring at the elevator, she willed the doors to open and discharge a company courier carrying a bright yellow envelope.

The final five minutes dragged by. No courier appeared. Mr. Trask arrived. Without looking in her direction, he stalked behind the teller windows to supervise the cash-outs.

Darcy popped into her office. She tilted her head, inspecting Tessa's face. "That must have been one nasty bug. You look as pale as Casper."

Tessa forced out the second smile in ten minutes for Darcy's benefit. "I'll be fine."

"That new guy, Bond? He's been absent, too. You know, underneath his nerdy clothes and Jerry Lewis glasses, he's not bad. If someone did a makeover on him, he'd be hot. He's got a really sexy tush. Course, he'd need braces."

To Tessa's immense relief, a young man wearing the office mail uniform rushed in. "Priority interoffice delivery."

Thank heavens. And just in time to head off a discussion about Gabe's sexy tush.

She sent Darcy on her way and signed for the envelope with trembling hands. After locking the evidence in her briefcase, she crossed the lobby. Pausing at the door, she scrubbed her sweaty palms on her slacks, took a deep breath and stepped warily outside.

Expecting a bullet to slam between her shoulder blades any moment, she scurried up the sidewalk. Her head swiveled as she tried to watch beside, in front, and behind her at the same time. Appearing nonchalant was difficult when she was quivering like a nervous Chihuahua. "Gabe trusts me," she muttered. "I can do this." The walk lasted an agonizing eternity. Finally, she reached the car. Heaving a huge sigh, she collapsed into the passenger seat.

Gabe's solemn, tense gaze studied her face. "You okay?"

Other than a close encounter with a nervous breakdown, no problem. "Yes. What happens next?"

He eased the car into bumper-to-bumper traffic. "We make sure Peter gets to the safe house, then we go back to my house."

A surge of triumph rocketed through her, and she grinned. She'd delivered the evidence Gabe needed to catch the bad guys. This spy stuff wasn't so tough after all. No wonder he got a kick out of it.

He remained quiet for the remainder of the trip, his vigilant gaze constantly checking the mirrors. She didn't interrupt his concentration, but sat silently, savoring her victory.

Once they arrived at the cottage, he performed a thorough search of the premises. "We're secure. I'm going to check the evidence and stash the envelope where no one but me has access. Then 'Val' will message Leo requesting a meeting to exchange evidence for money. I'll be back soon. In the remote chance anything should happen, use the emergency phone procedure."

Her euphoria withered. Gabe was going to blackmail the man who had killed both Gregson and Carla. And two other federal officers. She'd forgotten obtaining the evidence wasn't the end. The real action had only begun. With Gabe smack in the middle. Then he'd leave her.

If he survived.

Her chills rushed back with a vengeance.

He tucked the envelope inside his jacket. "You did a great job. Why don't you put your feet up and relax?" Giving her a jaunty wave, he strode out.

Fat chance. Hoping to warm up, she put on a sweater. She called Mel and satisfied her friend's questions with a wild story about a federal audit shaking up the bank, and Val needing support while he hid from a jealous lover named André. To Tessa's dismay, creating blatant lies off the top of her head was becoming so second-nature that the woman who knew her better than anyone easily bought her crazy tale.

For the first hour, she paced the floor. A headache began to chip away at her temples. The sweater didn't stop her chills, so she drank two cups of instant coffee, barely tasting the vile brew.

The second hour, she peered anxiously out the window every thirty seconds. Her head was ready to explode, her stomach twisted into knots. And she was still freezing.

Approaching hour three, she chewed her manicured nails to

the quick, drawing blood. She studied her ravaged hands in disgust. She'd conquered that bad habit in the third grade. How could she help but worry? The man she loved was out throwing himself to the wolves.

''This is ridiculous,'' she told her pale reflection in the mirror over the fireplace. ''He's a grown spy.'' Shivering, she rubbed her icy hands together. ''Brr. It's cold in here.'' She busied herself by building a fire.

Finally, the Corvette rumbled into the driveway.

Gabe strolled in the door, all masculine grace and power, as relaxed as if he'd been on a pleasure cruise.

''How did it go?'' she asked evenly, amazed when her voice didn't crack into a shrieking howl.

''Peachy. Any trouble here?''

''No.'' Unless you counted an even closer encounter with a nervous breakdown. If she was going to keep helping him, she better stock up on antacids, ibuprofen and acrylic nails. ''What now?''

He grinned. ''I ladled out the chum. Now we wait for the shark to bite.''

The following morning would have been Tessa's wedding day. Gabe had been watching the news for an hour when she walked into the living room. She was dressed in a softer style than her usual business suit, in a long dark green skirt and creamy blouse with a matching green sweater. Her standard pumps had been replaced by flat-soled black suede boots. He tried to ignore the catch in his chest at the sight of her. ''Nice duds.''

She looked down at herself. ''I like this skirt. The cut disguises my...'' She trailed off, color flooding her cheeks.

He let his admiring gaze deliberately stroke her from head to toe, and enjoyed watching her rosy cheeks redden further. ''No part of you needs camouflage, honey.'' He nodded at the TV. ''A big storm is barreling in off the Pacific. I guess it's not wise to make Steel Lucille angry.'' He grinned. ''We should have thrown a bucket of water on her at the church and finished her off.'' He sang a Munchkin chorus of "Ding-dong the witch is dead.''

"Not nice,'' she choked, swiveling toward the television. But he caught a glimpse of the smile that flitted across her face. He loved making her laugh. From what he'd heard about her childhood, she'd had far too little joy in her life. She coughed several times before speaking again. "Do you have provisions in case the electricity goes out?''

"A few. But stocking up isn't a bad idea. Storm's not supposed to hit until afternoon, so we've got time.''

To his amazement, the mundane chore turned into fun. He and Tessa bantered through the supermarket's crowded aisles, and teased each other while they waited in a mile-long checkout.

By the time he swung the car into the driveway, heavy black storm clouds blotted out the sun, turning the midday sky as dark as twilight. Droplets of rain spattered the windshield.

They struggled up the sidewalk with the first batch of groceries. He had to shout over the rising wind and pelting rain. "You start a fire and I'll bring in the rest.''

She staggered inside and dropped her bags on the dining-room table. "No, I'll help.''

"I'll get it. You put the milk and cold stuff away.''

She frowned. "I'm not some delicate pansy that can't handle a little wind and rain.''

Maybe so, but he didn't want her out in the storm. "Did I say that?'' He wiggled his eyebrows at her. "I'm starving. The sooner the food gets put away, the quicker we can chow down.''

"You've got a hollow leg, Mr. Bond. As much as you eat, you should weigh three hundred pounds. What sounds good?''

"High metabolism.'' Laughing, he dumped his load and strode toward the door. "Three or four sandwiches would be great.''

He brought in the remaining bags. After checking the flashlights, he positioned candles on the fireplace mantel. Then he kicked off his wet shoes and stripped off his socks, stretching his bare feet toward the warm, crackling flames.

Tessa had just set steaming bowls of tomato soup and a stack of grilled cheese sandwiches on the table when his cell phone chirped. She jerked upright, color leaching from her face. ''Leo?'' she whispered.

He pressed the phone to his ear, and his boss's gravelly voice rumbled over the line. Shaking his head no at Tessa, Gabe hurried to his bedroom to take the call. Her part was finished. He didn't want her sucked any farther into this mess.

When he returned, she stood frozen in the same spot.

''My boss with last-minute details.'' Her tense posture eased, but she was trembling. ''C'mon, Houdini, let's eat. That grub looks great.''

She relaxed somewhat over lunch, but her face remained ashen. The anticipated call from Leo really had her on edge. He stacked his dishes in the dishwasher, and she remained silent while doing the same.

He hated to see her all uptight and worried. Maybe he could distract her, cheer her up. ''Want to play a game?''

A wary expression creased her brows. ''What kind of game?''

''Oh, ye of little faith.'' He smiled with exaggerated innocence. ''There's a Monopoly board in the closet. What did you think I was going to suggest?''

A rosy blush pinkened her pale cheeks. ''After your handcuff stunt, who knows?'' She smiled back at him. ''Monopoly is fine. Nothing kinky involved.''

The next several hours passed in playful conversation and laughter while she ruthlessly drove him to bankruptcy. Finally, he threw down his last piece of property in mock disgust. ''I should have known better than to play Monopoly with a banker.''

The wind and rain had risen steadily all afternoon, and the day had darkened as black as midnight. Without warning, a heavy gust of wind slammed into the side of the house. An earsplitting boom exploded outside. Tessa nearly leapt out of her chair. The lights flickered, then went out.

''Whoa, we lost a transformer.'' He lit the candles over the mantel, grabbed two and carried them to the table. He studied her somber face. ''The storm bothering you?''

''No. The noise just startled me when the transformer blew.''

He slanted an assessing glance in her direction, wanting to

bring back the carefree, laughing woman from a few minutes ago. "Since I can't win at Monopoly, how about a game of poker?"

"I guess I could try it. Can you explain the game to me?"

"No problem." He fetched a deck of cards. "We'll practice with a dummy hand to give you the idea."

She listened with rapt attention to his explanation of the rules, and studiously wrote down the ranking. They played out the practice round, which she lost by risking everything on a pair of fours.

"I think I've got the idea. What shall we bet?"

An irresistible spark of mischief goaded him into a grin. He couldn't pass up the chance to bait her. "How about our clothes? Unless you're too chicken?"

Instead of huffily shooting him down as he expected, she appeared to consider the idea. His groin tightened. "I was kidding."

She tilted her head. "Backing out on me?"

Oh, hell. "You seriously want to play strip poker?"

"Why not? I'm open to new experiences these days. Strip poker might be fun. Unless you don't think you can handle it?"

Oh, hell on a Popsicle stick. He gulped. "I can handle it." How well could he play with his eyes shut? Because that's the only way he'd keep from jumping her if she took off her clothes. Maybe he should lose instead. How would she react if he got naked?

He dealt with unsteady fingers. As he reached to pick up his cards, she put her hand on his, stopping him. "How about altering the stakes?"

Uh-oh. "To what?"

"If I lose, I'll take off my clothes. But if you lose, you have to answer any question I ask. Truthfully. No waffling."

He'd rather stroll through Times Square at midnight, wearing only a pink tutu and lipstick. Sweat beaded on his forehead. "No."

"You're not afraid to bare your body but you're scared to bare your soul?" She slanted an inscrutable look from under her lashes. "I understand. If you're not up to the challenge..."

Damn it, the most conservative woman he'd ever met was willing to strip in front of him. He couldn't back out without looking like an idiot. Besides, he'd been playing poker for years, and with men who would sever his jugular without a second thought. How tough could beating her be? "Okay, I'm game."

He scooped up his cards, barely able to suppress a smile when he saw a pair of tens. He kept those, took three more and drew another ten.

She asked for four cards. She consulted her written sheet of rankings, and with a big smile produced a pair of aces.

"Nice, sweetheart, but not enough." He showed his triple.

With good humor, she removed a boot and tossed it aside.

His next hand produced a flush which beat her two pair. She tugged off the other boot, sending it to join the first. Man, this was like stealing Tootsie Rolls from a toddler.

The third round brought him a straight to her three jacks. He bit the inside of his cheek to keep from laughing at the dismay on her face as she unbuttoned her sweater, leaving her in the filmy blouse and green skirt. The image of her climbing down the drainpipe in her sexy purple skivvies burned across his mind. All the blood from his brain rushed to his groin, and his jeans grew uncomfortably tight. The urge to laugh died. He shifted.

She frowned. "I'm not doing very well. Maybe we should quit."

A wise man would agree. He had never been mistaken for a wise man. Besides, he wanted to linger in her bright, warm glow a little longer before walking away, into the dark. Into the cold. Alone. "No quitting now."

She chewed her lower lip. "All right. Then let's up the ante."

A very bad feeling crept over him. "Up the ante?"

"One final hand, winner take all. If you win, I take off everything. But if I win—" She fixed him with a calculating look that started his stomach churning. "You answer three questions, no holds barred."

He shook his head. "I don't—"

She smiled smugly. "Now who's the chicken? Baak-baak-baak," she taunted.

No red-blooded male could cave in to that and keep his self-respect. "Okay, Houdini. Go for broke."

She suddenly began shuffling the cards with the smooth expertise of a Vegas croupier. "My deal. The game is five card stud. One down, three up, one down. Nothing wild."

He swallowed down the lump lodged in his throat. "You said you didn't know how to play."

"I never said that." Her lips quirked into that smug smile again. "I asked you to explain the game."

"You little scammer." The urge to laugh warred with the desire to strangle her. He drummed his fingers. "I've been hustled."

She shrugged. "This was your idea, remember? You in or out, Henry Chicken Hawk?"

Yeah, great idea, Bubba. He clenched his jaw. "In."

She dealt a facedown card to each of them.

He lifted the edge of his card. A king, not bad. Next cards face-up. A second king for him, she got a queen. Then he received a third king and Tessa a two. His mood lightened and he grinned. "Better quit while you're ahead."

She calmly dealt the next cards face-up. He snagged an ace and she dealt herself another queen. Even if she managed a third queen, his triple would outrank her. "Last chance to bail."

She shook her head and dealt the last cards facedown.

He slowly lifted the corner of his final card. Another ace. Hot damn, a full house, aces high! His heart raced. Even if she got a full house too, he still outranked her. Unless she pulled off a miracle, she'd be naked in a few minutes. What then? *Don't kid yourself. You know what's gonna happen.* She deserved so much more than a meaningless tumble in the sack. But that's all he had to offer her. His suddenly queasy stomach rolled, and the game lost its appeal.

"Look, Tessie, this has been fun and all, but let's call it even. It's a draw, nobody loses face, and we'll switch to Gin Rummy."

"I'm not a quitter. Are you?"

"No, but—"

"Let's see what you're so worried about losing with, then."

Why was she pursing this? Sensible, ready-to-compromise Tessa was showing a rare ruthless streak she'd only exhibited once before—and he'd had to cuff her to the bed that time. He hated to admit it, but he was getting a kick out of her stubborn persistence in seeing this through. However, that didn't mean he'd let it go any further than it already had.

Reluctantly, he flipped his cards face up. "Full house. No way your queens can beat that. Hell, even if you have another queen under there, you lose. But you don't have to strip."

"True, I'd lose with three queens." She nibbled at her lip again. "I'm not a welsher, though. Are you a welsher, Gabe?"

The bad feeling he'd had earlier rushed back double time. The hair on the back of his neck prickled. "No."

"Glad to hear it." She turned up the third queen. "Never underestimate the power of a lady." With a flourish, she produced her final card. "Especially the queen of hearts."

Stunned, he stared at the four queens splayed on the table. "Exactly how much poker expertise do you have?"

"We played constantly at school. And don't forget, I was a math major. Statistics and probability are right up my alley. I hardly ever lose." She grinned. "Unless I want to."

Suddenly finding it hard to breathe, he shot her an accusing glare. "I need a drink."

"I'll put some water on the fire for cocoa. We can toast marshmallows, too." Deadly serious, her golden eyes locked with his. "Then, Mr. Colton, you will spill your deep, dark secrets."

Sweating like a galley slave, he sank to the carpet in front of the fire. What would she ask? His pounding heart tripped into a frantic beat. Thirty lashes with a cat-o'-nine-tails sounded like a picnic compared to the touchy-feely talk women always wanted.

Tessa set a pan of water in the coals. She handed him a straightened coat hanger and a bag of marshmallows and sat down beside him. Her brows arched. "Don't look so scared. I'm not going to draw and quarter you with a rusty pocketknife."

Another viable substitute. Damn, his guts hadn't jittered this bad when he'd made his first nighttime skydive. "Let's get this over with," he growled.

Chapter 16

"Question one," Tessa intoned.

Gabe braced himself. Holding his breath, he stared into the fireplace, at eager, hungry flames devouring the logs.

"Have you ever been in love?"

His breath whooshed out. Easy. And so typical. Women always wanted to know about relationships. "Yes. But we were torn apart."

Her eyes widened. "How?"

"Her mom caught us playing doctor in her tree house, told my mom, and I was never allowed over there again."

She huffed out an exasperated sigh. "Answer seriously!"

"I'm a hundred percent serious. We were four, her name was Susie and she had the biggest blue eyes you've ever seen."

"And you've never loved another woman since?"

That was before he'd learned how risky loving was. Before he learned how much it hurt. Before an unbearable, searing abandonment had literally robbed him of speech for an entire year. He swallowed hard. "Nope."

She speared a marshmallow on her coat hanger and held the candy over the glowing embers. The sweet smell of melting sugar mingled with tangy wood smoke. "Why did you quit the Navy? The truth."

A sharp arrow of pain. This question wasn't as simple. "Half my team got killed, the rest wounded. Nothing would have been the same."

Her eyes shimmered with sympathy. "Were you hurt?"

Not badly. Physically anyway. And he preferred a fractured ankle over the emotional wounds he'd received. His throat tightened. "We were ambushed during a covert op. I got off easy with a busted ankle. The other guys weren't so lucky. Banks lost an eye, Stevens, a leg. We hiked through the jungle to an alternate rendezvous point."

He didn't mention he'd charged into the middle of a firefight to rescue Stevens, then carried him thirty miles. Or that he'd realized, too late, how attached he'd become to his team, how much it hurt when they'd died. A realization that had caused him to have his ankle casted in the infirmary and then hobble out without looking back. He'd resigned the next day.

She touched his arm. "Is that what causes your nightmares?"

"No." He gritted his teeth against a backlash of pain. "Bet or no, I won't talk about the nightmares. Drop it."

"Okay." Her voice was low, soft. "Last question. Why did you grow up in foster care? What happened to your parents?"

"I never knew my father. I lived with my mother until I was five." He sucked in a shaky breath. "Then I went to a foster home."

"Did she abuse you? Is that why you were taken away?"

He shook his head. "Not technically. It was neglect. She was into partying, not taking care of a little boy." He'd learned from a very early age to take care of himself, rely only on himself. His stomach rolled again. Obviously, he hadn't learned enough, or he'd have been prepared for the crushing blow that followed. Maybe he could have stopped it. Maybe if he'd tried harder, done more. Been better.

"You said your foster parents loved you?" Tessa's gentle inquiry ripped his thoughts out of that miserable track. He'd been there, done that, agonized over the "what ifs" too many times. The past was best left in the past, dead and buried. Forget it. Live for now. Live in the moment.

"Jim and Elizabeth Sinclair. They were great. I lived with them until I was ten." His insides twisted. "Then I was bounced from home to home until I turned fourteen, when I said the hell with it and took off on my own."

"You lived on the streets?"

The pity in her voice made him wince. He couldn't bear for her to pity him. "On the beach. San Diego never gets all that cold—I loved the freedom. I worked odd jobs and stayed in school, because even then, I knew I wanted to go Navy SEALs and needed a diploma." He surged to his feet. "Interrogation over. I'll get the mugs."

Tessa watched Gabe stalk to the kitchen. Now she knew. No one had ever really loved him. At least not long enough for him to depend on. Maybe with time, he would learn to trust his heart to her.

Except she didn't have time. He'd told Peter he expected to catch Leo within days. Then he'd leave.

His face intent and shuttered, he returned with mugs half-full of dry cocoa mix. He poured boiling water from the pan simmering on the hearth, and handed her a steaming cup. "That's the one and only time we're cruising down memory lane. I hope you got what you wanted."

She accepted the mug, inhaling the dark, chocolate fragrance. The storm howled, slamming into walls, rattling windows. The fire popped and crackled, a warm counterpart to the strained silence between them.

What did she want? She mulled it over as she toasted a marshmallow to golden brown. She slid the gooey sweetness into her mouth, then took a sip of rich chocolate. She studied Gabe. Golden firelight danced off his black hair and tinted his strong, solemn profile to bronze. He was quiet, lost in his thoughts.

I love you. Her heart ached to say the words. But she couldn't tell him. He wouldn't be able to accept it. Maybe she could comfort him instead. "I'm sorry. I didn't mean to upset you. I just wanted to know you better."

He blinked rapidly. As if awakening from a dream, his glazed eyes refocused. "It's okay." His soft smile didn't hide the lingering sadness. "You have melted marshmallow right..." He reached out and brushed his thumb across her lower lip. "There."

On impulse, she closed her mouth over his thumb and tasted his warm, salty skin.

He inhaled sharply. His eyes darkened to emerald. "Tessie," he groaned. "Don't." He snatched his hand free and edged away.

She followed, crawling across the rug toward him as he back-pedaled. "Running away from me, Gabe?"

"Baby, you're playing with a live grenade." He held up his hands. "And you're gonna get hurt. Bad. Don't start something I might not be able to stop."

"That's what I'm counting on." She leaned forward, pushed his hands aside and touched his lips with her own.

He froze.

She cupped his face, slipped her tongue into his mouth and stroked, mimicking the way he'd kissed her when they were lying on the kitchen floor. Slow. Sensual. Persuasive. He tasted of marshmallow, chocolate and Gabe.

He stayed completely still for too many long, shattering heartbeats. Then he groaned. He thrust his fingers into her curls and pulled her into his embrace, deepening the kiss.

More at peace, more complete than she'd ever been, she slid her arms around him and tangled her fingers in his silky hair. Pressing close, she snuggled against his chest. She ran her hands over the soft cotton shirt stretched across his shoulders, then trailed her fingers down his wide back.

He broke the kiss. His breathing ragged, he rested his forehead against hers. "It's not right. I can't do this."

Keep things light. Otherwise, he'd feel threatened. Amazed at her own boldness, she reached down and lightly brushed the front of his jeans. "Seems to me you're up for the job."

A shaky laugh escaped him. "I want you so bad my teeth ache. But I won't make promises I can't keep. I can't stay—"

She stopped his words by placing two fingers on his lips. "I know. But I refuse to live the rest of my life wondering what could have been. I want you as much as you want me.''

He groaned again before hugging her close. He lowered his mouth to hers. ''You could tempt a saint, and believe me, I don't qualify for sainthood,'' he murmured against her lips. ''I've been fighting this for too long.'' His tongue making, then keeping exquisite sensual promises, he made love to her mouth until she was panting for air. His warm breath feathered across her cheek, and he nibbled on her earlobe. ''If you're going to stop me, Tessa,'' he whispered in her ear. ''Do it now.''

She answered by unbuttoning his shirt and gliding her hands across the hard, smooth expanse of his chest. The raspy dark hair tickled her palms. ''Your skin is so hot.''

He laughed shakily. ''I'm hot all over, honey. Inside and out.''

She smiled in return, sliding his sleeves down and tossing his shirt on the rug. ''In that case, maybe you'd better get rid of these clothes.'' She drank in the beautiful play of firelight over the bronzed, rippled muscles on his chest and abdomen. Her eyes followed the dusky trail of hair down toward the waistband of his jeans. The tight denim revealed how much he wanted her. A lot. A whole lot. Her eyes widened.

''Tessie?'' At the husky question in his voice, she raised her gaze to his.

''I suspect you don't have much experience. Are you sure about this?''

Being in his arms felt so right. She needed him. And he needed her, even though he didn't realize it. She nodded. ''I want to live. Really live, instead of merely exist. No regrets allowed.'' Her cheeks heated. ''But you're right. I have minimal experience. Zero experience, in fact. You might have to, ah, instruct me. I know the mechanics, but it's quite different in practice than in theory—'' She broke off with a nervous laugh. ''I sound like an imbecile.''

''In case you can't tell from my response—which you'd have to be blind to miss—'' A playful grin danced across his mouth. ''You're doing great.''

Her flush deepened and spread to her entire body. "Um, thanks."

He sobered, reaching out to cup her face. "But I don't want to take something precious from you, then leave. And I will leave, sweetheart. Staying is impossible."

"I know. I've held back all my life. No man was ever right before. Until you. You won't be taking from me, you'll be giving. And I want to give in return. I promise, *no regrets.*"

"As long as you're sure." He smiled. His nimble fingers worked open her buttons one by one. He smoothed the blouse off her shoulders, leaving her in a mint-green lace bra.

"Gabe?" she asked, her cheeks heating again. "Before things go too far, do you...have protection?"

He chuckled. "A Boy Scout is always prepared."

"We've already established you're no Boy Scout."

"I've got it covered." He wiggled his eyebrows. "Or I will at the right time. So relax and enjoy. Come here, sweetheart," he murmured, enfolding her in his embrace again.

His hard, heated chest warmed her breasts through the delicate lace as he captured her mouth in a deep kiss. His clean, male scent surrounded her. Her swirling thoughts were dizzy with need.

Heavens, the man could kiss. She loved his kisses, could go on kissing him forever and die happy. As their tongues mingled, he wrapped his arms tightly around her and lowered her to the rug. After kissing her breathless, he nuzzled her throat. His lips worshipped the tender, ticklish spot where her neck met her shoulder, then licked and nipped along the ridge of her collarbone. She shivered and her nipples beaded.

He trailed his fingertips across her shoulders, between her breasts, slid his caress to her ribs. His soft, warm mouth followed the sensitive trail his hands created, making her feel worshiped, treasured. He taunted and tantalized with delicate strokes and nibbles, down her body, then back up again, but didn't touch her breasts. The more he dallied, the more her nipples tightened, ached for his touch.

"Touch me," she murmured.

He blew softly against her throat, provoking another delightful shiver. "I am touching you."

"Not like that."

He propped on one elbow to gaze at her and circled his fingertip around the upper curves of her breasts. "Like this?"

"Yes, but more."

His fingertip drew a series of light circles on her bra, closer to her tingling nipples, but not making contact. "Better?"

She groaned in frustration. "I thought you knew how to do this."

He chuckled. "What? Aren't you having a good time?"

"Yes. No. This is torturous. I want...more."

"You want more torture? I'm happy to oblige."

"I meant—"

He grinned. "I know what you want, sweetheart." His warm hands cupped her breasts, gently cradling her in his palms. "And I'm gonna do my best to give it to you."

She arched into his caress. "Well, hurry up," she panted.

He burst into laughter. "Damn, you're bossy in bed." His fingertips grazed her bra. He rolled her aching nipples between his thumb and forefinger, teasing them through the lace. Electric shock waves zinged right to her center. A startled gasp burst from her lips.

"Some things are better if they're not rushed." His hands skated down her spine, and the zipper on her skirt parted with a soft hiss. He slid her skirt and slip off her legs. His low whistle echoed through the room. "I'll be a—" He arched his eyebrows. "I knew you liked fancy skivvies, but these..." His fingers traced the lace edge of her black thigh-high stockings, skimming over her bare thighs. "Are incredible."

The sensual brush of his calloused fingertips made her pulse race. His touch felt so perfect, so right, as if she'd been made only for him. "Panty hose are uncomfortable. I don't like them."

"I gotta agree with you, these sexy stockings are a definite improvement." He nipped the sensitive skin above the tops of her stockings, sending liquid heat streaming through her veins. Trailing butterfly kisses down her legs, he unrolled the filmy nylons one by one. Then he nibbled a languid journey back up to her stomach, his hot breath and tender lips melting her into languid softness, as sweet and warm as the marshmallows she'd toasted.

He stopped to bestow loving attention to her navel before claiming her mouth again. He kissed her thirstily, tenderly, as if she were his most precious possession and he couldn't get enough. Reveling in the feeling, she clung to his broad shoulders, never wanting to let him go. His hands traveled to her back, and her bra slipped from between them. Springy hair and hard, smooth muscle abraded her nipples, the delicious heat wringing another moan from her.

His fingers dipped inside the waistband of her panties, and he slid them off. He studied her intently, his smoky gaze flowing over her body, his intimate perusal scorching her skin as if he'd touched her. Self-conscious under his close scrutiny, she jerked her hands up to cover herself.

"Don't. You don't have to be shy with me." He tugged her hands away, kissing her upturned palms. "You're so beautiful."

"I'm not."

Tucking a finger under her chin, he tipped her face up and held her gaze. "Yes, you are."

"My eyes are a funny color."

He kissed her eyelids. "Those wide, honeyed eyes speak to me without a word."

"My nose turns up at the end."

He kissed her nose. "That pert little nose is extremely cute."

"My mouth is too wide."

He kissed her mouth. "Your lips are as lush and tempting as sweet, sun-warmed peaches."

She licked her lower lip, tasting him there. "I'm fat."

His gaze dropped to her bare breasts, and he reverently cupped them in his hands. "Your body is silky-soft and round in all the right places. Perfect. You're a beautiful woman, Tessie. You're also intelligent, brave, generous and compassionate. Any man would feel lucky to have you by his side." He raised his gaze to hers. The tender longing in his eyes held her spellbound.

Then something amazing happened. She saw herself through

his eyes, and the awkward, ugly specter that had haunted her since adolescence vanished as completely as fog burned away by sunlight. Scalding tears prickled her eyelids. "Thank you," she whispered.

His breath caught. "No more denials, sweetheart?"

She could barely speak around the lump in her throat. "I believe you."

His eyes warmed to soft green velvet before he lowered his lids, hiding his expression. Burying his face in her neck, he pressed a kiss to her throat. "It's about time, Houdini." His voice shook, and fine tremors racked his body.

"I know you've been hurt." She stroked his silky hair. "But I won't let you down; I won't hurt you. Don't be afraid. You can trust me."

He uttered a ragged laugh that didn't quite cover an edge of panic. "Isn't that supposed to be my line?"

"Love me, Gabe."

"I'm lost," he mumbled so low she could barely hear. His body tensed.

He was ready to bolt. She had to do something. Grasping his hand, she cupped his palm over her bare breast. "How about if I draw you a map," she whispered back.

After several anxious heartbeats, he relaxed. She felt his lips curve into a smile against her neck. He drew a shuddering breath and raised up to gaze into her eyes. "X marks the spot?"

She winked reassuringly, made her tone playful. "Buried treasure."

His smile broadened into a grin. "Pillage and plunder never sounded so good."

Delighted with her success at calming his fears, she answered with a smile of her own. Perhaps if he could trust her with his body, intimately joined with hers in lovemaking, he would learn to trust her with his heart. "Well, then Matey, raise the mizzen mast and full speed ahead."

He laughed again, full and throaty this time. "My mizzen mast has been on full alert since the minute we met, *Matey*."

"I think you're all talk and no action, Mr. Bond."

"You want action?" His eyes twinkled. "I'll give you so much action, you'll beg for mercy."

She heaved a melodramatic sigh. "All I get are cheap promises."

He lowered his head and his tongue flicked her nipple. She arched, and he closed his mouth over the taut bud, sucking hard. Coherent thought fled on a stream of bright sensation that pooled low and heavy in her abdomen. He suckled until she was mindless with pleasure before turning his attention to her other breast.

She breathlessly explored the smooth skin of his back, luxuriating in the strong muscles bunching under her palms. Her hands slid over the rough denim waistband of his jeans and cupped his buttocks, as hard and fit as the rest of him. "I want to see you, too."

"Aye-aye, ma'am. Your wish is my command." He levered upright. Kneeling above her in the flickering firelight, his hair tousled, his chest gleaming, his eyes dark with desire, he embodied pure male magnificence. One leisurely hand unsnapped his jeans. Slowly, ever so slowly, he worked open the zipper to reveal a lean, tanned abdomen and black briefs. He eased the denim over his hips, tossing the jeans to one side. A sensual smile flirted at the corners of his lips as he hooked his thumbs into his briefs. One teasing inch at a time, he tugged them down. The briefs joined his jeans on the rug.

She looked at the naked man smiling down at her. He was incredible. Beautifully tanned, ridged muscles, flat abdomen, sculpted male perfection, gloriously aroused. With desire for her. Her mouth went dry.

"Well?" His smiled widened. "Do I pass inspection?"

A moment ticked by, then another before she found her voice. "You're beautiful." She rose on her knees so they were face to face. She touched the fine whiskers on his cheek, traced his sensual lips. Unable to resist, she trailed her fingers down his neck to his hard shoulders and across his wide, satiny chest. His nipples hardened under her questing fingertips and he groaned.

Encouraged by his reaction, she leaned forward and licked. The smooth nub beaded under her tongue. His abdominal muscles clenched and the scorching length of him jerked against her stomach.

"Damn." He groaned again.

Realization of her feminine power flooded her in a heady rush as she kissed his hot skin, felt it ripple and jump beneath her lips. His breath rasped raggedly as she explored his other nipple. Intoxicated by his ready response, by his warm, unique male scent, she moved lower, kissing her way down his flat stomach.

"Sorry, sweetheart." He grasped her shoulders to draw her up eye level with him. "You've got to slow down, or you'll be left high and dry wondering what all the hoopla is about." He gently cupped her face in his big hands and captured her mouth with his.

She lost herself in the erotic wonder of his kiss. His fingers glided through her hair. He trailed his fingertips over her shoulders, stroked down her back, and then cupped her bottom. When she opened her eyes again, she was laying on the rug with his welcome weight covering her.

"Mmm. Your lips taste so sweet." He nuzzled her neck. "There's something I've been wondering." He moved lower, licking and teasing her sensitized nipples. His lips meandered a delicious, leisurely path to her ribs.

"What?" she managed to moan.

He nuzzled her navel with his nose, kissing her belly. "If the rest of you tastes as good," he whispered. Then he moved lower and his mouth closed over her in the most shocking kiss of all.

"*Oh!*" She gasped at the intimacy, the searing connection that arced between them. A ribbon of heat streamed through her, coiling into a sweet ache. Her hips rocked upward. Seeking an anchor, she thrust her fingers into his hair.

He slid his hands under her bottom and lifted, intensifying the glorious sensation. She clenched her teeth to keep from screaming at the bold strokes of his tongue. Tension thrummed inside her, twisting into a tight spiral. Then unbelievably, wound tighter, and tighter yet. Her head thrashed from side to side as her body quivered, straining toward completion. A whimper escaped.

He raised his head, leaving her aching and unfulfilled, and

lowered her to the rug. He kissed a return path up her body to her lips. She moaned into his mouth in taut desperation. "Please don't stop."

"I won't," he soothed as his hand glided down her stomach. He gently caressed an exquisitely sensitive spot. "I want to see your pleasure."

Pleasure, oh, yes. Pleasure surged, arched her against his palm. Panting, she closed her eyes as aching tension spiraled again.

One long finger slid inside of her. "You're killing my self-control here." He groaned.

She gathered the scattered fringes of her concentration enough to gasp out, "Sorry."

His soft chuckle feathered his warm breath across her lips. "Nothing to apologize for, sweetheart." Another finger joined the first, filling her with exquisite pressure, while at the same time his thumb steadily stroked her toward a mounting crescendo.

Fire blazed inside her, burning outward, scorching every nerve ending. Her heart galloped wildly, and her body went rigid. Throbbing need clenched deep inside, her inner muscles involuntarily contracting.

"Go with it, Tessie. Let it happen."

Shaking uncontrollably, she teetered on the brink of the chasm, clinging to the edge. She was afraid of the unknown. She was afraid of her intense feelings, both physical and emotional. She was afraid she'd fall and shatter into a thousand pieces. "No! It's too much!"

"Look at me," Gabe commanded.

She opened her eyes. Her panicked gaze clung to his, the smoky green depths inches from her own.

"It's okay. Jump, baby," he soothed. "I'll catch you."

Her fear vanished in a warm wave of trust and love. Holding his gaze—her lifeline—she let go. Instead of falling, she soared. Tremor after tremor of ecstasy exploded inside her, and her body rocked with sweet release. She flew higher and higher, to the starry edges of the universe and into the fiery sun.

Then she floated to earth, gasping and trembling.

A long, shuddering sigh slipped out of her as he gently withdrew his hand. His mouth curled into a slow smile of male satisfaction. Caressing her face, he cuddled her close until her trembling stopped. "Okay?" he asked, his voice roughened by passion, his tone tender.

Awed, she stared into his glowing eyes. This was as close to Heaven as she'd ever been. Her heart overflowed. The words welled up inside and spilled out. "I love you," she murmured.

Stunned shock, then fear slashed across his face. He recoiled as if she'd slapped him. Flat darkness killed the light in his eyes. His jaw clenched in a hard line as he wrenched away and snatched up his jeans. Jumping to his feet, he yanked them on. "For how long?"

Caught in an emotional hurricane, she shoved her own pain aside and narrowed her focus to the wounded man who needed her. "What do you mean? I'm not going anywhere."

He bowed his head. "I can't be what you want. Eventually, you'll leave."

"I want *you*, Gabe. Nothing more." She sat up. "I won't leave you, I promise."

"Your love is wasted on me." His raw, ragged voice was so low she could hardly hear.

Seeing Gabe stripped of his confidence, painfully vulnerable, caused a stinging ache in her throat. But in order to help him, she had to make him face the truth. She scrambled to her feet. "The adventurer, the adrenaline junkie, will risk his neck without a second thought. But he's afraid to risk his heart?"

He raised his head. The anguish in his eyes burned to her soul. "You don't understand."

"I'm here for you," she said gently. "Help me understand."

He raked his fingers through his hair. His throat worked. "You don't understand." Each word wrenched out of him. "I...can't...give you...enough."

Even after everything they'd been through, all they'd shared, he was afraid to trust her. She stepped toward him, hands outstretched. "I understand far more than you think. Talk to me. Trust me."

Were those tears glittering in his eyes? "I don't know how."

He strode across the room, jerked open the door. The raging storm burst inside, the cold blast making the fire tremble wildly.

Her heart breaking, she blurted out a desperate, last-ditch challenge. "You can run away from me, but unless you face your fears head-on you'll never be able to escape them."

Gabe couldn't bear to hear her say it. He flung himself across the threshold. Not fast enough. She shouted after him, "Under all the bravado, you're scared!"

He hurtled outside, slamming the door on Tessa's words just like he'd slammed the door on her love. His chest heaving, he lifted his face, exposed and unprotected to the storm's brutal fury. Icy rain pelted him. Soaked and shivering, he let the stinging drops pummel his face, his bare torso. But the rain couldn't wash away the facts. He *was* scared.

Scared? Hell, he was terrified. His hands knotted into fists as he strode down the driveway. His stride lengthened, then he broke into a run.

He ran until his lungs burned and his side ached. He ran until his muscles screamed for mercy. But he gave none. He didn't deserve mercy. Punishing himself, he pushed his body to the breaking point.

Tessa was right. No matter how far or how fast he ran, he couldn't outrun the truth.

She loved him. And God help him, he loved her, too.

How the hell had it happened? How had she breached his defenses, defenses that were so firmly in place, he usually didn't have to try to maintain them? He'd thought his heart was barricaded behind an insurmountable wall. Thought it was safe. His deepest, most primal instincts had recognized the truth the instant he walked into the bank, but he'd managed to cling to denial. Until now.

The day he'd kidnapped Tessa, she'd captured his heart.

But if this woman walked out on him, he wouldn't survive. She'd annihilate him. Destroy him once and for all.

He just couldn't take that chance.

Chapter 17

The storm had blown out hours ago, but clouds hung heavy and dark, merely changing the horizon to menacing gray with the dawn. Tessa peered out the window into the gloom, anxiously seeking any sign of Gabe. He'd been gone all night. Alone and hurting.

He'd return. His responsibility would force him to finish the case. Her stomach clenched. Knowing the master of emotional retreat, he'd probably dump her in a safe house at the first opportunity. But she'd fight him every inch. She would see this through to the bitter end. She trudged to the kitchen. Somehow, she'd get through to him. Somehow, she'd convince him to trust her. Somehow, she'd convince him that needing her wasn't a weakness.

After coffee and a shower, she dressed in black slacks and a cream sweater. Gathering her curls into a pearl clip, she wandered into the living room, and jerked to an abrupt stop.

Gabe had just walked in the front door. Wearing only jeans, he was soaked and shivering, his skin blue with cold. His torn feet oozed blood onto the carpet. He looked at her, his face shuttered. His taut, drawn features and flat gaze confirmed her worst fears. He'd shut her out. He'd closed himself off and locked away his soul.

Her heart aching, Tessa's throat tightened with unshed tears. She'd pushed him too far, too fast. And lost him. "You look like you need a hot shower, strong coffee, and breakfast." The effort to keep her tone casual cost every ounce of strength she possessed.

"Leo call?" he asked hoarsely.

"No."

He thrust his fingers through his wet hair as he brushed past her. The bathroom door slammed behind him. The shower kicked on with a hiss.

Her knees collapsed, and she sank to the sofa. She stared at the bloody footprints on the ivory carpet. He'd built a wall of ice between them, and she didn't know how to break through. Struggling for control, she sucked in deep breaths as she stumbled to the kitchen to make breakfast.

He's threatened, scared, and he's put up his defense shield. Give him time and space.

When he exited the bathroom ten minutes later, she'd herded her emotions into line. She turned down the heat under the scrambled eggs. "Breakfast will be ready in five," she called.

He strode into the kitchen wearing clean jeans and a black T-shirt, his hair still damp, feet bare. The sight of his bruised, torn feet nearly unraveled her, and she swallowed hard. "There's toast and juice, too." Again, it took every iota of self-discipline she owned, but her voice emerged level.

They ate in strained silence. He wolfed his food, but every bite stuck in her throat. They'd just finished when his phone chirped. He snatched it up and sprinted to his room.

Acid roiled in her stomach. To keep busy, she stacked the dishes in the dishwasher.

Five minutes crawled by before he returned. Stocking-footed, he carried his sneakers in one hand, a gun and a deadly looking notched knife in the other. He dropped the weapons on the sofa, sat, and shoved his feet into the shoes. The rough movements had to hurt, but he didn't seem to notice. "Time to go to work."

"Leo," she croaked. "Where are you meeting him?"

He didn't even look up. "That's on a need-to-know basis."

Ah, the warrior was charging into battle and the first order of business was to stash the lovesick woman safely out of the way. If she wasn't so worried, she'd smack him upside the head. "What if you need help?"

Gabe stood, shoved the gun in his waistband, then sheathed the knife at his ankle. He shrugged on his black leather jacket. "If you don't hear from me in two hours, call the number I gave you before. Say the package was damaged in transit. The routing invoice is fifty-one, twelve dash thirty-three. They'll know I'm in trouble and my location." He stalked to the front door.

"Wait."

He paused with his hand on the knob.

"Be—" She couldn't help it, her voice broke. "Be careful."

He stared at her, expressionless. Gabe, but not Gabe. With none of the warmth, none of the laughter. None of the vitality. None of the qualities that made her so desperately love the man who silently yanked open the door and walked away.

The growl of his motorcycle ripped the morning apart. The rumble grew softer, then faded. Fighting stupid, useless tears, she stared at the bloodstained carpet. Gabe's blood. *I should clean that before the stain sets.* As she trudged to the kitchen for cleaning supplies, Gabe's cell phone rang. She pivoted and sprinted down the hall to Gabe's room to snatch up the phone. "Hello?"

"Tessa?"

At first she didn't recognize the frantic whisper. "Peter? Is that you? What's wrong?"

"Stop your cousin," Peter's panicked words tumbled into her ear. "Don't let him meet Leo this morning."

Icy fear clawed up her spine. She dropped the receiver and tore to the front door, but Gabe had already disappeared. Breathless, she raced back to the phone. "He already left."

"Oh, no! I'm in a phone booth near the Blue Moon. I just met with Leo. I forgot my jacket, and when I went back, I overheard Leo and Vic talking. The meeting is a trap. They're going to kill Val."

The room spun, and she nearly heaved up her breakfast. She

thrust out a shaky hand to lean on the wall. "Did they say where?"

"A fishing trawler docked beside the Coast Seafood ware-house on the waterfront. The *Lady Liberty*. It's Leo's base of operations. I heard him say something about 'the boat,' so I'm sure that's it. I'm calling 9-1-1."

"Absolutely no police! They're involved! I'll go warn him."

"Tessa, no, don't! it's too dangerous!"

The phone went dead in her hand. She stuffed it in her purse, grabbed the Corvette keys off the dresser, and ran to the car. She sped through the dark, deserted Sunday morning streets without stopping for traffic lights. Her gaze darted from street to street, hoping desperately Peter had listened to her warning not to call the police. All the way to the waterfront, she searched in vain for a lone man on a motorcycle.

Tessa made a left turn onto First Avenue and cut the lights. Slowing to a crawl, she spied the Coast Seafood warehouse ahead. She parked behind a ramshackle sign boasting Live Nude Girls. Her purse clutched to her chest, she scurried toward the abandoned warehouse, keeping to the shadows. Though the buildings blocked her view of the river, the cold, damp air reeked of polluted water and rotten fish. The area appeared deserted. She tiptoed around the corner of the building, her breath rasping in short, harsh pants.

Without warning, a hand clamped over her mouth from behind. Instinctively, she squeaked. The fingers tightened, cutting off the noise.

"Shh. Are you trying to get killed?" The hand dropped away.

"Peter!" She whirled. "What are you doing?"

"I refuse to live with another Carla on my conscience. Quit the Wonder Woman act and call the cops."

"They're involved. We'll sign Ga— Val's death warrant."

"Leo and Vic sure as hell aren't going to play Chinese Check-ers with him." He sighed. "Do you have a plan?"

"Find Val and warn him."

"Do you have a weapon?" She shook her head and Peter frowned. "Maybe we can see the boat from inside the build-ing."

They tiptoed up the crumbling, rotted wooden steps and into the darkened warehouse. Peter picked his way across the debris-littered floor to an east-facing window. "Here," he whispered.

She warily circled tangles of broken wire and chunks of mold-encrusted cement to join him.

"The *Lady Liberty* is the black fishing trawler docked to the left." He scrubbed a hand over his face. "You stay inside and I'll go scout around. See if you can find a weapon."

She turned away from the window to examine the gloomy interior. A piece of iron pipe caught her eye, and she skirted a pile of rotted boards to pick it up. "How about this?"

He half turned from the window, then stiffened. He gasped and jerked his gaze back outside. "They've got him!"

The pipe clutched in her hand, she leapt over the pile of boards and ran to his side. She didn't see anyone. "You saw Val?"

"Vic just hustled him on board at gunpoint. They had his hands tied behind his back."

She thrust the pipe at him and yanked open her purse. She snatched out the cell phone. "I'm calling Ga-Val's boss." She pushed the power button. Nothing happened. Cold dread congealed in her throat. She pushed it again. "The battery is dead. Val got upset and was gone all night. He must not have realized the phone needed to be charged." Gabe's state of mind last night was her fault. Tears stung her eyes, and she started to shake.

Peter's fingers whitened on the pipe. "Now what?"

She stared at the pipe. Resolve stiffened her spine. Her shaking stopped. "Now we rescue him."

"Tessa, I don't think it's wise to—"

"We're his only hope. If you aren't going to help, shut up." She searched the garbage until she found a second length of iron pipe. She tested the heft against her palm. A crude, but effective weapon. "I'm going to get him out."

"I can't let you go alone. Let's split up. You find Val, and I'll create a diversion."

He hurried outside. She paused to rifle through her purse for anything useful and found a nail file, which she stowed in her sock. Scant help, but perhaps she could jab the point into an unsuspecting eye. She hid her purse in a corner. Gripping the pipe, she navigated the debris to join Peter.

Hidden in the shadows, they scuttled to the dock. She stared up at the tall black ship. *Lady Liberty* rolled as waves slapped against her side. Tessa's stomach pitched. She clenched her teeth and reached for the ladder. *Gabe needs you.*

Clinging tightly to the rusty metal, she climbed, stopping once to wipe sweaty palms on her slacks. She reached the top and peered over the rail. Not a soul in sight. She clambered aboard, and darted behind a huge pile of coiled rope.

Within seconds, Peter joined her. He glanced at his watch. "In five minutes I'll create a disturbance. If all goes well, I'll meet you back at the warehouse. If not, leave without me."

The deck swayed under her feet as she tiptoed to the doorway that led below. Her chest tightened. "Focus on Gabe," she whispered. She eased open the door. The rusty hinges squeaked, shattering the eerie silence. She froze, her hand on the knob. Only her own ragged breathing and racing pulse thundered in her ears. She crept on.

A twisted stairway opened into a cavernous room with a thick web of pipes snaking overhead. The dank, echoing enclosure reeked of fish. Her stomach roiled. Gagging, she breathed through her mouth in short bursts. Pipe at the ready, she edged along the wall, peering into the blackness.

"Gabe?" she whispered.

"Hi there, songbird."

A gasp burst from her, and she whirled.

Leo loomed behind her, an ugly smirk twisting his mouth.

She charged him, lifting the pipe. He barked out a laugh as he wrenched the weapon away as easily as if she were a child and slammed her up against the wall. The breath exploded out of her lungs and stars blinded her vision.

"You've been trouble since day one." He lowered his blunt face to hers.

Out of the corner of her eye, she saw movement. Peter was sneaking up on Leo, pipe raised. If she could keep Leo's attention... She fixed her gaze on his. "I have a lot of financial contacts. I can be an asset to you."

Peter crept closer.

Drumm snorted in disbelief.

She held her gaze steady, afraid she might give Peter away. "I could double your profits."

Greed sliced across Leo's expression. Then he laughed again, the evil tone raising the hairs on the back of her neck. "You don't know it, but you've already earned your keep."

Peter was almost there. Three more steps.

Silently willing Drumm's cold gray eyes not to sever the connection, she strove to stay calm. "What do you mean?"

Peter swung the pipe.

Vic stepped out of the shadows behind Peter. Before Tessa could shout a warning, Vic slammed his fist down on the back of Peter's head. Peter crumpled to the ground.

A scream burst from her throat, a second too late. Leo grabbed her arm. "C'mon, songbird. I've got a job for you."

Fear made her feet clumsy as he dragged her into the bowls of the ship. Her heart galloped painfully. Was Peter badly hurt? And where was Gabe?

Leo shoved her into a chair. He wrenched her arms behind her and wrapped a length of bristly rope tightly around her wrists, cutting off her circulation. She gritted her teeth to keep from moaning. She wouldn't give him the satisfaction. Leo roughly tied her ankles together, bound her to the chair, then slapped tape over her mouth. She blinked back tears of pain and terror.

Vic arrived with an unconscious Peter draped over his shoulder. He dropped him into another chair six feet to the left and tied him up, then taped Peter's mouth.

Arms crossed, Leo sneered at her. "Now we wait for Val. And he'll show. Because we've got irresistible bait."

No! She threw herself forward, straining against her bonds. The movement wrenched the ropes tighter around her chest. Her vision darkened and she sagged, weakly trying to suck in air.

Leo gestured at the burly man beside him. "I could use a drink while we wait for our guest. How about you, Victor?"

Vic grunted his assent, and the two men left without looking back.

She studied Peter's unconscious face. He didn't seem seriously injured. He'd said he'd seen Gabe forced onboard. Did Leo have another prisoner besides them? Or had Leo caught Gabe, but then he'd escaped? Some "rescue." She groaned. Speculation wouldn't help. Concentrate on escape.

She tested her restraints. If she could loosen the rope... She furiously twisted her wrists back and forth, ignoring the pain as the rough fibers sawed her tender skin. *Gabe,* she silently sobbed. *Be smart. Stay away.*

She struggled until her muscles burned with exhaustion. Until her arms and legs went achingly numb. Exhausted, she slumped in her chair. How long had she been here? With every passing minute, her fear for Gabe grew.

Peter emitted a muffled moan. His eyelids floated up, his unfocused stare traveling the room. He spotted her and his eyes widened. He thrashed against the chair. She tried to comfort him with her gaze, and he stilled.

The air grew stuffy. The fishy stench thickened. No sound penetrated the ship's bowels. Her shoulder joints throbbed as though they'd been ripped out of the sockets, and her wrists stung horribly. But the misery in her body was minor compared to her worry for Gabe. She would suffer forever to keep him safe.

She closed her eyes as her thoughts drifted back to last night. Gabe's warm mouth covering hers. His passion-filled gaze. His sensual lips curved in a grin of masculine pride. Tessa's heart contracted. She prayed harder than she ever had before. *Please make him stay away.*

Hands clamped down on her shoulders and she flinched.

"Easy, honey," Gabe's silky drawl whispered in her ear.

Shaking her head, she lurched forward, her voice muffled by the tape.

"Shh." He held her still. "Don't move. I'll cut you loose."

Cold steel slipped between her wrists. Her arms dropped limply to her sides. He moved in front of her, knelt, and then the knife sliced through the rope at her ankles. "I'm afraid this will smart," he whispered before gently peeling the tape off her mouth.

She barely felt the sting. The second the tape loosened, she hissed, "It's a trap! Get out!"

He chuckled, soft and low. "Leo and Vic are indisposed. By the time they wake up, we'll be long gone." Silent as a stalking cat, he glided to Peter, cut his ropes and then returned. He squatted, cupping her chin in his hand. His eyes narrowed. "Did they hurt you?"

"No. But I can't move."

"Give it a minute." He began to massage her shoulders.

"I walked right into their trap." Burning blood surged painfully into her arms, and her muscles clenched in agony. "This is all my fault."

"The fault is mine." He lifted her chin, holding her gaze. "I knew this was a trap from the bug in Leo's office. I should have told you I had no intention of honoring the meet. I planned to do a little recon and set a trap of my own." His gentle fingers slid to her elbows. "Can you move your arms now?"

Ignoring the pain, she gingerly raised her arms. "But Peter saw—"

"Damn it!" Gabe grabbed her hands, holding them palm up.

She stared in dismay at her shredded wrists. At the blood trickling in obscene scarlet trails down her arms. "I tried to get loose. I had to warn you—"

He swore violently and creatively as he stripped off his jacket, yanked his T-shirt over his head, and then used his knife to cut the fabric into strips.

"Really, it doesn't hurt all that much," she lied as he tenderly bound the throbbing wounds.

A growl rumbled low in his throat "If I had time, I'd kill the bastards. Lucky for them, getting you out of here is my top priority." He helped her to her feet. "One sec." Like a shadow, he cat-footed to the door.

Peter crept to her side.

"Are you all right?" she whispered.

He nodded.

Gabe gestured from the doorway. "All clear. Let's bug out."

Her knees weak with relief, she took a step toward him. Toward freedom.

Peter's arm snaked around her neck and yanked her backward. A cold gun barrel pressed against her temple. "I'm afraid not."

Through a shocked haze, she saw Gabe freeze. His bare torso tensed to steel. "If you want to live, turn her loose." His voice dropped, low and deadly. "Now."

"Peter, wh-what are you doing?" she managed to stammer.

"I should take my grieving lover act to Hollywood," he gloated. "Oscar material. You two played into my hands like pawns on a chessboard." The arm around her neck tightened. "Drop your weapons, Cousin Val, and have a seat."

A muscle twitched in Gabe's clenched jaw. The knife thudded to the floor, point down. Fingers splayed, he pulled the gun from his waistband and slowly eased it down beside the knife. Expressionless, he stalked to the chair and sat.

Peter thrust a rope at her. "Tie him. And do a good job, so I don't have to shoot him."

On shaking legs, she stumbled forward to kneel at Gabe's feet. She tried to be gentle, but fear for his life made her obey Peter's command to tie him tightly. "I don't understand. You told me to call the police, and you watched me try to summon help on the cell phone."

Peter shifted, keeping her between him and Gabe. "If you had called the cops, Vic would have arrived. Of course that's not his real name. But he is a real cop. And I wouldn't have let you complete the cell call. Luckily, the battery was dead. Having you rush to the rescue was much easier than dragging you aboard unconscious. One way or another, you'd have ended up as bait."

A betrayal worthy of Judas. She swallowed down a wave of nausea. After Gabe's ankles were bound, she moved behind him to tie his wrists. "I thought we were friends."

"Friendship pales next to getting out from under Leo's thumb. Not to mention the money. When you and Val stuck your noses in, you provided me with the perfect opportunity. With Leo occupied by Val's interference, Vic and I planned a hostile takeover. We pretended I was helping you, then we turned the tables. I'll own the whole operation. With inside information from my position at the bank, I'll make millions. Nobody can touch me.''

Gabe tensed. ''Release Tessa. Name your price.''

Peter smirked. ''Cousin Val, with the mysterious contacts. We'll discuss that later.''

While Peter was distracted by Gabe's offer, she slid the nail file out of her sock and laid it in Gabe's palm. His fingers closed over it.

Peter waved the gun at her. ''Hurry up.''

''I'm done.'' She stepped away from Gabe.

Holding her breath, she watched Peter test the ropes. Gabe's clenched fists didn't give away their secret.

Peter tied her to the other chair, then strolled to the door. ''I'll be back. Don't go away.'' The door slammed behind him.

''Gabe, I'm sorry. This is all my fault.''

His gaze held warm admiration. ''You came after me, even though you're terrified of the water. That took major guts, Houdini.''

''I'd walk barefoot into hell for you,'' she whispered. ''Maybe now you'll believe me.''

''Nobody has ever—'' He swallowed hard. ''When we get out of here, we need to talk about last night. For now, focus on escape.''

Her heart stuttered. A bud of hope blossomed inside her. She and Gabe might have a future. If only they could get safely away. ''Will that file work?''

He chuckled dryly. ''Weakening this rope is gonna take a while, but you've tilted the odds in our favor, Houdini.''

Peter sauntered in beside Vic, who carried an unconscious Leo over his shoulder. Peter rubbed the back of his neck. ''Damn it, Vic, I've got a headache clear to my toenails. You were supposed to give me a convincing-looking tap, not cave in my skull.''

Vic shrugged. Leaving a bound Leo on the floor, they left.

''Leo's been cradling an asp in his bosom,'' Gabe drawled.

''How can you be flippant at a time like this?'' But that was his way. He covered deeper, dark emotions with humor. Underneath, he was probably as scared as she was. Now there was a comforting thought.

He arched a brow. "It would hardly help if I freaked and starting screaming, 'we're all gonna die.'"

She shuddered under a sharp onslaught of fear. "Are we?"

His gaze caught and held her. His warm regard stroked her like a caress, melting away some of her fright. "Not if I have a say. Especially not now. Not when I finally—" He cleared his throat and looked away.

The bud of hope blossomed into a glorious bouquet. "What, Gabe?" she whispered.

Uncertainty creased his forehead. "I...I have some stuff to tell you." He swallowed again. "I don't know how you'll feel about me afterward, but—" He heaved an exasperated sigh. "Oh, hell! Wrong time, wrong place. It's complicated, and we can't get into it now."

Her stomach flip-flopped. He was finally going to open up! "Okay, I'll take a rain check. But no matter what you have to say, nothing will change the way I feel about you." She gave him a reassuring smile. "Back to the situation at hand. I thought you knocked out Leo *and* Vic."

"The guy must have a cast-iron skull under that buzz cut."

A loud clank sounded from outside, then a rumble, and the engine throbbed to life. A giant chain scraped the hull, creaking upward, then the swaying increased. She stiffened. "What's happening?"

"They're moving the ship." He shot her a sharp glance. "Don't go ballistic on me, Tessie. Hang in there."

"I w-won't." She forced her rigid muscles to relax. "I'm focusing."

Gabe smiled encouragingly. "That's my girl."

The possessive endearment sent a warm flood of reassurance through her. He was so strong, so in control. So capable. Surely they'd get out of this. She watched him and concentrated on not panicking.

His shoulders and biceps bunched as he worked the file against his ropes. He looked up, smiling. "Are you humming?"

"Sorry. Habit."

"What song?"

Her cheeks heated as she realized what she'd been murmuring. "I Can't Help Falling In Love With You."

He cocked his head, his smile widening into a grin. "Sing out. Might help pass the time."

Leo moaned several times but didn't regain consciousness. She'd nearly reached the end of her Elvis repertoire when the engines stopped. The chain rattled, screeched, and a huge splash rocked the ship.

Gabe's head jerked up. "They've dropped anchor."

"How are your ropes?"

He grimaced. "Fraying, but not enough to break free yet."

"What do you think they're going to do to us?"

He didn't quite meet her gaze. Not a good sign. "If we're lucky, they only want what I took from Leo's office." Her stomach bottomed out. He didn't say what would happen if they weren't lucky. He didn't have to.

The door opened and Vic barged inside, followed by Peter. "Day of reckoning, ladies and gents." Peter untied Tessa's ankles. Leaving her wrists bound behind her, he hauled her to her feet. He again wrapped his arm around her neck, the gun barrel pressed to her temple. "You don't want me to put a bullet in this lovely lady's brain, Val, so you'll behave, right?"

Gabe shot a murderous glance at Peter, but nodded.

Vic freed Gabe's feet, leaving his wrists bound behind him, and slung Leo over his massive shoulder. Shoving a gun in Gabe's spine, Vic followed him out the door. Peter tugged her along behind.

On deck, one sight of the lashing waves spiked choking panic into her throat. She couldn't breathe, couldn't get enough air.

"Tessie," Gabe's soft voice commanded. "Look at me."

She ripped her gaze from the dark water and met his tender smile.

"Keep cool, sweetheart," he murmured. "C'mon, you've done great so far. I need you to stay in control."

She gulped, forcibly swallowing down her fear. Losing her head could get them both killed.

Vic slammed Gabe against the cabin wall. The fresh air revived Leo, and Vic shoved him next to Gabe.

Peter dragged her to the rail. Terror again seized her, and she trembled. He shook his head. "The ocean always did terrorize you, didn't it? Don't worry, you'll soon be out of your misery." He pursed his lips. "Who would like to go first?" Peter pointed the gun at Gabe.

Tessa's pulse crashed into a frantic rhythm.

Peter slowly swung the gun toward Leo. "Wait. Leo, you know Vic, aka officer Mac Marshall, Riverside PD. But with Carla using a phony last name, you didn't know she was his baby sister. He's a little ticked that you offed her. I'm not happy about it myself. She was great in the sack, and I was quite fond of her. But family has priority."

Without any warning, Vic put his gun to Leo's forehead and pulled the trigger.

Tessa screamed. Desperately trying not to retch, she slammed her eyes shut, trying to block the nightmare image. Her hope that Peter couldn't actually hurt anyone died along with Leo.

There was an ominous dragging sound, then a loud splash. She opened her eyes to see Gabe standing alone, Leo's gory remains staining the bulkhead beside him. Was Gabe next? Agony pierced her chest. How close was he to breaking the ropes? His stony expression didn't give any clues. She couldn't stand here and watch him die. Her mind whirled.

"Now you understand we're serious," Peter said, his voice horribly calm and even. He waved the gun at Gabe. "You must realize by now the copies I gave you were bogus. Completely useless. How much do you know?"

Gabe's eyes narrowed. "I have enough real evidence to put you away for life. You kill us and it gets sent to the D.A."

"A predictably clichéd response. Doesn't matter what you've got, I've covered my tracks. Dearly departed Leo will get the blame for everything." Peter threw her a smarmy smile. "Don't go anywhere, Tessa. Not that you could." Confident that her phobia would keep her paralyzed, he strolled to Gabe's side. Vic lumbered over to join him. The three men stared each other down.

She broke out in a cold sweat. Frantic, she wrenched her wrists back and forth. The rope bit through the makeshift bandages into her already shredded skin, but she ignored the pain.

Peter pointed his gun at Gabe's head. "How about it, Cuz?"

Gabe arched a mocking brow.

Vic drove his meaty fist into Gabe's stomach. Grunting, Gabe doubled over. Tessa's muscles contracted and a sympathetic ache streaked through her abdomen.

Peter yanked Gabe upright by his hair. "Be reasonable. Vic is a maestro. We can keep you alive for days, but you'll long for death. You'll spill your guts. They always do."

"Better men than you have tried," Gabe gasped out. "Even if I sang—which I won't—you'll kill me anyway."

"True. But your death will be fast and merciful."

"Go to h—"

Vic again smashed his fist into Gabe's stomach. Tessa's nails dug into her palms. She bit her lip to keep from crying out, and tasted blood.

"Hold on." Peter raised his hand. "Cousin here thinks he's a tough guy. We'll waste our time and energy beating on him all day." He turned a calculating look on her. "Perhaps there's a quicker, less tiresome method. I wonder..."

Her heart lurched. They'd never break Gabe. He'd take what they dished out, even if it brought a slow, painful death. And they knew it. They were going to kill him.

Peter turned back and pointed his gun at Gabe's head. "Maybe you're not afraid to die, but how do you feel knowing Tessa is going to watch me spatter your brains all over the wall? We don't need you. She's been in on it all along. We'll simply get our information from her. It will be much less...arduous."

"She doesn't know squat. Let her go." The pulse in Gabe's throat hammered and the muscles in his shoulders and arms bulged as he strained to break free. How much longer? What if the rope didn't break?

"If you kill him, Peter, I won't tell you a thing," she vowed.

He laughed. "Oh, you'll tell me. Before Vic and I are done, you'll tell me everything." He watched Gabe closely. "Too bad you won't be able to join us. The three of us are going to have quite a party.''

Every muscle in Gabe's body bunched, and his eyes glittered with fury. He snarled. ''You hurt her and there's nowhere you can hide. I'll find you if I have to follow you into hell.''

She didn't care about Peter's threats against her. Nothing they did would be worse than seeing Gabe die. She glanced over the rail into the deep green water. She'd never noticed before how much the emerald waves resembled Gabe's eyes.

''It's a date. You go first.'' Peter drew back the hammer, the click obscenely loud in the quiet morning.

She swiveled back to look at Gabe. His gaze held hers, his expression oddly wistful. His eyes conveyed yearning, sorrow and bone-deep regret.

She wouldn't just stand here and watch him die! Her gaze spun wildly over the deck. Suddenly, she knew exactly what to do. Deadly calm settled over her, cloaking her in warmth.

She looked at Gabe one final time, drinking in his face. Tucked the memory deep in her heart. *No regrets.* She stared into his eyes, telling him without words. *I love you.* The silent message arced between them.

Peter and Vic were watching Gabe, and didn't see her hoist herself onto the rail. For a sickening heartbeat, she stared over her shoulder into the roiling water.

Gabe's eyes darkened in horror as he realized her intent. He lunged. ''No!''

She narrowed her focus to the huge metal crane in front of her and kicked with all her might. The bar slammed into Peter's back. He hurtled to the deck, his shot going wild.

She'd done what she could for Gabe. The rest was up to him. She managed a triumphant smile at him as the momentum threw her backward over the rail.

''*Tessa!*'' His anguished cry rang in her ears.

Then the icy water swallowed her alive.

Chapter 18

A white-hot flash exploded inside Gabe's head, burning out every thought except one. *Save Tessa!*

Roaring, he tore apart the ropes shackling his wrists and whirled into a roundhouse kick that slammed into Vic's head. Vic staggered forward at the same time Peter stumbled to his feet, drunkenly waving the gun. Gabe shoved Vic into Peter. Peter fired off another shot, which hit Vic in the chest. Vic crumpled, and Gabe leapt over his body. Grabbing Peter's arm, Gabe jerked it back, then down across his upraised knee. The bone snapped like a dry twig, and he shrieked. Gabe picked him up and threw him over the side. He'd yanked off both shoes before he heard the splash.

He dived over the rail, ignoring the icy shock. Plunging deep, he searched the murky water for a glimpse of Tessa. With her hands tied, she would have sunk like an anchor. He swam until his lungs begged for air. Rocketing to the surface, he gulped in three breaths, dived again.

Over and over, he dived. His skin turned numb from the cold, his chest burned and his arms and legs ached like lead weights. But he continued the frantic search.

He'd known the instant he'd seen her tied up in the bowels of the ship that she'd come to help him. And why. He'd decided then and there that if she could face her worst nightmare for him, he sure as hell could meet her halfway. He'd been ready to reach out, only to have her snatched from his grasp.

His mind screaming that she had been under too long, his lungs screaming from lack of air, he hit the surface, gasped in a huge breath, and again dived into the dark ocean, replacing his desperation and terror with resolve. By damn, he wasn't having it! Either he was coming back with her, or he wasn't coming back.

Finally, he spotted a blur of white far below—her sweater! He swam toward her. At the sight of her closed eyes and deathly pallor, his racing heart nearly burst from his chest. He grasped her limp, unresponsive body under the arms and dragged her to the surface. Quickly, he swam to the ship.

Throwing her over his shoulder, he climbed the ladder. He lowered her to the deck and put his cheek next to her nose. She wasn't breathing. His fingers pressed into the icy skin at her throat. No pulse.

Dark horror clawed at the edge of his mind, threatening to tear away his reason. He ruthlessly shoved his clamoring emotions down. If he lost it, Tessie would die. He forced himself to view her crumpled body as nothing more than a training mannequin as he tore the ropes off her wrists.

On automatic pilot now, he tilted her head back, pinched her nose and gave her his breath. He began chest compressions, counting until he reached fifteen, gave her more breaths. He repeated, pausing to check her pupils. They were dilated—bad, but reacted to light—good. Again, he pressed his fingers to her ice-cold neck. No pulse.

He repeated the CPR cycle, checked again. Nothing. ''Come on, baby!'' he muttered. More breaths, more chest compressions. His arms trembled and his head spun. Exhausted from the search, he was also shivering violently from his too-long immersion in the frigid Pacific. But he wasn't about to give up on her.

Breaths, compressions, check pupils, feel for pulse. Over and over. Somewhere along the way he started to shout. "Breathe, Tessa! Come on, sweetheart, breathe, please!"

More breaths, more compressions. No pulse.

"Damn it," he roared. "Don't you leave me!" Beyond reason, he grabbed her shoulders and shook her roughly.

She coughed, then wheezed in a slow, shuddery breath. Relief threatened to render him weak and useless, and he shut off his feelings completely, as he'd been trained to do in these situations. He couldn't help her if he didn't stay rational. He touched trembling fingertips to her throat and counted. Her pulse was thready, barely there. She was still unconscious.

He tore into the cabin to use the radio, then ransacked the room to locate a blanket and flare gun. He raced back to Tessa and checked her pulse. Her heart had stopped again.

He fired off the flare. He restarted the breathing and compressions, but couldn't get a steady heartbeat. He was doggedly performing CPR when the chopper arrived. As the aircraft hovered overhead, a medic dropped onto the deck beside him.

"I can't get her stabilized," he yelled over the rotors.

The medic motioned upward, and a woman landed on deck. Gabe continued compressions while the woman slid a ventilator tube down Tessa's throat. The man ripped open Tessa's blouse. He placed defibrillator paddles on her chest. "Clear!"

Gabe raised his hands. Tessa's body arched as the electric current charged through her body. The second the paddles lifted, he searched for a pulse. *Damn it.* "Nothing!"

They shocked Tessa twice more before finally establishing a weak heartbeat, then loaded her into the chopper. The medics stripped off her wet clothes and wrapped her in blankets. Refusing a blanket for himself, Gabe focused his entire being on Tessa, silently willing her to live. Her core temperature was so cold, the thermometer didn't register a reading. She flatlined twice. Twice the medics shocked her back to life. The twenty-minute flight lasted an eternity.

Seconds after the chopper touched down, Tessa was placed on a stretcher and hurtled toward the emergency room. When they reached the E.R., a gray-haired doctor took one look at her

and turned to Gabe. The doctor's grim face spoke volumes.
"You family?"

His pulse jackhammered. Unable to speak, he shook his head.

"Get her family here. In a hurry."

A nurse slammed the doors in Gabe's face. He forced his
leaden feet to the phone where he managed to call Melody. He
trudged into the packed waiting room, to two vacant seats under
a wide bank of windows, and collapsed into a chair. He rested
his elbows on his knees. Covering his face with his hands, he
began to shake. No matter how hard he willed it, he couldn't
stop.

He wasn't sure how much time passed before a small, warm
hand touched his bare shoulder.

"Val?"

He looked up wearily and saw Melody bent over him. "The
name is Gabe Colton. I'm FBI," he rasped. "Sit down."
Wracked with violent tremors, he stared fixedly at the wall as
he told her everything.

When he finished, Mel remained silent. Gabe didn't dare look
at her. His control teetered on a razor edge. If she fell apart,
he'd break down like a baby.

Her hand patted his shoulder again. "I'll be right back."

He didn't really care. A distant part of his mind recognized
the symptoms of adrenaline crash. He'd trained himself to function normally when the adrenaline overload dropped, but this
time he couldn't pull himself together.

He didn't know how many minutes ticked past before Mel
returned. She grabbed his unresisting hand and tugged him up.
Body aching, mind numb, he let her lead him down the hall and
through a door. She gently touched his bruised ribs. "Does this
hurt?"

He shook his head.

"I don't suppose you'd see a doctor." He shook his head
again and she sighed. "I didn't figure." She slipped a shirt on
over his head and worked his arms through the short sleeves.

When she slid down the zipper on his jeans, he snapped back
to reality. "Hey!" Gabe jerked her hands off his fly. Dazed, he

stared at the porcelain urinals lining the wall. "Are we in the head? Are you taking off my pants?"

The tiny blonde planted her fists on her hips. "You got a problem with that?"

He looked down at the green cotton shirt she'd put on him. She had matching pants draped over her arm. "Surgical scrubs? Where did these come from?"

"Sometimes you're better off not knowing." She arched her elfin brows. "You're freezing, your jeans are soaked and necessity is the mother of invention. You going to shuck those pants, big guy, or do you need help?"

"This isn't an audience participation event."

"If I recall, you didn't have any qualms about hanging around in the ladies' room." In spite of the pain shadowing her eyes, she smiled. "All right. If you can handle this on your own, I'll be in the waiting area."

She left, and he changed into the scrubs. She'd even found him a pair of those slipper-type shoes surgeons wore into the operating room. Feeling a little warmer and less stunned, he trekked back to the waiting room. "Any word about—" His throat closed up.

"No." She rose. "Sit down, before you fall down." She stood on tiptoe, placed her hands on his shoulders and pushed him into a chair. She shoved a steaming cup of coffee into his right hand and a giant-size candy bar into the left. "Drink. Eat."

"Bossy little thing, aren't you?"

"Tess needs us. We've got to be strong for her."

His throat constricted again. He'd seen drownings before. He knew what happened to the brain when the body was deprived of oxygen for too long. Bile churned in his gut. He carefully set his coffee and candy bar on the table beside him.

"She *will* make it." Melody's chin wobbled, then firmed. "I refuse to believe otherwise." She thrust the coffee back into his hand. "You look terrible. Get something in your stomach or I'll rustle up an IV. I'm quick to pick up new skills, but I'd probably have to jab you at least half a dozen times."

"Aye-aye, ma'am." The corner of his mouth quirked. "Far be it from me to take on the pint-size blond tornado who whipped Steel Lucille's butt.'' He managed to drink the coffee and choke down half the Snickers bar. ''Did you—'' he swallowed down a lump that wasn't a peanut. ''Call her mother?''

''Yes. She was in L.A.'' Melody's fists clenched in her lap. ''She's *too busy* to come. She said the doctor can phone her.'' Her slender body vibrated with fury. ''She doesn't care about Tessa, she never has.''

He covered her hands with one of his. ''Tessie has us. We're here for her.''

''But, Gabe. I am—was—an attorney.'' Melody bit her lip. ''Vivienne is the only person legally entitled to make decisions regarding Tess. And she won't hesitate to put her convenience first. If Tessa's situation deteriorates to a life-or-death decision, Vivienne will be the one making it.''

He squeezed her hands reassuringly. ''We won't let that happen.''

''We can't stop her.''

He narrowed his eyes. Nothing was going to happen to Tessa on his watch. Especially not when he'd finally realized that his fear of loving her was minor compared to the soul-shattering agony of losing her. He inhaled a ragged breath. He couldn't lose her. Not now.

She'd stared at her worst fear when she looked over the railing into the cold, unforgiving Pacific Ocean. Yet she hadn't hesitated. She'd gone over…with remarkable courage, and a message of love in her eyes. A message for him.

I love you.

Facing down his own fear was the only way he would be worthy of her love. He was willing to bear any kind of pain, willing to risk anything—risk everything—to be with her. ''I'll handle Vivienne if the need arises.''

The E.R. doors swung open and a young, dark-haired nurse walked toward them, her face carefully neutral. Gabe started to shake again.

''You're the man who brought in Tessa Beaumont?''

At his nod, she continued. ''We still can't get a core temperature, and her heart won't establish a regular beat.'' The nurse gave them a sympathetic look. ''We're not giving up, but I have to be honest. Even if she rallies, there's a chance of brain damage. We'll do all we can, but you should probably prepare for the worst.''

All the air slammed out of his lungs, and the room spun. Through a thick, red haze of pain, he watched the nurse hurry away.

Melody grabbed his hand. ''Are you a praying man, Gabe?''

''I am now,'' he whispered.

Sixty endless minutes crept by.

Then sixty more.

Gabe sat frozen in the uncomfortable chair, bargaining with God, not sure if he wanted the doors to open again or not. As long as they stayed closed, it meant Tessa was still fighting. Still alive.

Three of the longest hours of his life dragged by before the doors opened and the same nurse approached. Her facial expression revealed nothing, but instinct warned Gabe she brought crucial news. He dug deep for every ounce of strength he possessed. He stood to meet her.

The nurse stopped in front of him. ''We managed to raise Tessa's temperature. At four-thirty, we got one heartbeat. After more effort, we got a few in a row, then at four-forty, she developed a pulse.'' She smiled. ''Your friend is quite a fighter. She surfaced briefly, but not long enough for us to determine if there's any brain damage. Her lack of consciousness is due to a concussion and not a coma, and she is breathing on her own, which is a very good sign. We're moving her to intensive care.''

Gabe's knees gave out and he collapsed into the chair. Melody burst into tears. He slid his arm around her slender shoulders. He couldn't distinguish her tremors from his own.

The nurse sat down beside them. ''Tessa's not out of the woods yet. We're going to have to watch her carefully for the next few days until she's stable. There's a good chance she'll flatline again.''

''But she's alive,'' Melody sobbed. ''She's not in a coma. She'll beat this.''

Gabe swallowed the panic the nurse's words had caused. ''I

want to see her.'' He'd drag her back to him with both hands. With everything he had.

The nurse nodded. ''ICU is on the fifth floor.''

Melody headed upstairs, and Gabe spent a few minutes in the head to splash cold water on his face and get a grip on his shredded equilibrium. As he strode into the elevator, he continued bargaining with God. *Please. Please let her be all right.*

He watched the red numbers flash in the panel above his head. Tessa had said she loved him. After everything he'd put her through, after he finally came clean, would her love still stand? His gut clenched. In his experience, words didn't mean anything. People said *''I love you,''* then strolled away without a backward glance. Leaving you mute with pain and terror.

But damn it, he'd kept love at arm's length all his life. It was time to take a stand, to stop running away from love and run toward it. Living without Tessa just wasn't an option.

The elevator glided to a stop and the doors slid open. Determinedly setting his roiling thoughts aside, he strode to the nurses' desk at the end of the corridor where Mel waited. She looked up at him, her elfin face pinched. ''They're only allowing one visitor at a time, for ten minutes. I thought you might want to see her first.''

He patted her slender shoulder. ''Once I get in there, they're not going to be able to blast me out with C4. I know how close the two of you are. Go ahead, Mel. I can wait a few more minutes.''

She gave him a wobbly smile. ''You know, for a Y chromosome carrier, you're pretty sweet. I might even have to change my lowly opinion of the male species.'' She stood on tiptoe, bussed a light kiss on his cheek, and then hurried down the hall.

Gabe again walked to the windows, staring out at the gray landscape. Menacing clouds hung over the city, bringing premature twilight. Sharp wind gusts drove spatters of rain against the windowpanes like shrapnel. Yet lights from downtown office buildings pierced the gloom. Small, bright beacons of hope in the darkness. Tessa was a fighter. Not bold and in-your-face, like Melody, but with a deep, quiet strength. She possessed an inner core of iron-clad resolve. She *would* make it.

"Gabe?" He turned in response to Melody's shaky inquiry. Fresh tears shimmered in her solemn blue eyes and clung to her blond lashes. "Your turn. But be prepared. She drifts in and out, but she's not fully conscious." Mel swallowed hard. "She looks awful."

He drew the trembling woman into a hug. "That's to be expected after what she's been through."

Steeling himself, Gabe gathered his courage in both hands. He stalked down the corridor and pushed open the door to Tessa's room with the same resolute purpose as when he'd followed her over the ship's rail. Either he was walking out of here with her, or he wasn't leaving.

In spite of Melody's warning, he took one glance at her and dropped into the chair beside her bed, his knees wobbly, his chest tight and aching. God, she looked like someone had beaten her nearly to death. Her auburn lashes fanned over pale cheeks whiter than the pillowcase. Deep purple shadows smudged her closed eyes, and tiny, ruptured blue veins traced under the swollen, frail skin of her eyelids. Blood had seeped through gauze bandages wrapped around her torn wrists. IV tubes had been stabbed into her badly bruised right arm, clear liquid dripping into her veins from a bottle overhead. Mottled bruises ringed the tender skin at her neck where a faint pulse throbbed in her throat. A heart monitor beside the bed beeped in the same slow rhythm.

Fragile and broken, against formidable odds she clung stubbornly to life. Her even, persistent pulse gave him hope, gave him strength.

"Hey, Houdini," He leaned forward, his voice unsteady. "You're taking this power nap to extremes. How about if you wake up and I'll get you a nice cup of Earl Gray tea? I'll even bring it in your Elvis mug." He grasped her limp hand in his, caressing her silky, cool skin. Too cool. "Tessa? Can you hear me?"

She didn't respond.

"Come on, sweetheart. Come back to me."

Not a breath of sound, not a whisper of movement.

"I'm here for you. Everything is going to be all right." He continued speaking quietly and stroking her hand.

All too soon, a young blond nurse slipped inside the room. "Time's up."

He stood and walked to the doorway where she waited. "I'm not going anywhere. There's no harm in letting me stay."

The nurse, whose name tag read Hailey Matthews, frowned. "If you don't cooperate, I'll have to call security. You seem like a nice guy. I know you don't want to cause a scene and upset your friend."

"Look, I understand you have rules and all, but I'm not leaving." He held her gaze, his own steady and determined. "I owe this woman my life. In more ways than one. I won't do anything to endanger her care or get in your way, but *I will not leave her.*"

Ms. Matthews hesitated. She studied his face for several tense heartbeats, then nodded. "All right. As long as you're quiet and don't obstruct us in any way. And if she flatlines, you get out immediately and let the team do their work."

"You got it." She left and he returned to Tessa's bedside.

He talked for nearly an hour, pleading, cajoling and downright threatening dire consequences if she didn't wake up. She stirred and whimpered a few times, but didn't open her eyes. Wanting to howl, he tipped his head back, swallowing his anguish.

Finally, he took a deep shuddering breath and gripped her hand more tightly. "No way, baby! I am *not* gonna let you go. I won't sit here this time, helpless and mute. I've never told anyone about this, but..."

Desperation drove the words out of him. "You wanted to know about my nightmares? This is it. My worst nightmare come true." He stopped to clear the thickness from his throat before continuing. "One summer morning when I was five, I got up, and my mom told me we were taking a trip. I'd never been anywhere except around the block, so I was thrilled. I ran and got my red backpack, and she packed my things."

He took another fortifying breath. "I remember that day so vividly. The clear blue of the sky, the bright sunshine, the birds singing in the trees. Mom was real quiet. I stopped to pet Mrs. Mendoza's black Lab and asked if I could have a puppy when we got home. Mom said sure. It was a long way, and my legs got tired, but she said we didn't have enough money to take a city bus. I held her hand all the way to the bus station.''

Gabe stared blindly at the wall, seeing it all again, living it all again. ''When we got to the bus station, she sat me on a tall wooden bench. My feet didn't touch the floor. The hard wood hurt my back. She looked down at me and said, *'Stay right here, Gabe. Don't move. No matter what happens, don't move from this spot. And don't talk to anyone. Anyone, you hear?'*

''Then she stared at me for the longest time. She finally said, *'I have to do this, because I love you.'* Her face looked blank. It made my stomach ache.''

His voice dropped to a whisper. ''When she turned away, I knew. Somehow I knew she was never coming back. I didn't say anything. I couldn't. Inside, I screamed and screamed. But I watched my mother walk away and didn't say a word. I just sat there. I sat there all day on that hard bench, clutching my backpack, hungry, thirsty and so scared I wanted to die. I didn't move an inch. I didn't cry. But she didn't come back.

''And I didn't speak again for over a year.''

His voice broke. ''Maybe if I'd been able to call out to her. Maybe if I'd been different, been better, she would have stopped. Turned around. Stayed.'' He squeezed her hand. ''I'm calling out to you, Tessie. Don't walk away from me. Don't leave me. Please.''

His heart shattered inside of him, fear and hurt and betrayal that had been locked up hard and tight and safe for so many years. ''If you come back, I promise I'll be with you, always. I'll spend the rest of my life making you happy.'' He clenched his teeth against the pain, but a helpless cry broke from the back of his throat. ''Fight, Tessie. Find your way back to me. I need you.''

Shaking, he buried his face in the blanket. He battled the white-hot torment, but he had no defenses left. Sharp claws shredded his insides, ripped him open. His body shuddered. The tears he'd refused to shed all those years ago leaked out and spilled onto the delicate, limp hand under his cheek.

He didn't know how much time passed before he finally realized someone was stroking his hair. "Mel?" he rasped. Ashamed she'd caught him crying, he jerked upright.

And met Tessa's amber gaze.

Clear and lucid, her gaze clung to his. His heart bucked into a wild gallop. "Tessie! Oh, God, you're awake!" He cupped her face in his hands and kissed her cheeks, her forehead, her mouth. "Do you know who I am?"

Her lips wobbled in a crooked smile. "Bond," she whispered, her voice weak. "Gabe Bond."

His spirit soared. He grinned at her. "Hang on, honey." He turned toward the door. "Somebody get in here," he roared.

Gabe's bellow assaulted Tessa's tender eardrums and she flinched. Confused, she squinted at the jabbering crowd that swarmed over her, poking, prodding and peering. A blond woman flashed a bright light in her eyes, sending white-hot spears through Tessa's brain. Her head throbbed as though someone had slammed a sledgehammer into her skull. "Gabe," she cried.

"I'm right here, baby." He stayed by her side, adamantly refusing when one of the women tried to force him to leave.

"Where? What?"

"You're in the hospital. You're going to be fine."

She clung to his hand. "Make them stop."

He stroked her face. "I wish I could. But you've got to let them do their job."

"Get Mel. She'll stop it."

He gave a crack of laughter. "I'm afraid even Mel is outranked this time. The tests will be over soon."

Voices babbled, the bed shook and lights whirred by overhead. She focused on Gabe's face, her only security in a sea of confusion. Suddenly, her bed slid forward. She lost sight of him and found herself entombed in a tiny metal chamber. "Gabe?"

His voice answered. "I'm with you on headphones. They're doing a CAT scan. You'll be out in no time." His voice crooned into her ears.

"Are you singing?"

"Yeah."

"Thought they were scanning the cat. Not killing it."

His rich, warm chuckles filled her ears. "Hey, don't knock my rendition of 'Blue Suede Shoes.'"

Tessa closed her eyes.

"You still with me, Tessie?" Gabe's whisper was soft in her ear.

She forced up her heavy eyelids and saw his face hovering over her, his eyes dark with pain.

"You're back in your room." He stroked her hair. "I'm sorry if I disturbed you. But I wanted—I needed to see you awake. I was so afraid—" his husky voice faltered.

"What happened?"

"Do you remember anything at all?"

She sorted through the blurred images in her mind. "Peter tried to kill you. I stopped him. Fell into your eyes."

"You fell into the Pacific Ocean." He choked. "With your hands tied behind you." His hand at her forehead started to tremble. "You scared forty years off my life."

"I hurt. All over. A lot."

Gabe's breath caught. "I know. But you'll be fine, I promise." He smiled at her. "You'll be tap dancing before you know it."

Scared, dazed, she stared at him, trying to make sense of the information bombarding her. "You're not hurt?"

Gabe's smile wobbled. "No. You saved both of us, Houdini."

He was all right and they were together. Beyond that, her mind refused to function any longer. "I'm so tired."

"Go ahead and sleep. But promise you'll wake up real soon."

"Promise." She closed her eyes and everything went black.

Some time later, Tessa floated to awareness. She heard Mel and Gabe talking, their voices pitched low.

"The CAT scan showed no brain impairment, thank God." Gabe murmured. "The frigid water sent her body into hibernation, so the lack of oxygen didn't affect her as severely as it could have." Humor lightened his tone. "She's sharp as ever.

She gave me what-for about my singing when they did the scan.''

Mel chuckled. "How long is her estimated recovery?"

"The doctor told me she'll probably be out of here in less than a week."

Mel sniffled. "It's a miracle."

"It is at that. Our own personal miracle."

"Hey, stop talking about me," Tessa said, her voice still too feeble for her own liking. "My ears are burning."

Gabe and Mel rushed to her side. "Hi, there, Houdini. Welcome back." Gabe tenderly smoothed his hand over her hair. "How do you feel?"

"Like Wile E. Coyote after a hard day's night."

Gabe chuckled. "Yeah, and no wonder."

Mel enveloped her in a gentle hug, then drew back, tears shimmering in her eyes. "I love ya, kid."

"I love you, too, Mel." Tessa smiled at her friend. She tried to marshal her scattered thoughts and frowned. "What happened to Peter and Vic?"

Gabe and Mel exchanged a silent communication. Gabe took her hand. "They—" He cleared his throat. "It's all over. They're dead. They didn't leave me any choice."

She nodded. Gabe would have helped Peter escape from Leo, but Peter had sealed his own fate when he chose money and power instead. Considering he'd nearly succeeded in murdering them, she couldn't feel much regret.

"Did you call my mom?"

Gabe's Adam's apple bobbed as he swallowed hard. "Yeah, Mel called her. She couldn't come."

"Let me guess. Too busy."

"I'm sorry, honey." Gabe scowled. "I know how much your mom's attitude hurts."

It didn't hurt nearly as much as it should, which surprised her. "I should be used to it by now."

"She's the one who lost, sweetheart. She's missing out on you in her life."

She firmly put the final cruelty behind her. She wouldn't waste any more time wishing for Vivienne's affection. Gabe was her future. She channeled every ounce of strength and determination she possessed toward recovery. "I want to sit up."

Gabe pursed his lips. "Probably not a good idea just yet. Give yourself time."

"I'm sitting up, with or without your assistance, Mr. Bond."

"Stubborn wench." He shook his head. "If you weren't so bruised and battered, I'd spank you."

She knew darn well he'd never do such a thing. Unless she asked him to. She grinned at him. "Pervert."

He grinned back. "And don't you love it?"

For the next five days as she recovered in the hospital, Gabe thoughtfully attended her every need. He supplied fresh apricot roses daily. The place looked like a florist's shop. In cahoots with Mel, he brought her snacks, magazines and movies. He joked and laughed and kept her spirits high. But he studiously avoided talking about anything personal.

She ached for his warm embrace. For his tender kisses. For his love. Even though he seemed to be avoiding intimacy, every time he thought she wasn't looking, she'd catch him staring at her with desire so intense, so hungry it made her shiver.

On the ship, he'd told her he had something to confess. She yearned to know, but refused to bring it up first. Pushing him had resulted in disaster before, and she wasn't about to repeat the mistake. He had to conquer his own demons, just as she'd vanquished hers.

She would never again settle for less than complete commitment.

At the end of the week, the doctor gave her a clean bill of health and scheduled her for discharge the next day. She lay awake during the long, empty hours, listening to Gabe's quiet, even breathing from the cot next to her bed. He'd refused to leave her side, even at night. Surely that was a good sign.

But what would happen when she went home?

Chapter 19

The next morning, a rumpled, yawning Mel arrived at the hospital extra early bearing a sapphire-blue silk lounging outfit with matching panties and hard-soled dark blue slip-on mules. Tessa warmly embraced her groggy friend and thanked her for the twofold gift. Mel wasn't a morning person under the best circumstances, and ever since she'd lost her job as an attorney, she'd been strapped for cash.

Giving Tessa privacy to change, Gabe steered Mel out the door, promising to return her thoroughly caffeinated.

Dressed and ready, Tessa perched on her bed, the combination of leaving the hospital and the long-awaited chance to be alone with Gabe tying her stomach into conflicted knots of anticipation and dread. A knock sounded on the door. "Come in."

Her favorite nurse, Hailey, entered, pushing a wheelchair. "Good morning. I know I don't have to ask if you're happy to be leaving us."

Tessa eyed the wheelchair warily. "What's that for?"

Hailey's smile morphed into her no-nonsense-nurse face. "It's policy."

Tessa wrinkled her nose. "I'm strong and fit, and can walk just fine."

Gabe and Mel breezed in, Mel restored to her bubbly, cheerful self. Gabe's glance swept over Tessa's mutinous expression, and he laughed. "Causing trouble again, I see." He tweaked a curl that trailed over her shoulder, his knuckles brushing enticingly close to her bare breast under the sapphire silk. "Plant your cute little six in the chair, Houdini, and let's get the hell out of here."

His touch made her breath hitch in her throat. She was going home. With Gabe. She obediently sat, no longer bothered by the wheelchair.

When they reached the car, parked outside the front door, she was surprised and touched to see her doctor and nurses had turned out to see her off. They gathered on the curb, bestowing hugs and encouragement. Everyone voiced amazement at her "miraculous" recovery.

Tessa knew better. Gritty determination and gut-wrenching courage deserved the credit. And she didn't discount divine intervention. She had survived because Gabe needed her. She knew for a fact the Man Upstairs understood that.

The ride went by in a blur. As each familiar street passed, her tension grew. Would she finally be able to get Gabe to talk? What did he have to say? Did she really want to hear it? He unlocked the door, and she walked inside. Mel followed with armloads of apricot roses.

Tessa breathed in the fresh, lemony scent of her apartment. "Home, sweet home."

"Sit down and take a load off, Houdini." Gabe's voice sounded gruff.

"I'm not tired. I'm so glad to be here, I could leap tall buildings in a single bound." She kicked off her mules and strolled to the window to gaze at the dreary winter skyline, her happiness at getting out of the hospital outweighing her anxiety over Gabe. "Have you ever seen anything so gorgeous?"

Mel wrinkled her nose. "I thought you quit the pain meds."

Tessa chuckled. "Days ago, and you know it." She flung out her arms. "It's beautiful. Life is beautiful." She turned just in time to see a crooked grin waver across Gabe's face.

He cleared his throat. "Some chow sounds beautiful to me."

Mel laughed. "Now that he has his appetite back, good luck keeping the big guy here full. That's a project in and of itself." She laid the roses on the counter. "I wish I could stay, but I have to get to work."

Tessa hurried to hug her friend. "I feel guilty about you missing so many shifts at the cannery to be with me."

"Hey, you were there for me in spades when my life blew apart. The cannery can get anyone to stir vats of Hood River peas." Melody returned her hug. "Besides, Gabemeister loaned me enough to get by. I *will* be paying it back however."

Gabe extracted three large vases from the cupboard. He turned to the sink to fill them with water. "I already told Trixie Tornado that's not necessary."

"And I told you—"

Laughing, Tessa held up her hand. "You two sound like Bert and Ernie."

Mel gave her another squeeze. "I gotta go. I'll see you tomorrow, though. You, too, Tyrannosaurus Rex." Waving, she breezed out.

Gabe picked up the roses. "What do you want to do this afternoon?"

She arched her eyebrows at him. "We could play poker."

He laughed. "No way, Houdini. Fool me once, shame on you, fool me twice…" His gaze held hers, and his eyes darkened.

Was he remembering the results of their poker game? Her pulse quickened.

He tore his gaze away and stuffed the roses into the vases. "I rented some videos and we could order pizza."

Her fears and doubts rushed back with a vengeance. She fidgeted with the hem of her shirt. "Actually, I'd rather talk."

He stiffened, his expression scared. "Okay."

Even on the ship, when Peter had held the gun to Gabe's head and he was about to die, he hadn't shown any fear. But he sure looked afraid now. Her stomach pitched. "It's time, don't you think?"

The pulse in his throat throbbed rapidly. "Past time."

She leaned against the kitchen door for support. "Spill it."

He sucked in a deep breath. "I'd feel much better if you sat down."

"I've done enough sitting this week to last a lifetime. I'd rather stand."

He swallowed hard. Swallowed again. Stared at his feet. "When I was a kid, my mom abandoned me at the bus depot."

"Yes, I know. I heard. In the hospital."

His head jerked up. "So you did hear me."

"Every word," she whispered. "One minute, I was alone, lost in a pain-filled gray void, then I heard you. I focused on your voice. Suddenly, all the pain disappeared, and I was floating near the ceiling. I could see you by my side, see myself in the bed, you holding my hand. Only a thin, fragile thread bound me to earth. It was about to snap, but I didn't care. I wanted to break free, embrace the peace that beckoned so close."

The color drained from his face. "Oh, God, Tessie." He squeezed his eyes shut, opened them again. "I knew I'd almost lost you, but—"

"I heard everything. You said you needed me, begged me not to leave. Your tears fell on my hand, and then I knew where you were. At that moment, I was given a choice. Go or stay. Peace or pain."

She touched his pale cheek. "I chose to stay. I fought to get back to you, fought hard. I hurtled violently back to my body. The pain was intense, but when I opened my eyes and saw you, I knew even if my body never healed completely, I'd never regret my choice."

With a choking sound, he reached for her and buried his face in her neck. His fists clenched in her curls. "You won't. I promise, you won't."

She stroked his silky hair. "You're afraid of love because she abandoned you. But you don't have to be afraid anymore. I'm not like her."

He trembled in her arms. "Oh, baby, I know about your devotion better than anyone. You willingly gave your life for mine!" He let go of her and eased away to look into her eyes. The torment swirling in the jade depths made her throat ache.

"Remember I told you I lived with my foster parents until I was ten, then bounced from home to home?"

She nodded.

"I loved the Sinclairs, started to feel secure. Then the state removed me, some idiotic bureaucratic mix up. Losing two homes in as many years terrified me. I didn't let myself stay with the next family long enough to get attached. I ran away. When the authorities caught me, I refused to go back."

"Oh, Gabe, I'm so sorry. No wonder you were scared."

"I've been running ever since. I never let myself get close to anyone. You know why I really left the SEALs? When half the team died and Banks and Stevens got wounded, I carried them to the infirmary, then walked away without a goodbye. Half our team had bought it. My buddies needed me. And I deserted them. Because I let myself care, it hurt too much to stay."

Her heart stopped. He'd been through so much. Maybe he'd been scarred too badly. Maybe the damage cut so deep he just couldn't trust, no matter how hard she tried. She clenched her fists against a soul-searing agony far worse than any physical pain she'd suffered. "That's why you kept insisting you weren't the man for me."

He grimaced. "I knew I would hurt you, too. Like good old Mom, I didn't have the guts to stick around. Whenever I started to care for anyone, I ran—before they could walk out on me. I've made a career out of retreat. I was afraid to trust you, and I couldn't trust myself. I was convinced I couldn't do forever. But you don't deserve anything less."

Oh, no. Her chest tight and aching, she stared at the floor. Every muscle in her body tensed as she braced herself for the *I care about you so much, I'm leaving for your own good* speech. She had to try twice before she could force words past the lump in her throat. "I'm well, now. You can go."

He cupped her face in a shaky hand. "The jig is up. No matter how hard I tried, I couldn't keep you out of my heart, Tessie. You're always with me. In my thoughts when I'm awake and in my dreams when I sleep. I have no desire to run. In fact, if you had slipped into a coma or suffered brain damage—" his voice caught. "I would have provided for you the rest of my life."

Her heart started beating again, trying to pound out of her chest with wild, painful thrusts. Hope ignited inside her. She again raised her gaze to his.

His eyes darkened. "I fell in love with you the first instant I saw you, standing by the vault with your golden eyes all wide. Jumping out of a chopper into a firefight or dodging missiles never gave me a second's hesitation. But loving you scared the hell out of me. I hung onto denial until that night when we almost made love. When you said you loved me, I went into a tailspin."

The flicker of hope burst into flame. She began to shake, too. *He loved her!*

But was his love strong enough to overcome his past? She rested a reassuring hand on his chest. Beneath the soft cotton, his heart thundered under her palm. "I was scared, too, Gabe. I've never felt this way about anyone."

"I know what you mean. I never realized how empty my life was, how superficial, how much I was missing until I met you." He covered her hand with his own. "When I saw you tied up inside the *Lady Liberty,* I knew you'd fought your worst nightmare to help me. I realized I had to face my own fears, meet you halfway, to be worthy of your love." He sucked in a ragged breath, his chest jerking under their joined hands. "Then I nearly lost you. That's when I learned the meaning of real terror."

She nodded. "I had a few awful moments when I thought Peter was going to shoot you."

His expression fierce, he gripped her upper arms, tugged her close. "If either of us had died, we would have been separated forever, without you ever knowing how I feel. Never again. I'm through running. I'll risk anything, risk everything to be with you. Tessie..." He held her gaze. "I love you. I need you. I can't imagine living the rest of my life without you."

Relieved, happy tears spilled down her cheeks. He'd done it. He had overcome his fears and freely admitted his love. "I was beginning to think you didn't want me."

"Don't cry. Oh, baby, please don't cry." He wiped away the

wetness with his thumb. "I'm so sorry. I didn't want to start our life together without clearing up the past. I was waiting until you got stronger. I needed to confess, and ask for a new start. But I knew you were already dealing with a lot, both physically and mentally, and didn't want to mess with your recovery."

He gave her an unsteady smile. "Constantly fighting the urge to strip your clothes off and make love to you until neither of us could walk didn't help, either. I was trying to be noble and self-sacrificing."

She couldn't hold in a ragged laugh. "Noble and self-sacrificing don't become you, Mr. Bond."

"Can you forgive me?" His wary expression made him look like a stray dog who hoped for a handout, but expected a kick. "I'll love you to my dying day. And I swear on my life, I'll never leave you."

"We've both been hurt. Because of our pasts, both of us expected the worst. Both of us expected pain. Both of us expected rejection. But the past is over." She brushed a soft kiss across his lips. "You belong to me, and I to you. You're forgiven. And I'll hold you to that promise."

Still trembling, he dropped to one knee and took her hand. "Tessa, will you marry me?"

She stared into his eyes, the warm green depths overflowing with promises. Joy flooded through her, and her spirit soared. "Yes!"

His trembling increased. His smoky gaze roved over her, and her body tingled under his heated regard. "The day I stole you out of the bank, you stole my heart. You don't know how much it means to me to receive yours in return, freely given."

"My heart belongs to you. It always has." Pure, golden happiness bubbled inside her. She smiled at him tenderly. "Make love to me, Gabe."

Gabe slowly rose to his feet. He stared into Tessa's beautiful, glowing eyes and the desire to make her his slammed into him. He sucked in a shaky breath, fighting for restraint. Ripping off her clothes and taking her against the door would not be cool. He bent his head and kissed her.

Her lips parted, welcoming him inside, and he lost it. The

long hours when he didn't know if she would live or die, the torturous week of hospitalization, the silent message of love in her eyes right before she fell off the ship swirled through his mind.

He shoved her against the door, and drank in the heady, drugging taste of her. Mindless with the need to touch every inch of her precious body, to reassure himself after the nightmare of nearly losing her, he arched his hips into her welcoming softness. He ran his hands over her breasts, the small of her back, the curve of her bottom.

Her fingernails dug into his shoulders, and she moaned into his mouth. The pain and the soft sound jarred him out of his sensual haze. He jerked back. Planting his hands on either side of her head, he leaned against the door. Gasping, he struggled for restraint. "Oh, hell. I'm mauling you like a high-school sophomore. My control goes AWOL when I'm with you."

Her lips curved into a sensual smile. "I liked it."

He sucked in more air, trying to regulate his breathing. "I need you so much," he admitted shakily. "I need to be inside you, be a part of you. But this is your first time, sweetheart. We have to go slow."

She slid her arms around his waist and pressed full-length against him. "I need you, too. I've waited so long. I don't want you to go slow."

He didn't dare touch her again until he'd regained a measure of control. He kept both hands on the door. *Breathe.* "Trust me on this one, Houdini."

"I trust you," she murmured against his chest. "With my heart. My soul. And my body."

A groan slipped out. "Heaven help me." He wrapped her in his arms and kissed her again. Her vanilla fragrance dazzled his senses as he savored her sweet mouth. He turned and began edging them to the far end of the loft toward the bed.

They'd progressed as far as the piano when he had to stop and kiss her again. Locked in the sensual dance, her tongue flirted with his. He threaded his fingers in her hair, drawing her closer, his thumbs stroking in reverent wonder over the baby-fine skin of her temples and cheekbones.

Her hands slipped between them to unbutton his shirt. She hastily tugged it off and boldly explored his shoulders and his chest before moving to his abdomen. At his sharply indrawn breath, she smiled and cupped his buttocks. Then her fingertips brushed over his jeans to tease his straining fly. "I love touching you."

Perspiration dampened his skin. He groaned again and grabbed her wrists. "I'm real happy to hear that, but you're killing me, honey."

Her husky laugh arrowed straight to his heart. She arched her hips into him. "You feel like you're enjoying it."

He clenched his jaw. *Dredge up that famous self-discipline, Colton.* He spanned her waist with his hands and sat her on the oak piano. Stepping between her thighs, he cradled her against him, kissing her cheeks, her nose, her eyelids. He nibbled the tender spot where her neck met her shoulder, and she shivered. Under the silky blue top, her beaded nipples grazed his chest. He palmed her breasts, thrilled at the sound of her breath catching in her throat.

He bent his head and suckled her nipples through the silk. Her throaty moan speared through him, pumping scorching blood through his veins like lava. He stroked the cool, slippery pants and matching panties down her slender legs, delighting in her sensual shivers as he bared her lower body. Taking his time, he unbuttoned her shirt, revealing her creamy ivory skin inch by inch. The silk whispered off her shoulders and rippled into a sapphire pool on the lustrous oak.

Awed, he devoured the sight of her naked beauty, memorizing every lovely curve. He lifted his gaze to hers, her shimmering golden eyes reflecting his own passion. So this was what it was like to make love. Really make love, not just have sex. Another miracle. His heart thundered in his ears. "My beautiful Tessa, I love you."

"I love you, too," she breathed. "So much."

He sipped again and again at her sweet lips before he tasted the line of her jaw, her earlobes, her neck. Marveling at her satiny smooth breasts, he drew her nipple into his mouth and

circled his tongue tantalizingly around the velvety tip before
suckling hard.

Quivering, she thrust her fingers into his hair, pulling him
closer, her gasps choppy and ragged. "Oh!"

He gave the other nipple his careful attention, and then moved
lower, kissing her soft belly. He moved lower still, tasting her,
sweet and feminine, leisurely flicking his tongue across the
small, swollen bud. She moaned, trembled under his hands.
"Wait. Don't. I want you inside me first."

He stripped off his remaining clothing. Gazing into her pas-
sion-dilated eyes, he smoothed her tousled curls from her forehead. "There's no hurry. We've got all night. And a lifetime
after that." A lifetime with this remarkable woman. His heart
soared.

"I know." She rained impatient little kisses all over his face.
"But I want you now. Right now. No more waiting."

He smiled at her uninhibited eagerness. "I'm yours. Now and
always."

Without hesitation, she opened her thighs wide, giving him
unquestioning access to the most vulnerable part of her. At her
trust, warmth curled in his chest. He wouldn't betray her faith.
Not now, not ever. Lifting her bottom, he nestled between her
thighs. Holding his breath, he eased into her soft, damp heat.

She wrapped her arms around his neck and pulled him closer.
"I want to give you everything."

Tenderness washed over him. He clenched his jaw at her urgent movements, resisting the pleasure that urged him to race to
the finish. As her sleek warmth encircled him inch by inch,
sweat pooled in the small of his back and beaded on his forehead. "I want to give you everything, too, sweetheart. The best
of everything." He closed his eyes, fighting the temptation to
thrust in to the hilt. Encountering resistance, he stopped at the
fragile barrier. He opened his eyes to look at her.

"Mmm. More, Gabe." She wriggled against him.

He clung to the razor edge of sanity. "Trust your pilot, honey.
This won't hurt if we take our time."

"It doesn't hurt. It's wonderful." She arched her back. Her

abrupt movement pushed him deep, and the barrier between them gave way. She gasped and went rigid in his arms.

Rattled and as unsure as an inexperienced virgin himself, he froze. "Tessie? You okay?"

"Yes." She sighed. "Go ahead."

He rubbed her back until the tension eased from her muscles. "Relax, honey. From here on, it only gets better." Carefully, he slid nearly out of her sweet warmth and then in again, searching her face for signs of pain before continuing.

"This is amazing," she whispered, her body rising to meet him with each stroke. "The way you feel inside of me. You fill me, complete me."

He felt that way, too, as though he'd found the piece of his heart that had been missing all these years. Blitzed by both the emotional and physical bombardment, he was perilously close to climaxing. He groaned. Gripping her bottom, he held her in place. "Stay still. I need a minute."

She froze. "Is this hurting *you?*"

"No, sweetheart." Chuckling, he rested his forehead against hers. "But you're blowing my self-control all to hell. And I want your first time to be great."

"I'm making love with the man I love. How could it get any better?"

He grinned at her innocence. If he had his way—and he would—she'd soon know. Once again, he gently began to thrust. "Okay?"

She instantly picked up the rhythm, her body as in tune with his as if they'd been lifelong lovers. Trembling, she rocked her hips faster, increasing the pace. "Yes. Oh, yes."

Watching her closely, he matched her quickening movements, their passion quickly escalating.

Her heart thundered against his own. "In my wildest dreams, I never imagined—"

Fire licked through him. "Fly with me, honey," he gasped. Pure sensation took over. He wrapped his arms around her, thrusting hard and fast, glorying in possessing his woman, and her wild response. He lifted his gaze to hers. Her eyes were alight with amber fire, glowing with fierce adoration.

She brought her mouth to his, her warm, ragged breaths feathering over his lips. "You'll never be alone again, Gabe. I love you. Forever."

His entire being exploded with a surge of love so intense, so bright, he shook. She cherished him. He never thought any woman would. She loved him. He'd never thought any woman could. And he never thought he'd be capable of loving and cherishing in return. He surrendered, willingly giving her everything. Even the part of him he'd always held back. Sweet, hot pleasure rocketed through him as he poured himself into her.

She quivered, her inner muscles contracting around him again and again. His gaze embraced her soul, and he cradled her body, protecting and treasuring her as she found fulfillment in his arms. The intense emotions that swept through him rocked him to the core.

Tessa blinked rapidly. Lights, colors, sparks swirled in her vision. Gasping for breath, she held fast to Gabe's gaze, the center of her spinning universe. His body was shuddering violently. She gripped his damp shoulders as he took her impossibly high, then higher, to paradise. Soaring, she rapidly crested a second time, crying out as ecstasy again flooded her.

Aftershocks rippled through her. Dazed, she clung to him. Tenderly he urged her closer. Murmuring encouragement and praise, he prolonged her pleasure by slowing to a gentle glide, drawing out the sensations. Sheltered in the safe haven of his embrace, she floated back to awareness. She didn't want their connection to end. She wanted to stay here forever, with his hardness and strength filling her, with his body enveloped in hers.

Staggering, overwhelming love for him welled up inside. Trembling uncontrollably, she buried her face in his neck, her ragged breaths inhaling his unique male scent, hot and damp with arousal.

He went still. "Damn it! I did hurt you."

"No. Making love to you is—" she gulped. "When you're inside of me and you look at me, I see, I see your soul. We're as close as two people can be, one person, one heart."

He dragged in a deep breath. He was trembling, too. "Heart

of my heart, soul of my soul.'' His strong hands stroked her back in a soothing caress. ''I'm sorry about this, sweetheart.''

She pulled away to give him an incredulous look. ''Whatever for? You just gifted me with the most incredible experience of my life.''

''I wanted your first time to be special. Dinner, love songs, dancing, candles.'' A wry grin tilted his lips. ''A bed.''

She grinned back. ''This is the most beautiful music I've ever made on a piano. We can make love in bed the second time.'' Her grin widened. ''Speaking of which, when does the next flight leave on Colton Air?''

It was his turn to look incredulous. ''You've got to be kidding.'' He pressed a gentle kiss to the corner of her mouth. ''You must be sore.''

''Only a little tender. Not enough to keep me grounded.'' She rocked against him, exulting as he instantly hardened inside of her. ''Again, Gabe.''

He laughed. With their bodies still joined, he lifted her and carried her to the bed. He gently lowered her to the plush yellow comforter. ''Anything you say, sweetheart.'' He began to stroke, slow and deep.

''Mmm. There's only one thing I want to know.''

''What's that?''

She slid her hands down his back, enjoying the play of hard muscles under his smooth, heated skin. ''Does this airline give frequent flyer miles?''

Chapter 20

Three incredible, passion-hazed days later, Tessa woke to Gabe's soft kiss. "Wake up, sleepyhead."

"Uh," she groaned, reveling in the strong thud of his heart under her cheek. She'd slept with her head on his broad chest all night. When they'd slept, that is. "What time is it?"

"Noon. And we have an appointment."

"Noon? Good grief! What kind of appointment?"

He hugged her. "It's a surprise."

She rolled over. Her body protested, reminding her of the hours of paradise spent in Gabe's arms. He made love the way he did everything else, with uninhibited playfulness and abandon. His blatant delight and reverent absorption in her body had unleashed a wild, unrestrained streak in her she hadn't even known she possessed. He enjoyed looking at her, touching her, and he'd openly reveled in her fiery response.

Their life together would be one roller-coaster adventure after another. Especially in the bedroom. She groped for the clock and another, louder groan escaped.

"Muscles a little stiff this morning, hmm?" One dark brow arched in amusement. "I tried to convince you those last two times were too much, but little did I know I'd pick a genuine flying ace.''

She gave him a wicked smile and slid her hand down his body. ''Speaking of stiff muscles.''

He sucked in a breath. ''As you can tell, I'd love to rocket into the wild blue yonder with you again, but no time for that.''

She took a quick shower, then drank a cup of tea and ate a slice of toast while he showered. He hustled her downstairs and into the Corvette.

''Curiosity is killing me. Where are we going?''

He grinned. ''You'll find out.'' Fifteen minutes later, he dropped her off at an exclusive spa. ''I'll see you in a while.''

She entered the spa and found Mel waiting for her, wearing a neon lime-green pantsuit and a beaming smile.

She eyed her best friend. ''Okay, what's up?''

Mel laughed. ''This is so much fun.''

An attendant ushered them to a back room where she served them a large platter of fresh fruit and cheese. They were treated to massages, facials, manicures and pedicures. Then stylists did their hair and makeup. Gift-wrapped dresses with matching lacy undergarments arrived. Soft apricot for Mel, glowing emerald-green for Tessa.

Tessa looked at the accompanying heart-shaped box of imported chocolates, and grinned. ''Wow, does Gabe do it up in style or what? He's the most incredible, wonderful man on the planet.''

Mel rolled her eyes. ''For a testosterone jockey, he's tolerable.''

When they stepped outside, relaxed and pampered, a gleaming black limo awaited. An uniformed chauffeur snapped to attention. He touched the brim of his cap. ''Miss Beaumont. Miss Parrish. I'm Giles, at your service.''

Giggling like schoolgirls, Tessa and Mel slid into the luxurious ivory leather interior. Surround-sound speakers played Elvis hits as the limo wove through the city streets. Tessa looked at Mel. ''Want to clue me in?''

Mel gave her a pixie grin. ''Nope.''

The limo meandered down familiar streets, finally stopping in front of St. Michael's Church. Tessa's heart lurched. "Mel?"

Melody took her hand and tugged her up the stairs, through the vestibule and down the hallway to the bride's dressing room. Her friend pushed open the door.

Tessa entered, then stopped short. The candlelight satin-and-lace Victorian gown from Bernard's Bridals hung in front of her. Gabe stood beside the gown, wearing a tux.

"Happy wedding day, sweetheart."

Her stomach flip-flopped. "You're wedding-phobic."

"I've been miraculously cured." He grinned at her.

"But you came unglued over my wedding to Dale."

"Exactly. Which I'd never done before. Granted, I abhorred commitment, but I'd never freaked out. It doesn't take a rocket scientist to figure out my over-the-top reaction was due to the fact that you were marrying another man."

Her eyes filled with tears. "I don't know what to say."

"How about *I do?*" He kissed her tenderly. "I'll be at the altar. Don't make me wait too long."

Mel helped her dress in the lace gown, adjusted a wreath of apricot rosebuds on Tessa's hair, and then stepped back. "You're a beautiful bride, Tess." Teary-eyed and sniffling, her friend handed her the matching bouquet.

Arm in arm, they walked to the vestibule. When they arrived at the rear of the sanctuary, the organist began the wedding march. Tessa followed Mel down the aisle, glancing around in amazement. Apricot roses spilled from every nook and cranny. Her friends filled the pews, their faces smiling as she passed.

Then she looked at the front where Gabe waited, gorgeous in his tux. Her stomach fluttered in response. He flashed her his five-hundred-watt grin, and her soul soared. The ceremony flew by in a blur of happiness.

He'd even provided a gold band for her to slip on his finger. A symbol of his commitment, and a counterpart to the heart-shaped diamond he placed on hers. She blinked back tears as his strong, even voice pledged her his love, his life, and his sacred honor. Forever.

Afterward, he escorted her down the aisle accompanied by a triumphant organ refrain and a shower of rose petals.

Inside the limo, he handed her a fluted crystal goblet brimming with champagne. "I've been thinking—"

"Uh-oh. That's always dangerous."

He laughed and tweaked a wayward curl peeking beneath her veil. "We make a great team. What would you say to opening a private investigation business? Agency work has lost its shine. Being away from you for months at a time is highly unappealing. And I don't want to get caught in a bad situation and leave you a young widow."

Her heart leapt into her throat. "If anything happened to you—"

He slid his arm around her shoulders. "Exactly why I'm 'retiring.' I can run the P.I. firm on my own if you want to stay with the bank."

"Oh, right. I'd miss it horribly. I'll pine away if Trask isn't dumping all his work on me and chewing out my fanny day after day." She took a sip of cool, tart champagne, enjoying the tingle. "After this last month with you, Mr. Adventure, banking seems as dull as dishwater."

He laughed again. "I guess that's settled, then." He raised his goblet. "To my partner in crime, and Houdini Private Investigations."

She clinked glasses with him. "We're going to be solving them, not committing them. And speaking of crimes, don't turn in your handcuffs. I need them."

"How come?"

"I still owe you for that highhanded stunt at your place. One of these days, when you least expect it, you're going to wake up and find yourself cuffed to the bed, naked and helpless." She arched her brows at him. "Then, Bond, Gabe Bond, it will be payback time."

He inhaled sharply. "Promise?"

She smiled. "It's a promise. Remember, I never break my promises."

Desire glittered in his eyes. "And I always pay my debts,

sweetheart.'' He gave her a wolfish grin. ''I look forward to paying this one. With interest.''

With the sensual vow glittering between them, the limo arrived at the banquet hall. Gabe held her arm and escorted her inside. She glanced around at the room overflowing with more apricot roses and turned to her husband with a smile of pure bliss. ''Did you wipe out every apricot rose in the state?''

He grinned. ''Darn near.''

Buffet tables off to one side practically groaned under heaping platters of food, and a huge wedding cake topped with a tiny, perfect, auburn-haired bride and raven-haired groom sat at one end. ''How did you do all this, contact my friends, know the exact dress and size, order the cake?''

''I was with you when you finalized the arrangements before, remember? I saw what you wanted. Plus, I confiscated your daily planner.''

''But how did you have time?'' Her cheeks heated. ''We've done nothing but make love for three days.''

''You slept in between. I didn't. Mel and I nearly went insane secretly getting everything ready. That is one determined pixie. Remind me never to stand in her way.'' He chuckled. ''The honeymoon is up to you. Where would you like to go?''

''How about three or four months sunbathing naked in the Caribbean? On the *Serendipity*.''

He frowned. ''What about your fear of water? And you can't swim. You can't be on the boat if you can't swim. It's not safe.''

''My phobia got cured, too. The hard way. I found out there are worse things than dying. From now on, I'm living every moment of my life to the fullest.'' She gave him a tender smile. ''You can teach me to swim. Along with tutoring me in a few other skills. Like in the bedroom.''

He snorted. ''Hell baby, you've taught the tutor a thing or two in that department.'' He cupped her face in his big, warm hand. ''Are you sure? I've never spent even a fourth of my paycheck. I invested it all these years. We've got a nice fat nest egg. We can go anywhere, do anything you want.''

''Positive.'' She glanced at the door as the guests began to drift inside, then back up at him. Her soul mate. ''I'm overwhelmed.

I love you so much, Gabe. I don't know how to thank you for all this.''

"I love you, too." His lips curled in a sensual grin that sent heat sizzling through her from eyelashes to toenails. "I'm sure you'll think of a way to thank me."

When the receiving line ended, he led her to the dance floor. He held up his hand for silence. Expecting a dance, she glanced at him in puzzlement.

"I'd like to present my bride with her wedding gift."

A side door opened, and a stocky man carried in a piano bench. Two others wheeled in a piano. The piano wasn't new. The wood was scratched and battered, the keys yellowed and worn with age. The old instrument looked achingly familiar.

Her breath jammed in her throat.

"Look under the keyboard," Gabe murmured.

Trembling all over, she bent down. The wood bore a tiny handprint in black marker with a larger hand drawn beside the little one. In between was a heart with initials. Hers and her father's. "Dad's piano," she choked. "How?"

"I've been searching for weeks, practically since the day you told me about it. The writing made it easier to track down. I found it in a retirement home in Sacramento." He slid his arm around her and nudged her gently. "Go on, honey. Play something."

Trembling harder, she seated herself on the bench. Gently, reverently, she placed her fingers on the worn keys. Remembering her past, anticipating her future, she played from her heart.

Love Me Tender.

* * * * *

SILHOUETTE *Romance* ®

From *New York Times* bestselling author

DIANA PALMER

CATTLEMAN'S PRIDE

(Silhouette Romance #1718)

He was strong, seductive and set in his ways. She was shy, unassuming and achingly innocent. Together, next-door neighbors Jordan Powell and Libby Collins were like oil and water. Yet when Jordan made it his personal crusade to help Libby hold on to her beloved homestead, everyone in Jacobsville knew it was just a matter of time before romance ignited between these sparring partners. Could Libby accomplish what no woman had before and tame this Long, Tall Texan's restless heart?

LONG, TALL *Texans*

An enchanting new installment in the legendary *Long, Tall Texans* miniseries!

Available May 2004 at your favorite retail outlet.

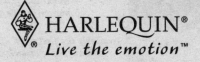